PRAISE FOR MARIANO'S CHOICE

Mariano's Choice *is one of those rare, wonderful books that sticks in the mind and heart long after you've read the last page. The story, masterfully paced and filled with fascinating historic details, offers an intriguing snapshot of the West through the eyes of characters largely ignored by mainstream fiction: fur traders, Indian captives, dislocated Spanish settlers, horse trainers and trail blazers. The underlying themes of honor, compassion, revenge, and the power of love and friendship, transcend setting and genre. The book shines brightly because of a vulnerable, wily, complicated Spanish Mountain Man—one of the most interesting protagonists I've encountered in a long time. Highly recommended.*—**Anne Hillerman**, *New York Times* best-selling author of *Spider Woman's Daughter* and *Rock With Wings.*

David M. Jessup adds flesh and blood to the bones of one of the West's legendary mountain men. Mariano Medina has not one choice, but many, as he stands up to violence and prejudice—and to his own cowardice. He must choose between fear and friendship, safety and honor, and loyalty and love in this tightly wound novel of the Old West. —**Sandra Dallas**, *New York Times* best-selling author.

Jessup is a master historian and writer—and this gorgeous novel proves it. What mesmerizes most is the depth of understanding and love of the West, which therefore includes the untold stories, the filling-in of an incomplete history. In Mariano's Choice, *we discover the peoples who are often minimalized by mainstream historical fiction but which are essential to an understanding and love of the real and varied West. In vivid and gorgeous prose, we encounter the world of the late 1800s and the men and women who literally shaped the West. We also find a tale of love and the power of redemption. History, place, love, forgiveness, healing: this book has it all. I loved it.* —**Laura Pritchett**, winner of the PEN USA Award for Fiction, author, *Red Lightning.*

Mariano's Choice isn't your typical Western. And Mariano Medina isn't your typical Western hero. Rather than fearless and invincible, he is timid, often uncertain, and occasionally cowardly. Medina and other historical Westerners serve author David Jessup well as he spins a gritty, sometimes painful tale of an ordinary man facing unwelcome change as the fur trade era gives way to immigrant wagons and the United States seeks increasing influence on the Mexican frontier. This book reveals the Old West through the eyes of a regular frontiersman and the result is a richer, more realistic interpretation than the overwrought, myth-driven view we see in so many Western novels.—**Rod Miller**, three-time winner of the Western Writers of America Spur Award.

Mariano's Choice continues the saga of Mariano Medina, a man both ordinary and extraordinary. Author David Jessup's fluid, compelling prose takes the reader back to another time, to share Medina's adventures and adversities. I hope someone has the sense to produce this as a mini-series. It's too rich and complex to fit into a two-hour movie. —**Lucia St. Clair Robson**. *New York Times* best selling author of *Ride the Wind*, and winner of the Owen Wister award of the Western Writers of America.

Mariano's Choice is a bold story about the West as it existed before the Western, a story about a raw land populated by rugged folk, men and women, native and immigrant, living alone and in community. Jessup's cinematic eye for detail and his gift for gut-wrenching, heart-pounding storytelling pulls us seamlessly into a world of danger, beauty, and unbounded possibility—for success and failure, for betrayal and redemption, for love and hate, and for life and death.—**Gary Schanbacher**, author of *Crossing Purgatory*, winner of the Langum Award for American Historical Fiction.

What strikes me first about Mariano's Choice *is David Jessup's writing. Elegant isn't a word one would usually associate with a novel of the 1800s, yet that's the word that comes to mind. Next, I'm taken by the pace of the story, and the authenticity of the characters. It moves, and they're so believable. Finally, the plot is riveting. The historical basis just adds to it. If Mariano's Crossing was an award-winning first effort, Mariano's Choice should join it on the judges' stand.—* **Denny Dressman**, author of eight books and President of the Colorado Authors' League.

PRAISE FOR MARIANO'S CROSSING
David M. Jessup's award-winning first novel
to which this book is a prequel

*Winner of the Rocky Mountain Fiction Writers Contest
Finalist, Colorado Book Award for Literary Fiction
Finalist, Pacific Northwest Writers Contest
and the Santa Fe Writers Project*

*What a vivid piece of writing! The craftsmanship is most impressive. And the multiplicity of perspectives makes the truth tantalizingly elusive. Great stuff!—***Louis Bayard**, *New York Times* bestselling author of *Mr. Timothy* and other historical mysteries.

Mariano's Crossing *is a beautiful, exciting, wonderful novel... I couldn't put it down.... It does what good historical fiction should do—places me in what John Gardner calls the 'vivid and continuous dream'.—***Laura Pritchett**, recipient of the PEN USA Award and the Milkweed National Fiction Prize, author of *Hell's Bottom, Colorado.*

Based on real characters and the mysteries connected with historic events, author David Jessup has woven a mesmerizing tale of people struggling to find their places in the rapidly changing landscape of post-gold rush Colorado. —**Page Lambert**, author of *Shifting Stars*, featured in *Inside/Outside Southwest Magazine* as one of the most notable women writers of the contemporary American West.

Fine writing throughout, with many dynamite scenes and fascinating characters. The descriptions of landscape and the natural world are marvelous, and there's a lot of great history here, along with a complex psychological dimension and a touching relationship between the characters.—**Paulette Alden**, Stegner Fellow, author of *The Answer to Your Question*, winner, Kindle's Best Indie Book Award.

Mariano's Crossing *is smoothly paced and taut with drama. The internal conflicts of the characters pull them all forward through the story to its dramatic conclusion. The major characters are well rounded, each with a unique voice, as well as faults and virtues that determine their paths along the way.*—**Teresa Lewis**, *Flatirons Literary Review.*

A great character driven work of historical fiction! —**Meg Wessell**, *A Bookish Affair* book review.

Reading this novel set in the Old West, I was reminded at times of two other historical novels, Snow Falling on Cedars *and* The Kite Runner. *Neither of those books are westerns, but they deal with similar themes—racial and ethnic bigotry and relationships across class boundaries. In all three, there is also a thread of menace.* —**Ron Scheer**, *Buddies in the Saddle* book review.

Historical fiction that reads like a true story. Told from multiple points of view, Mariano's Crossing *is a convincing historical treatment. Each character has his own voice and is so believable the reader is convinced each one told his version to Jessup in person.* —**Patricia Stolty**, *Chiseled In Rock* book review.

For way too many years, the incredible accomplishments of the Hispanic community have gone untold. Finally, David Jessup illuminates the life of Mariano Medina, a very important Colorado Hispanic pioneer. I very much enjoyed reading his historical novel, Mariano's Crossing, *and I know you will as well.*—**Cecil Gutierrez**, Mayor, City of Loveland, Colorado.

I loved hearing David Jessup tell the fascinating story and details behind his book Mariano's Crossing. *Just like James Michener's* Centennial, *Mr. Jessup weaves the story about individuals with their own unique personalities, including strengths and character flaws. To say that this is "history come alive" is an understatement. I cannot wait to take one of David Jessup's tours of the locations he describes in the book.*—**Susan Dominica**, member, *The Breakfast Club* book club.

MARIANO'S CHOICE

A Novel

David M. Jessup

PronghornPress.org

For Linda, the Choice Lady

ACKNOWLEDGMENTS

My thanks for in-depth critiques from Laura Pritchett, author of one of my favorite books, *Hell's Bottom, Colorado*, Liane Ellision Norman, poet, literary professor and author of *A Stitch in Time*, Paulette Alden, author of *The Answer to Your Question* and workshop leader at the Key West Literary Seminar, Suzanna Banwell, Kim Johnson, Annette Chaudet, editor of Pronghorn Press, and my own talented wife, Linda E. Jessup, author of *Parenting with Courage* and *Uncommon Sense*.

For historical insights and information about Old West customs, prices and clothing, I'm indebted to Mike Guli, of River Crossing and Michael J. Guli Designs, Bill Meirath of the Loveland Historical Society, and the generous folks at the Fort Bridger and El Pueblo Museums.

I'm grateful to members of book clubs and participants in my book tours for their enthusiastic interest in the life and times of Mariano Medina.

There is a pain—so utter—
It swallows substance up—
Then covers the Abyss with Trance—
So Memory can step
Around—across—upon it—
As One within a Swoon—
Goes safely—where an open eye—
Would drop Him—
Bone by Bone

—Emily Dickenson
unpublished poem
about summer 1863

PART 1

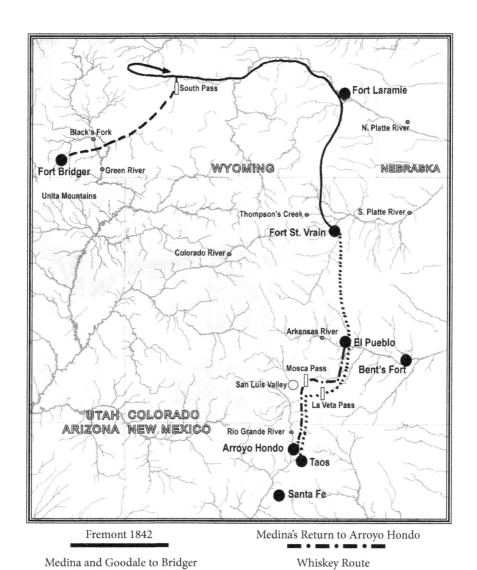

Fremont 1842

Medina's Return to Arroyo Hondo

Medina and Goodale to Bridger

Whiskey Route

1

FILI'S POOL

Taos 1827

She flashed into Mariano's world like a meteor on a starry night. Wavy brown hair, startling blue-green eyes, dimples that magically appeared at the corners of her mouth whenever she smiled. Nothing in his fifteen years of life had dazzled him as much as the arrival of Señorita Filomena at the *Hacienda de los Árboles* a year ago. Hers was a brightness intense and unapproachable.

When Omar, the grizzle-browed stable manager, ordered him to serve as her groom on that glorious April morning, Mariano's pulse raced.

"She will be here soon, after breakfast," Omar said. "The Don has called me to the *casa grande*. Remember all I have taught you. The Don expects the best for his daughter."

"Yes, sir." Mariano straightened in response to Omar's rheumy-eyed stare, but as soon as the stable manager hobbled out of the barn, he practically danced his way to the stall where the *señorita's* horse, a bay gelding named Prince, stood chewing hay. The horse cast a startled eye toward him as his hands fumbled to untie its halter rope. He led Prince to the tack room, opened the door, and stopped short.

Two days ago, while repairing a bridle inside that very room, he'd overheard the girl's half-brother, Ricardo Castillo, call her an *hija de puta*. That snake-bite slur provoked uneasy laughter from Ricardo's two crony cousins lounging next to the stall where Ricardo's horse was kept. For Mariano, the venom—more than the words themselves—scared him. He had pressed himself against the tack room wall, scarcely breathing, until the three swaggered out of the barn.

Daughter of a whore? The girl had been brought to live in the big house by her doting father, Don Diego Castillo, when she was sixteen. "Fili," the Don called her, the affection in his voice matched by the lavish gifts he gave her. No one knew who Fili's mother might be, but she was certainly not the Don's sickly wife, who ventured out of her room in the *casa grande* only often enough to scold her maid. Servants whispered about a beautiful Spanish woman kept in luxury at some secret location Don Diego visited during his trips away from the *hacienda*. But to call her a whore?

Mariano glanced around. What if the señorita's half-brother wandered into the barn just then and asked him what he was doing? He would not want to explain to Ricardo Castillo why he was taking so much time trimming Prince's black mane and tail, blackening his hooves and grooming his dark brown hide to the point that not one hair was out of place. Or explain why he wanted everything to be perfect for her.

The big gelding craned its head around to stare at him, as if to ask the same question.

"Because the Señorita Filomena is coming to ride you," Mariano whispered, stroking the horse's velvet nose.

He led Prince out of the barn's inner gloom into the bracing light of the corral, where he administered yet another round of hide brushing and saddle polishing. Sun gleamed off the saddle's leather pommel. The deep blue sky, washed clean by yesterday's spring rain, promised an outing worthy of his preparations.

A movement at the front of the big house caught his eye. Mariano's father stepped through the ornate double door and signaled to him. Even at fifty paces, his father appeared nervous. Mariano sighed. The Don's house servant, Antonio Medina always appeared nervous. His graying head came close to scraping the ground as he bowed to usher Señorita Filomena through the open door and down the path toward the stable. After she passed, Father waggled a finger at his son. A warning?

Mariano untied her horse, walked it a few steps from the tie rail and stood at attention, willing his hands to be still, stifling his own fluttering pulse.

Her step had a spring to it, the long straight riding skirt no match for her body's fluid energy. Rolled-up sleeves allowed him to glimpse her bare arms. Her torso, shaped into an hourglass by one of those mysterious, lace-up undergarments that rich women wore, pushed her young breasts alarmingly close to the opening in her blouse. Mariano tore his eyes away from the unnerving sight.

As she drew near, dimples announced the beginning of a smile.

Smiling at me? He swallowed hard. *No, at her horse. She is pleased.*

She stopped beside him and reached out to stroke the gelding's neck. Her scent floated to him, some exotic perfume.

"My, how handsome you look, my Prince," she said.

She turned to Mariano. He could not—dared not—meet her eyes. Staring down at her riding boots planted in the dust of the corral, he caught sight of his own manure stained toes, strangers to shoes, splayed out toward the polished tips of her boots like shabby subjects groveling before royalty. He stood only two steps away. It might as well have been two miles.

He risked a quick glance into the startling turquoise pools of her eyes.

"*Señorita, perdóname...*" He hesitated, then plunged ahead. "I am wondering, with your permission, of course, if I might ride along with you. Your horse might need attention, or your saddle cinch might, you know..." His voice trailed off. He wished his Spanish were more refined.

Her laughter, to his relief, sounded kind.

"Thank you, but I'll be fine." She cocked her head and added, "I'll ride up into the canyon. Back after lunch." She held up a small cloth sack that smelled of freshly made tortillas and tucked it into a saddlebag. "That pool just below the falls."

He knew the spot.

"Fili's pool," he said, then caught himself. Reckless of him to speak the diminutive of her name.

Smiling, she raised her foot. He enfolded the soft boot with the enlaced fingers of his hands and boosted her up. Her leg, warm to the touch, brushed his arm. She settled onto the sidesaddle and hooked her right leg over the pommel. After adjusting her skirt, she lifted her hand in goodbye and reined away toward the canyon in the low hills to the south.

Her slender figure, long hair lifting in the breeze, held his gaze. He remained rooted in place, even after she disappeared behind a copse of trees that lined the creek's twisting turn into the mouth of the canyon. A thin plume of dust marked her progress. On the dry hillside to the west, a second plume spiraled up and followed hers, as if in pursuit.

A dust devil. Common enough in the desert, but not this early in the day. He frowned, wishing it away.

Mild apprehension tugged at him. It was unusual for a rich man's daughter to ride without an escort. It was the kind of behavior that raised eyebrows. But her father, Don Diego, seemed to indulge her.

Is that why her half-brother hates her? Mariano pictured Ricardo Castillo's narrow eyes, the twist in his thin lips whenever he looked at his half-sister.

Words like "inheritance" and "illegitimate" floated through the servants' quarters whenever they spoke of Ricardo's animosity. Mariano had pestered his father for explanations. He was told to mind his own business lest his curiosity about the young woman come to the attention of the Don. Or Ricardo.

Mariano forced his gaze away from the moving wisps of dust, hefted a spade from its resting place against the barn and began scooping horse droppings into a wheelbarrow. The rhythmic swing of the shovel calmed him. He smiled at how far he had come since starting work in the stables two years ago at age thirteen. Under Omar's tutelage, he discovered he was good at handling horses, loved horses, in fact. From cleaning stalls and feeding them, he'd moved on to grooming, helping with their training, and eventually to serving the Don and his guests when they came to ride, adjusting their stirrups and cinches and helping them mount and dismount.

Back inside the barn Mariano began grooming the sorrel stallion that Ricardo rode. As he worked, stroking the animal's thick neck and taking in its rich horse smell, he imagined himself as a person of consequence, worthy of respect, instead of the invisible son of a humble servant. Would a time come when he might leave the *hacienda* and become his own man? A trainer of horses, perhaps even the owner of a livery stable in Taos, catering to the *Americanos* traveling to New Mexico along the Santa Fe Trail?

He wanted to be different from his father, Antonio Medina, who seemed resigned to being a *peón*, bowing his head, humbling himself, ever fearful of offending his *patrón*. Father had left Spain in 1810 to seek his fortune in the New World. Settling in Arroyo Hondo, a small town north of Taos, he had found only poverty and hardship. "Never forget, we are Spaniards," he would say, clinging to that scrap of dignity as a beggar might hang onto his last, worn-out shirt.

Mariano's mother died in Arroyo Hondo when he was five years old. Thinking of her drew a blank, a hole in his memory, little more than a warm feeling tinged with hurt and a strange kind of dread. He shook his head to clear it of any lingering thoughts of her.

The sorrel stallion winced and sidestepped, causing Mariano to pause in his brushing. His fingers found an open sore, a wound from Ricardo Castillo's spur. Mariano spat. *Piss on him! He treats his horse as bad as he treats his half-sister.* He daubed some of Omar's healing salve on the wound and walked back outside.

Something gleamed on the ground where the *señorita* had mounted. A fine ivory comb studded with small jade stones. It must have fallen from her hair as she rode away. He picked it up, brushed away the dust and smiled in anticipation of returning it to her. He tried to think of a story, or a little joke, that would dimple her face when she returned. He took a deep breath of desert air and said her name aloud.

"Fili."

David M. Jessup

A loud voice came from behind him, interrupting his reverie. "*Peón*, our horses."

He whirled around to see Ricardo opening the gate to the corral. Mariano thrust the comb behind his back. Had the patron's son overheard him say her name aloud? Seen him hide the comb? He held his breath. The comb bit into his hand.

The Don's son rooster-walked into the corral. Through the crown of his dark brown hair ran a red streak that drooped over the right side of his head like a cock's comb. His mouth twisted into the kind of smile that made Mariano want to hide under a rock.

Ricardo's two cousins sidled up behind, tailored riding pants tucked into shiny boots, quirts dangling from their belts, hands unscathed by work. One was short and thin, like Mariano. The other was husky, with bulging forearms, his fine felt hat held aloft by ears that stuck out like signposts. Red-top, Skinny and Big Ears. Nicknames spoken aloud only when Mariano talked to horses. Their arrival twisted his stomach into a knot.

Ricardo Castillo turned to watch the thin spiral of dust left by Fili's loping bay gelding. Then he pointed a manicured finger toward his sorrel stallion inside the barn.

"Mine," he said. "Those two, there and there, for my *muchachos*." He beckoned and the three moved over to wait against the corral fence.

Mariano thrust the comb into his pants pocket. He trotted to the stallion's stall, his feet stirring up dust and horse smells. The stallion winced as he swung the blanket and saddle into place, grazing the still-oozing spur wound. He slipped on the bridle, led the horse out to the corral fence and tied the reins to the top rail.

The second horse, a rangy paint gelding, resisted the bridle, raising and lowering his muzzle to avoid the cold iron. Mariano paused to warm the bit with his hands.

"Hurry!" Castillo said, his voice a knife edge. He pushed away from the fence, strode over and grabbed the paint's halter rope, jerked its head down and snubbed it to the corral rail. The horse's eyes rolled white. "The whore's daughter will get away."

There it was again. Mariano willed himself to stay calm, to stop his hands from shaking. The pinto finally took the bit, mouthing the intruding metal with a slobber of greenish foam.

The third horse made no trouble, and the three young men mounted up. They tested the stirrups, lifted their legs so Mariano could adjust the straps and check the cinches. They paid him no more attention than they would a fence post. Their eyes were fixed on the disappearing dust cloud. They dug their spurs into the horses' ribs and took off, sending their own powdery cloud into the pale blue sky. The dust blew back into Mariano's face.

Mariano rushed to saddle a fast buckskin mare. Instead of following the riders, he loped toward a trail that cut across the piñon-juniper flats to the shallow canyon's rim above Fili's pool. He reined in, tied the heaving mare to a squat pine and darted onto a rocky outcrop on the slope above the canyon's floor.

Peering between two boulders, he spotted Señorita Filomena sitting on a flat rock next to the pool about fifty paces below, her face upturned, her bare feet drying in the sun. She wiggled her toes, closed her eyes, and leaned back on her elbows. Beside her rested the cloth lunch bag. Prince, picketed a few paces away on a small streamside meadow, yanked on a tuft of bunch grass, pulled it up by the roots and started chewing. Suddenly the bay's jaw muscles paused, its ears jumped to alert, pointing downstream where the water left the pool and trickled down through stair-steps of stone into a thicket of willows.

At the sound of bodies pushing through bushes, the clink of spurs, Fili sat up, twisting around. From his perch, Mariano saw them before she did—Ricardo's red cock's comb, the tight-lipped smiles of his two cousins. They strode out of the willows and clambered up over the rocks to surround her.

Fili pushed to her feet, backed up a step, then caught herself, planted her fists on her hips and looked her half-brother in the eye.

She pointed her finger at him, shouted, "Leave me alone," and something else Mariano couldn't quite hear.

Castillo stepped forward, gave her a shove. She staggered back and teetered on the edge of the pool. One more push and she toppled in. She went under briefly, then gained her feet on the smooth rock bottom. The water came up to just above her waist.

She clambered out of the pool, water flying off her hair, fists swinging. One caught Ricardo on the shoulder. He tried to duck, slipped, fell.

"*Perra*! Daughter of a whore," he shouted.

She swung a foot at his head. He grabbed the hem of her skirt, throwing her off balance. Big Ears grabbed her shoulders from behind. She wrenched away, her blouse and *camisa* tore, her breasts quivered into view, pale, exposed. She shouted something more rage than words.

Mariano's fingers dug into the rocks until his nails bled. He wanted to yell, run down the slope, throw a rock—anything.

Castillo reached for her waistband and gave it such a vicious tug the buttons flew off. He yanked her skirt all the way down to her ankles and grabbed her flailing legs. Big Ears pulled her backward and she went down onto the hard surface. Castillo scrambled to his knees, leaned over her, slapped her face. She clawed at him, tried to kick him in the groin. They were on her now, all three of them, like coyotes diving in for a kill.

Mariano jumped to his feet, forced out a "Leave her be." His voice came out as an inaudible croak. He picked up a rock.

They tore away her blouse and camisa, unhooked the front of the undergarment that bound her torso, and cast it aside. She writhed naked in their hands as they wrestled her to the pool's edge. Her body twisted in mid-air before splashing down in a silvery spray. She sputtered up from the depths to a standing crouch, tried to cover herself with her hands, and searched for a way to escape.

Mariano scrambled down the slope, rock in hand, stomach in a knot. Fili's frantic eyes found his. She screamed, rage replaced by fear.

Those eyes! Haunted, pleading, terror-filled. Mariano's impulse to rescue her evaporated under that panicked gaze. Inside his head a voice screamed, *"Run! Get away!"* He turned and bolted. His calloused feet leapt across the rocks and carried him out of the canyon onto the flat where his horse was tied. Fear gave him wings. Shame gave him speed.

At his frantic approach, the buckskin mare pulled back on the halter rope. He managed to calm her, swing aboard and gallop back toward the barn. He shook his head to dispel the choking, baffling panic that had seized him when Fili's frightened eyes had found his. But dread continued to flicker through the dark folds of his brain, spurring him on, sapping his will.

Fili! He must find someone to help. But who?

Omar. He spotted the barn manager's hunched form by the

corral gate as the mare burst out of the sagebrush flats and raced toward the barn. Mariano pulled up in a haze of dust and flung himself out of the saddle.

"Help! The *Señorita*! They are…she is… You must go to her…."

Omar gripped Mariano's shoulders, steadying him long enough for his story to spill out.

"Did they see you?"

"I don't know…I think so, yes."

Omar's faded brown eyes bored into him, then shifted away toward the arroyo.

Mariano followed his gaze, stiffening at the sight of three riders galloping toward them out of the trees. He pushed away from Omar and leapt onto the winded mare.

"Help her. Tell the Don."

His throat burned. He wheeled the mare onto the road heading north. He rode for his life, his mind clotted with images of what might have happened to Fili, each made worse by not knowing. And by guilt, for leaving her. He looked back. The distance between him and his pursuers was slowly closing.

They caught him as he rode into Arroyo Hondo, his buckskin mare spent. Red-top thundered up beside him, jerked him out of the saddle and flung him on the ground. They leapt from their mounts to surround him. Mariano scrambled to his feet and tried to run, but Big Ears grabbed one arm, El Flaco the other.

Ricardo Castillo pulled on gloves, drew back his fist and slammed it into Mariano's face. The blows came fast, one after another, into his face, his gut, his groin. Just before he lost consciousness he heard a shout, in English, from somewhere behind him. The last thing he saw was Ricardo's fine glove spattered with blood.

Then blackness.

David M. Jessup

PART II

David M. Jessup

2

FREMONT
Fort St. Vrain, 1842

Fifteen years later, Mariano Medina stood inside an adobe room at Fort St. Vrain on the South Platte River, some three hundred miles north of Taos and half a lifetime away. He withered under the hard-eyed stare of Captain John Charles Fremont, who sat with his boots propped up on the crude wooden table that separated them. The boots of fine polished leather, gleamed at him. Medina—that's what people called him now—stood ramrod straight, trying, and failing, to meet the Captain's steady dark eyes.

"I hear you Mexicans are good with livestock." Fremont blinked as a bead of sweat dropped from his eagle-beak nose onto his well-trimmed black beard. He flicked it away in the manner of a man annoyed by small things.

I'm a Spaniard, not a Mexican, Medina wanted to say. He shuffled his feet and glanced toward the door that opened onto the plaza. In the west, the top of Long's Peak rose above the plain. He fought back a strong impulse to walk out the door and flee into the mountains.

His friend, Tim Goodale, broke the uncomfortable silence.

"Captain, Medina here is the best mule-skinner you'll ever find. I can vouch for him. Used to haul Taos liquor for Charlie Autobees all the way up from the Arkansas." Goodale stood off to Medina's side, smiling underneath a hairy overhang of mustache, revealing two broken, tobacco-stained teeth.

Charlie Autobees. Medina had first seen Charlie's thin face frowning down at him when he struggled back to consciousness after Ricardo Castillo's beating. Charlie had lifted his broken young body off the Arroyo Hondo road as easily as he might lift a sack of brittle bones and placed him atop a wagonload of tanned cowhides, woven blankets, silver conchos and skeins of sheep wool. He'd hauled him out of Mexico to El Pueblo, just over the Mexican border on the Arkansas River. Autobees had saved his life.

Goodale went on, one hand on his long rifle, the other cutting the air in short hatchet strokes to punctuate his words.

"I been with him some five years now, and he's never let me down. Best if you call him a Spaniard, though. Where he's from, down in Taos, Spaniard is more respectful. Mariano Medina is pure Spanish stock. He don't like being called a durn Mexican."

"Is that so." Fremont's head jerked eagle-like toward Goodale then back to Medina, eyes boring in from beneath dark brows. His lips parted into the kind of smile that an indulgent father might bestow on an unreasonable child. "Fine. Spaniard it is."

To Medina, Fremont's voice came across as a sneer. He wanted to shrink away, become invisible. Why did he feel cowed in front of this man? Something about those polished boots, maybe. He felt Goodale's restraining hand on his shoulder.

Goodale said, "Kit here can vouch for him, too." He nodded toward Kit Carson, who stood at Fremont's side.

Wrinkles fanned out from the corners of Carson's pale blue eyes when he glanced at Medina, a subtle signal of approval.

Carson turned to Fremont.

"He can handle mules and horses better than most," he said. "Good guide, too. He done some trapping with me a few years back."

Tension lifted from Medina's shoulders. He had trapped beaver with Carson on two occasions during the 1830s. Señor Kit was only a couple of years older than Medina's thirty winters and not much taller, but to Medina he seemed almost father-like. He had that air of confidence, of coolness in dicey situations, that Medina lacked. Qualities his own father lacked.

Fremont jerked his head back toward Medina. "That true?"

"Si, Señor." Medina returned his gaze to the floor.

"We'll have two wagons and five pack mules when we link up with the rest of my crew," Fremont continued. "Some are loaded with the latest surveying equipment. Sextants, barometers, telescopes...but you probably don't know about...well, it doesn't matter. The thing is, it's valuable stuff. *Muy caro*. You *sabe*?"

Medina felt Goodale's prompting elbow in his ribs. *"Si, Señor."*

"We use a two-mule team for the small wagon, four mules for the big one. What size teams have you driven?"

"Four, six, eight...everything."

Fremont frowned. "Speak up. Can't hear you."

"He's driven all-sized teams, plenty of them," Goodale said.

"Good." Fremont nodded, appearing satisfied. "Oh, and the horses. We'll have thirty, half to ride and half for replacements. You and the other Mexican will..." Fremont caught himself, winking at Goodale. "You and the other Spaniard. You'll be taking care of the string when we stop. Grass, water, a little grain. Go easy on the grain. Save it for when, you know, the grass gets thin."

Fremont went on about the fancy equipment he had in tow, how carefully it would need to be treated, and how the mules and horses would have to be cared for. He spoke as if to a child, or to a greenhorn fresh from the states, which fueled Medina's urge to walk out. Medina wasn't sure why he recoiled from this dandy so much, with his shiny boots, expensive tailored pants, and well-trimmed beard. Or maybe what he despised was his own feeling of servility the man seemed to provoke in him.

The Captain went on to explain that the President of the United States had commissioned the topographic expedition and was relying on him, John C. Fremont, to explore the land and its resources and write a report about the first part of the Oregon Trail which would pave the way for westward expansion, and how this year, 1842, would go down in history as the beginning of the country's manifest destiny.

There was no doubt that he expected to go down in history as well. Finally, he lifted his boots off the table and stood up.

By that time, Medina had stopped listening. Those boots... Shiny, with inch-high heels, pointed toes and high tops. They stirred a memory from his childhood.

He'd been only seven at the time, two years after his mother's death. He and his father were walking through the Taos plaza toward his Aunt Esperanza's house. Father was lecturing him about minding his manners, shaking his shoulder to make him pay attention, when they nearly ran into Don Diego Castillo, the owner of the biggest *hacienda* in the valley.

Don Diego had loomed over them like the feudal lord he was, the *patrón* whose whim could decide the fate of *peónes* like them. Castillo's quirt tapped slowly, languidly, against his shiny black boot, which reached nearly to his knee. His upper lip lifted, revealing fine white teeth under a thin, hawk-beak nose. Mariano shrank away from that smile, clutching at his father's frayed cotton trousers.

Don Diego lifted the quirt and flicked the hat off Father's head. The wide *sombrero* flopped to the ground like a gunshot grouse. Sweat pooled along the brim line on his father's forehead and trickled into his downcast eyes. He quickly bowed, then lowered himself to one knee in front of the Don. He pushed Mariano behind him.

Don Diego bent close, his face inches from Father's forehead.

Softly, almost like a caress, he said, "Please be so kind as to remove your hat the next time you pass by a Spaniard." He flashed another wolf smile and sauntered off tipping his hat to two passing ladies.

Father reached down, plucked his *sombrero* out of the dirt and cast a stricken eye at his son.

"Mariano, my son..." he began, reaching out. But Mariano stepped back, afraid, embarrassed. "Mariano, do not worry...we are Spaniards, too..." Mariano spun away from those pleading eyes and walked out of the plaza, ashamed.

Shortly after that encounter, Mariano's father became the Don's servant. Perhaps the Don remembered his father's quick bow, his unquestioning subservience, and approved of it. Or maybe it had been his father's light skin, which was why, he claimed, the Don liked having him be the greeter of guests. His father had always taken pride in the fact that they were pure Spanish, not Mexican or Indian like most of the other servants.

Medina tried to forget about his father, but memories like this one ambushed him now and then. He wondered if his father was still alive, if he still polished Don Diego's boots. Was Don Diego still alive? Or had his accursed red-topped son, Ricardo, taken over as patrón? And what of Fili? Even after fifteen years, that look of fear in her eyes sometimes popped into Medina's dreams like a striking snake, jolting him awake, sweating and panicky. Had Omar been able to rescue her? He felt a flush creep into his face and neck.

Fili had witnessed his weakness, his failure, his spineless scramble to run away. And that knowledge, more than his flight from the *hacienda* and his narrow escape from Castillo's gang, more than the beating he'd received from Ricardo Castillo, was what had driven him to seek a new life for himself whenever he'd shivered awake from one of those dreams.

In the north, where mountain men trapped beaver and roamed free, he had found a place where there were no *patrónes* with privileged children. A place where no one knew him. A place where he could start over and prove to himself that he was not a coward. Backward, whether in dreams or his job, was not where he wanted to go.

"That will be all."

Fremont's curt dismissal brought Medina back to the present. He bowed low at the waist and, eyes on Fremont's boots, backed out of the room into the packed-earth plaza of Fort St. Vrain. Waves of heat rose around him. Sweat pooled in his armpits.

Goodale caught up with him and grabbed his arm.

"You cussed little hoss! What the hell got into you? I had to talk for the both of us. We durn near lost this chance to get some coin."

Medina shook him off.

"Sorry. I…" He couldn't finish. He lacked words to explain his reaction. There was no reason to bow and scrape and act like he was still a *peón*. He was a grown man now, a survivor of thirty winters. It was as if his past life—his boyhood—had reached out like a hand from a dark cave and yanked him back into the shadows.

"He's too big for his britches, I'll admit," Goodale said, voice softening. "Eyes dart around like a durn rooster's. I feared you was going to fight him n'spoil our chances."

But fighting had been the farthest thing from Medina's mind.

"The mules. I go to them now, to have a look."

He left Goodale there in the middle of the plaza, shaking his grizzled head.

Medina hadn't wanted this job. Not that he wasn't good at it. He had a knack for training mules and horses, putting them in harness to haul freight. Charlie Autobees had taught him well during the ten years he hauled whiskey for the man. Had taught him English, too. Given him a tent and blanket. Made him feel part of El Pueblo, that rough little settlement of *Americano* traders and their Mexican women hunkered on the north bank of the Arkansas, out of reach of Mexican *hacienda* owners and their sons.

He once asked Charlie Autobees why he and his friends had bothered to rescue him from Ricardo Castillo.

"Didn't like the odds" was all Charlie'd said.

Medina glanced back at Goodale with a little nod of thanks. Another man he owed much to. Five years ago, Señor Tim had talked Charlie into letting him leave the freight hauling trade to join Goodale's band of fur trappers. He taught Medina the ways of the mountain men, introduced him to that far-roaming fraternity of people like Kit Carson, Jim Bridger, and Louis Vasquez, took him into the vast reaches of mountains to streams where beaver obsessively toiled to dam the flow of running water. With Goodale he had the easy comraderie of men who knew each other's quirks, who could depend on each other in a scrape. Their cobbled-together mix of Spanish and English was a language unto itself.

Medina loved his five years as a free trapper. But ever since the beaver trade had gone to the devil in 1840, the trappers he knew had to find other ways of making a living. Some, like Jim Bridger, were setting up trading posts along the path of the new migrants bound for Oregon. Others, like him and Goodale, had hired themselves out as guides. In this case, he'd settled for a muleskinner job, an *arriero*, a step backward.

Medina's pace slowed as he approached the pole fence corral at the far end of the adobe fort where Fremont's mules were kept. Some twenty of the flop-eared animals crowded into one partly shaded corner. They looked as hot and tired as he felt.

Goodale sidled up beside him.

"It's only short-term work. Fremont told me he'd be heading back to the states in September, soon as he gets to South Pass. Then you and me, we can go on up to Jim Bridger's new trading fort on Black's Fork, soon as we cross Green River."

"Why there?"

"We'll do some trading. Resupply ourselves with the money we plunder from Fremont, then head into the Uintas for some winter beavering."

Medina studied his friend's face. He looked serious.

Goodale nodded, reading his thoughts.

"The beaver trade'll come back. You'll see." It came out a little too forcefully.

Medina wished it were true, but he had doubts.

"Besides, my Jenny will be there, with some of her Shoshone kin." Goodale winked, setting one of his bushy brows in motion. He slapped Medina on the back and grinned. "Been a while since I had me a woman to warm my arse underneath the buffler robes."

Medina smiled at the memory of Goodale's woman, short, plump, always welcoming. He turned to Goodale.

"Let us go then, before she finds some other arse to warm."

Goodale laughed out loud, a hearty haw-haw-haw that Medina enjoyed provoking.

"Better not be yours."

No danger of that, Medina thought. He had known the pleasure of several Indian women whose lodges he shared during the past five winters. But he hadn't grown attached to any of them in a way that Goodale seemed attached to Jenny.

"Maybe you'll find yourself a purty woman to warm your robe at night, too," Goodale said.

"Maybe."

Medina shrugged and crawled through the corral rails. He shook his head to dispel the image of turquoise eyes and dimpled smile that crept unbidden into his mind's eye.

3

GHOST EYES

Medina felt the squint leave his eyes the moment they alighted on the woman. Slender, with narrow nose and high cheekbones, she was unlike any other Indian he had seen in five years of roaming the fur country. Her face stirred memories of his native Taos, of *señoritas* promenading the plaza, of dancing, of flashing smiles.

This woman didn't smile. She seemed not to notice them at all, despite being only ten paces away. She sat astride a gray gelding on the other side of the narrow creek where he and Goodale had pushed through the willows to water their horses. Her gaze angled down to where her gelding, nose nearly submerged, sucked water out of the creek. Her neck was unusually long; her slender frame angular, shoulders squared off under her shirt—so different from the curved roundness of women he had come to know in lodges where he'd wintered.

Two sorrel horses on lead ropes stepped forward to quench their thirst beside the gray. Magnificent animals, high in the shoulder, well-muscled. Medina took them in, but only fleetingly. His own mount, a big roan he named Don Justino, whinnied a greeting and waded a few steps farther into the gravel-bottomed stream until water flowed half way to its knees. Small clouds of silt rose around its hooves and drifted downstream in lazy swirls. Ahead, the gray gelding raised his head to look at them. Jewels of water backlit by the westering sun dripped from his mouth and plinked onto the water's smooth surface.

Finally, the woman looked up. No hint of surprise crossed her features, nor fear, nor any modest dropping of the eyes. Those eyes! Spectral gray, riveting. She stared straight at him—through him, it seemed. Seeing, but not really seeing. A ghost stare.

The hairs on Medina's neck rose. His Aunt Esperanza, were she alive, would call it *el mal ojo*, the evil eye. He didn't believe in such things but crossed himself, just the same.

An image of Señorita Fili's terrified eyes came to mind. Whatever it was that lurked in the pale eyes of the woman on the gray gelding was not fear, but some deep sorrow. Her ghost stare triggered something in Medina that came not from his ordeal with Fili, but from some deeper, shadowy place. He blinked it away.

The woman's horses raised their heads, thirst quenched. She turned away, and tugged the other two horses into line behind her. Unhurried, she moved away through the willows toward the Bridger camp which Medina figured was located just upstream.

He marveled at the ease with which she rode, the measured grace of it. *Ai, that woman knows horses. But why such a haunted stare?* He detected no curiosity in those eyes, which seemed beyond caring.

Beside him, Tim Goodale shifted in his saddle and breathed out a low whistle.

"Amigo, you best fetch your eyeballs back out of the creek less they become fish food."

Medina turned toward his grinning companion and crinkled his eyes back into a squint just as a mosquito stung his hand.

"Maybe you best close your big mouth before one of these mosquito people flies in," he suggested.

Goodale's smile widened beneath the hairy mustache.

Medina tilted his head as if to examine his friend's mouth.

"You are safe, Señor Tim. No little bug will risk going in that cave of death vapors."

At that, Goodale laughed out loud. "You're just testy 'cause I cotched you thinking impure thoughts." He tilted his chin toward the willows where the woman had been. "That one shines, sure enough. Strange eyes. Wonder who she is?"

Medina wondered, too, but not aloud. The woman was beautiful. Tawny skin, wide-set eyes. But what she stirred in him was more than desire. It was something elusive, flickering on the border between past and present—a kind of kinship, perhaps. The woman seemed overwhelmed by sadness. Why would he feel drawn to her?

He reined up, turned his horse away from the creek, and headed back to the trail that wound its way upstream. Small pools—mosquito nurseries—flanked the creek as it meandered in easy twists through the flat willow bottom into which the woman had disappeared. It was late in the season for the annoying bugs. Most likely there hadn't been a hard freeze yet.

Two months had passed since they signed on with Fremont. They had guided the Captain north from St. Vrain's Fort along the edge of the mountains to Fort Laramie on the North Platte. After linking up with another part of Fremont's group led by a queer little German named Preuss, they pressed west past Independence Rock, through the cleft at Devil's Gate, then up the Sweetwater to the flattened crest of South Pass. By mid-September, Fremont had called a halt to his expedition and turned back toward the States. Having no further use for the mountain men, he dismissed them with a small sack of dollar coins, fifty for Medina and one hundred for Goodale.

Medina had felt like a free man again, out from under the burden of Fremont's orders. He'd stashed his earnings in a pouch sewed to his belt and turned to face Goodale.

"We go now to Jim Bridger's new trade post?"

Goodale had grinned. "Yep, we'll go spend some of this plunder."

His friend's hair reminded Medina of windblown bunches of buffalo grass, but his buckskin shirt reeked of buffalo grease.

"I will ride in front, if you don't mind," Medina had said, suppressing a smile.

David M. Jessup

Six days later they had reached Black's Fork of the Green River. A mile or so short of Bridger's place, they stopped to water their horses in the shallow stream. The willows on the other side of the creek stirred. Something, or someone, approached. A soft horse whinny floated out of the bushes. Medina tensed, his hand automatically finding the stock of his Hawken Rifle. They pushed through the willows. That's where they encountered the woman with the ghost eyes.

Medina guessed she must be living in one of the tipis that clustered around posts like Bridger's. Indians, the dignified ones, would be there with robes and pelts to swap for guns, powder and ball, or, if enough was left over, for pots and beads that the women coveted. "Foofaraw," Goodale called it.

There would be other Indians as well, the *sin vergüenzas*, shameless thieves, dirty, scrabbling for handouts, falling down drunk. They would slit each other's throats or sell their sisters for a taste of the Taos Lightning that Medina used to haul to the Plains tribes along the Platte River and on to Fort Laramie. He grimaced at the thought of Indians enslaved by whiskey. Wished he'd never involved himself in the firewater trade.

There would be trappers, too, settling in for the winter with their squaws. Was the tall woman a mountain man's squaw?

"There's the fort," Goodale sang out from behind.

The roofline of Bridger's Fort, a flat dark shape with edges gilded by the sun's last rays, came into view above the willows. As they emerged into a meadow surrounded by trees, they saw it clearly: two flat log structures joined by a rough pole corral, on a low bluff above the stream. A shabby-looking affair, thrown together in a hurry. Hardly a "fort," in Medina's view.

He wondered if they would find work there. Although it was late in the season, maybe they could hire themselves out as guides to a passing wagon train headed for Oregon. Goodale would have to do the talking. Goodale knew how to pass himself off as a lead guide, while Medina posed as his faithful assistant who mainly tended the animals.

Goodale could talk his way into, or out of, almost any situation, but without Medina, he couldn't find his way out of a box canyon with a wagon road down the middle of it. That's why they made a good pair. Goodale would do the talking, Medina the finding.

It galled Medina to play the subservient role. But the *gringos* didn't have much truck with a Mexican, which is what they insisted on calling him. Among trappers he had gained respect, become part of their fraternity. But as a guide and muleskinner for outfits like Fremont's, he was dismissed. He was small, looking younger than his thirty years, with a face that was nearly hairless. He wished he had a more commanding presence, like Kit Carson.

One good thing was his gift for languages. Fluent in Spanish, adequate in French, with enough Ute, Navajo and Cheyenne to get along when combined with the universal sign language of the fur country. His English was getting better, allowing him to earn a living as a guide and teamster with those *Americano* caravans coming across the prairie. But he yearned for the day when he might become his own boss.

Medina and Goodale drew close to the trading post. Judging from the uneven daubs of mud chinking slung between ill-fitting logs, the cabins had been thrown together by men in a hurry. Outside the corral fence stood some twenty lodges, mostly Shoshone, glowing with firelight. Here and there a person could be seen moving about. In the twilight it was hard to tell whether they were white or Indian.

Goodale spotted Jenny's lodge with a red buffalo painted on the right side of the tipi opening.

"Thar she be! Made it here just fine, just like I told her." He urged his horse forward. "See you in the morning."

Medina pulled up, wondering if he would ever have a woman with a lodge to welcome him. As the darkness gathered, he selected a campsite in a small aspen grove, and set up his traveling lodge, a rude square of canvas folded over a rope tied between two aspen trees. He tossed his blanket and gear beneath it, then picketed Don Justino in a nearby patch of grass.

Other horses grazed among the lodges surrounding the trading post. His eyes searched for a gray and two sorrels until it became impossible to see.

4

THE RITUAL

Medina fell asleep quickly enough, only to be awakened by a recurring nightmare: a copper-colored hand holding a bone-handled knife dripping with blood. The blood flowing—gushing!—covering the knife, the hand, rising to engulf him, choking him. Then a voice in his head screamed, *"Run! Get away!"*

He lurched upright, covered in sweat, gasping. Looking out of the tent, he peered into the night sky, rubbed the rough canvas between his fingers, saw his horse picketed, and collected himself. The nightmare had occurred less frequently as he grew older, its power diminishing over time. Yet now and then, like some wolf skulking in the trees, it lunged into his slumber and raised havoc. He lay back, tried to sleep. His mind roamed. Thoughts of his father, hazy glimpses of his long-dead mother.... At last, God knew at what hour, he managed to drift off.

A shaft of rising sun, lancing its way through the tent opening, struck Medina's face. He muttered, rolled out of his blanket and crawled from under his canvas shelter. He stood, stretched, looked around. Nothing moved. Jenny Goodale's lodge poked above the willows. No smoke wafted from its top. *Still asleep.* No doubt Señor Tim had a better night than he did.

Medina scrubbed a mint leaf over his teeth, chewed it awhile and spat. Goodale teased him about this, but Medina liked the cleansing taste it left in his mouth. He walked a few paces to a small stream, one of several that braided through the willow flats, and cupped icy water onto his face. Later he would look for a place to bathe, another habit that arched the eyebrows of the mountain men.

The morning chill drove him back for his blanket. He wrapped it around his shoulders, mouthed a morning prayer and crossed himself. Frost wouldn't be long in coming. He scooped a fire pit into the soil, gathered sticks and kindled a small blaze with flint and steel. He tossed a handful of raw coffee beans into his roasting pan. From the nearby aspens his horse, Don Justino, snorted and waggled his nose.

Medina bowed in mock servitude. "Well pardon me, *jéfe*, for wanting coffee before you have eaten." The big roan nickered and pawed the ground.

Medina smiled. For five years the horse had been with him. In addition to having the endurance of a mule, Don Justino was smart. Medina had trained him to sidestep, bow on one leg, and move along in a smooth trot that ate up the miles without vexing Medina's legs and back. Fast, too. Medina had won several racing wagers with him. He'd trained the horse to feign a slight limp before bets were taken, an illusion which had separated more than one greenhorn from his money pouch.

Medina scooped a handful of grain out of his saddlebag. Don Justino arched his neck.

"Proud, just like your namesake." Don Justino Melgar, an elegant dancer at Taos *fandangos*, had come to mind when Medina named his horse.

Medina stroked Don Justino's glossy neck. When the grain was gone, he picketed the horse in a new patch of grass. Don Justino moved with a grace that Medina never tired of watching.

How would it look, he wondered, if the woman at the creek rode this horse? He conjured her image. The woman's ghost eyes stared back at him. He wondered what secrets might be hiding behind those eyes.

He brushed a few clinging oat grains from his palm and finished roasting his coffee. The hot liquid warmed him. He cast off his blanket and retrieved his Hawken rifle from beside his bed. Old Lady Hawken spends more nights with me than any woman, he mused. Its wood stock was rubbed and polished with oil, its brass patch box dulled with a file to avoid sunlight reflections that might reveal his location to unfriendly eyes. The gun might as well be made of gold for all it had cost him. The model was new to the frontier; it announced its owner as no ordinary muleskinner.

He rested the weapon in the crook of his arm and set off upstream. The water twisted through the willows in countless meanders on its way east to the Green River. Some of its watery coils doubled back on themselves so far that only a few feet of bank separated them. In places, the spring surge had cut off loops from the main channel, like amputated sections of a lizard's tail.

Ahead on the left he spotted a low ledge slanting down into the stream. Water snaked around the end of the ledge and splashed a couple of feet down into the streambed below. Above the ledge, water backed up into a pool deep enough for a bath.

He slipped off his moccasins, stripped, and draped his deerskin pants and shirt over willow branches next to the stream. From his possibles bag he drew out a chunk of yucca root harvested the day before. Soapweed, Americans called it. He broke it up and pounded it into a pulp with a rock, then wet and squeezed it until it began to foam. With a sharp intake of breath, he stepped into the pool, lowered himself into the chilly water and began to scrub. After rinsing, he lay down on the riverbank to dry.

The grass on the bank was still brilliant green, an emerald set in a ring of faded upslope vegetation. Evaporation raised bumps on his skin. He glanced at his wiry frame, flat belly, and stringy muscles, wishing he saw more bulk there. Still, his body was better than when he was a weak and skinny boy.

The sun warmed him. What a luxury, he thought, after two months packing mules and enduring orders from a trail boss who knew nothing about the animals, or the people, under his charge. He stretched, took in the clean smell of his skin, the freshness of the air, the sound of water swirling past the rock ledge, the *tsee-tsee-ti-ti-wee* of yellow warblers flitting through the willow branches.

And suddenly, something else. From below the ledge came the faint sound of footfalls swishing through the grass then crunching softly in the gravel. Medina rolled onto his hands and knees. After a brief silence he heard clicking sounds, stone on stone. Another pause, then what sounded like wood hitting against metal, and finally, a voice singing low-pitched words in some Indian tongue, vowels that flowed like water—*Salish, maybe*—sad and slow.

He peered over the rock ledge. Ten paces below on the opposite bank he saw the woman with the ghost eyes. She knelt on a gravel bar that elbowed into one of the stream's many loops. Before her stood a small stack of river stones holding a foot-high wooden cross. Dangling from its horizontal bar was a smaller silver cross on a chain. The woman's body swayed in time with her song. One braid hung loose, swinging like a pendulum; the other lay along her back. Eyes closed, she fingered a rosary, the beads clicking in time with her keening. Teardrops left dark spots on the leather of her shirt. Her voice rose, her swaying increased.

Just when it seemed she might topple over, she stopped swaying and pulled her right sleeve to her shoulder, tucking the buckskin fringe under her chin to hold it in place. A horizontal welt scarred the otherwise perfect skin of her upper arm. With her left hand she drew out a black object from the pouch attached to her waist. She raised it to her upper arm and pressed it into her flesh just below the scar. An obsidian blade. She lowered the black stone and watched as a grin of blood widened on her arm, pooled at one end and dripped onto a stone beside her. She scooped up some river sand with her fingers and rubbed it into the wound.

Lowering her sleeve, she turned back to the makeshift altar, crossed herself and began praying. Medina recognized the Lord's Prayer in French and mouthed an "amen" with her. She pulled the cross out of the pile of stones and set off upstream. In a few paces she would round the bend and step over the rock ledge where Medina crouched, naked.

Diós! Medina ducked down and scrambled to where his

buckskins hung on the willow bushes. He snatched up his shirt, wrapped it around his waist, tied its sleeves in a hurried knot behind his back, turned, and found himself staring into the woman's strange, gray eyes.

5

FIRST MEETING

Other than a slight arching of her eyebrows, the woman's face gave no hint of surprise or fear. Medina felt his face flush. For a long moment they stared at each other across the stream.

Then he pointed to the pool and blurted "bath," in Spanish, then "wash," in French, then signed the word for "bathing."

She looked at the pool, then at him, and nodded once. With her hands she replied, "The men go upstream, there, past that big pine tree." Her slender finger pointed the way. "This pool, for women."

Her hands moved with the effortless grace of a swallow in flight. She gave no hint she knew he had witnessed her strange ritual, although she must have suspected. The despair that had clouded her face only minutes before had lifted, replaced by matter-of-fact blankness.

Up close, her face was even more beautiful than Medina realized. Even the tear stains were strangely compelling. Her gray eyes, wide and grave, held him without making real contact.

He asked her pardon and told her he would leave as soon as he could dress.

Then he added, speaking in Spanish as well as signing, "I arrived here only last evening. You saw me at the stream farther down, yes? When you watered your horses." He pointed at himself. "Mariano." She gave a slow nod. He pointed at her, questioning.

"Takánsy," she said aloud.

He repeated the word as best he could. *Tah-káhn-see.*

She started to go around the rocky ledge and pass him by.

"Wait," he said, then signed, "I have interest in your horses. Sometimes I buy, trade horses."

She paused. "The horses belong to my husband, Papín." She said his name aloud, accenting the last syllable with a nasal "a," like the word pan. He recognized the name: a French fur trading family from St. Louis.

Once again she started to leave.

He held up his palm. "Wait. That gray horse, very fast, yes? A race horse?"

Her lips tightened. "Yes, race horse." Stepping forward, she strode around the rock ledge and headed upstream, the wooden cross clutched under her arm.

Medina stared after her. Was that a look of pain that twisted her face when he mentioned a race horse? He hastily pulled on his clothes, started to follow her, then paused.

"Don't be loco," he muttered aloud. The strange ritual, the scar on her arm, the hint of trouble—bad medicine. Not to mention she had a husband. Leave her be. Yet the impulse to see her again welled within him.

6

WANDERING FORT BRIDGER

The following day Medina groomed Don Justino, checked his bridle and saddle for repairs, then rode upstream to hunt for game. He shot a two-point mule deer buck and slung its gutted body over Don Justino's back. He gave most of the meat to Jenny, save for two strips of back meat. Maybe he would give those to the woman with the ghost eyes. He wondered what Takánsy's lodge was like. Rich? Poor? Who shared it? *Tah-káhn-see* . He rolled her name silently on his tongue. *Get her out of your mind.* He gave the venison strips to Jenny.

After returning to his lodge, he cleaned and oiled his Hawken, checked to see if the gunpowder in his buffalo horn was dry, and counted the lead rifle balls in his pouch. He heated three squares of char cloth inside a tin box to flammable blackness and tested one of them with a shower of sparks struck from his flint and steel, blowing on the cloth edge until it glowed. He finished a new pair of moccasins with a sheath in the top to hold his dagger, and used the excess sinew to sew up a tear in his leather pants.

Make work. It failed to quell the restlessness that drew his eyes toward the surrounding forest of cone-shaped tipis. He rose and walked into the camp, as if he were out for a casual, late afternoon stroll.

In the sun's slanting rays, the so-called fort of Jim Bridger and Louis Vasquez looked even punier to Medina than when he'd first seen it. The logs of the two buildings might not survive the winter, and one section of the connecting corral was missing a top rail. To the south, the sun gilded the edges of the Uinta peaks, already covered in snow. *Ute country.* He shivered and set out along the bank of Black's Fork, which headwatered in the Unitas before braiding its way through Bridger's camp and turning east on its way to the Green River.

Between the fort and the stream rose some twenty lodges, their pointed cones poking above the willows growing in the flood plain. Most of them belonged to the squaws of mountain men, he guessed, some there to trade, some to spend the winter.

He passed two Shoshone women scraping a buffalo hide stretched out in the sun. Backbreaking work, to be followed by rubbing with brains. When finished, the supple robes would sell for a pretty price, more than beaver plews. It paid to have an Indian wife. More than one. He nodded toward them as he passed by. They stared at him with black, questioning eyes.

At the next lodge sat three Indian men, Bannocks from the look of them, and three mountain men, squatting in a circle. Medina recognized Uncle Jack Robinson, Pegleg Smith, and Hungry John. Pegleg patted a couple of blankets folded beside him, and gestured toward a copper pot and a basket with trade goods, probably powder and ball, needles and thread, maybe beads. The tallest Bannock man pointed to a stack of buffalo robes. Medina smiled. They had obviously finished the smoking and gift-giving rituals and were into the bargaining phase. Soon the Bannocks would return to their tribes for the winter. They weren't whiskey-addled beggars, he was pleased to note. They were dignified. They commanded respect.

Medina tried to slip past them, but Uncle Jack waved him down.

"Want to join us for venison at Jenny's lodge?" he asked.

Medina shrugged and looked at the lodges he had not yet visited.

"We're about done here," Uncle Jack insisted.

Medina nodded and waited until the trade was completed.

That evening after eating with Goodale, they smoked tobacco, drank whiskey, gambled and told lies long into the night. It usually felt good to be included in their banter, but tonight Medina mostly kept quiet. He sharpened his skinning knife with a honing stone, then took out the double-edged dagger hidden in the top of his right moccasin.

"You sure take care of them knives," said Pegleg.

"You wouldn't want to be in a knife fight with him," Goodale said.

Medina shrugged and sheathed his knives. Strange how in his nightmare, the knife in the copper hand aroused fear, while in his own hand, it meant safety. He rose, mumbled a goodbye and backed out of the tipi opening.

On the third morning, Medina set out early and circled the encampment. The horses picketed around each lodge would soon be led out to the sage flats to graze, watched by a handful of Indian and half-breed boys. On the far western edge he spotted Takánsey's gray gelding and two sorrel mares tethered beside an unusually tall tipi with several large bundles of trade goods stacked outside. Gray wisps rose above the smoke flaps, smelling faintly of cooking meat. He stepped behind a willow bush to watch, but approaching voices propelled him upstream, away from the encampment.

At the edge of a small clearing he squatted behind sagebrush to watch three Indian boys stalking through the grass. Naked from the waist up, painted with mud streaks in imitation of warriors, they held bows in one hand and fingered arrows in their quivers with the other. Breechcloths flapped against their bare legs. Owl feathers wobbled in their headbands. Medina smiled. Boys becoming men.

A fourth boy, smaller than the rest, maybe six winters old, hung back. A frayed rope cinched his rough cotton pants and threadbare calico shirt. His hair was chopped off like carelessly stacked hay.

The tallest boy motioned for the others to drop down and lie prone in the grass behind him. He inched forward, bow thrust out ahead, stringy muscles flexing in his skinny arms. The other two, one shorter, the other still pudgy with baby fat, mimicked his movements. Their quarry stood on the far side of the clearing, an oblong cotton bag stuffed with dried grass propped up with four sticks. Aspen twig antlers sprouted from its head.

The lead boy signaled a halt. They rose to a crouch, laid arrows across their bows, drew them back and let fly. The arrows thumped into their target. Tipped with deerskin bags, the arrows were hard, but not lethal. Medina's eyes widened at the boys' fluid, blurred swiftness. Those boys would be able warriors.

The boys leapt to their feet, whooping. The pudgy one, who had missed with his first arrow, scowled. They picked up their arrows and turned back toward the clearing. Stringy Arms pointed at the small boy and barked out a command.

The little one's eyes rounded into startled orbs. He flinched as one arrow bounced off his head and another thudded into his shoulder. He jumped up and ran, short legs pumping.

Before he could reach the clearing's edge, Stringy Arms clubbed him in the head with a hide-wrapped version of a war club, knocking him to the ground, counting *coup*. Pudgy huffed up and delivered a vicious kick in the boy's ribs. The small boy screamed and clutched his side. Stringy Arms straddled the child, grabbed a tuft of hair and drew a knife.

A blade in a copper-colored hand...*Run! Get away!*

Medina jumped up, pulse racing.

"*Diós mio, no!*" he heard himself shout. Three pairs of eyes widened as he bounded into their midst. He swatted Stringy Arms in the chest, sending him staggering. The other two jumped back, crouching before him. Their silent, dark eyes stared, unblinking.

"*Salvajes! Pendejos!* Get the hell out of here!" His voice hoarse, he reached for his tomahawk with shaking hands.

The boys backed away, eyes wide, until they reached the edge of the clearing and disappeared into the sagebrush.

Medina knelt beside the child, who was now sitting up, rubbing his side, gasping. Tears channeled rivulets through the dust on his cheeks.

Medina fought to bring his own breathing under control. What had come over him? Why had he exploded into the middle of this rough boys' game as if lives were at stake, when all they were doing was pretending?

"You are hurt?"

The boy answered in Spanish. "*Estoy bién.*"

Medina studied the child more closely. His chopped off hair was not shiny black like the Indians, his eyebrows fuller. His forearms sprouted a fuzz of fine hair.

"You are from Mexico!"

The boy nodded.

"Where is your mother?"

The boy shrugged.

"How did you come to be here?"

"Utes."

"Kidnapped you? From your home?"

Another nod.

"But those boys...Shoshone, yes?"

"Yes."

"Bought you from the Utes? A slave boy?"

"Yes."

Medina shook his head. Such kidnappings were common where he grew up. Utes, Navajos, sometimes Comanches, would raid small hamlets and big *haciendas*, killing men, stealing livestock, and carrying off women and children for the slave trade. In retaliation, Mexicans organized militias to attack Indian villages and capture their own slaves. There had been two slave children in Don Diego's *casa grande*, one of whom Medina had befriended, a boy they called Negrito. Negrito's job included emptying and cleaning Don Diego's chamber pot. From that sorry lad, Medina had picked up rudiments of the Ute tongue.

"Your mamá. She is alive?"

Medina read the answer in the child's stricken eyes. He brushed dirt off the boy's cheek.

"Your hair. They chop it off?"

Another nod.

"A scalping game," Medina said, as much to himself as to the boy.

The child pulled away and struggled to his feet. He brushed himself off, wiped his runny nose with the back of his hand.

"Your name?"

"Pedro. I have to go. Don't tell anyone." The boy turned and walked away.

Medina rose and took a deep breath. A slave child with no mother. Tormented by bullies. He'd had his own encounters with bullies.

7

BULLIES

He was seven years old, playing with his little friend Chepe Luis, in a pasture next to Don Diego's horse corral. Dust swirled around them as they scuffled in the sparse grass for possession of Chepe Luis's new leather-stitched ball. The ball was given to the small boy by Mariano's father after Chepe Luis's father was crippled in a wagon accident and lost his job as a wagon driver for the Don.

Mariano rolled the ball just out of reach of the younger boy's swinging foot. Chepe Luis broke into a joyous laugh. In this game, losing was an honor for his six-year-old friend, whose open adoration both pleased and worried Mariano. He liked being admired, enjoyed the silly games they played together, took guilty satisfaction in the way he could get Chepe Luis to do almost anything he asked, like putting a horned toad into Señora Wilamena's cooking pot. Beneath the fun lurked a nagging anxiety that as the older of the two, he was responsible for his friend's safety.

Chepe Luis finally connected, kicking the ball into a lazy wobbling roll. Giggling, he ran after it. Twenty paces away he stopped, his smile fading as the ball neared the edge of the pasture and came to rest against the upturned sole of Ricardo Castillo's boot.

Medina hadn't seen the patron's son approach. Yet there he was with two of his swaggering friends, older boys with hands jammed into pockets, faces agleam with malice. Castillo brushed his hair back, red streak flopping.

Castillo rolled the ball with his toe, lofted it into the air, bounced it on his knee, then kicked it to his heavy-set friend, who rolled it toward the third member of the gang, a short, thin boy with close-set eyes. They passed it back and forth, moving closer to Chepe Luis, eventually surrounding him. Suddenly, Castillo drilled the ball straight at the small boy. It caught him on the back of the shoulder with such force that Chepe Luis staggered and fell on all fours. He looked up at Medina with pleading eyes.

"Get out of the pasture, you're in our way," Castillo said. His friends laughed.

"My ball..." Chepe Luis' voice barely rose above a squeak.

"Your ball? I don't see your ball." Castillo shaded his eyes with his hand, pretending to look around. "You muchachos *see this little goat's ball?"*

The ball rolled in a tantalizing triangle around Chepe Luis.

"Maybe the Spaniard over there has your ball." The word "Spaniard" came out as a sarcastic drawl.

Mariano couldn't move. Sweat dripped under his arms. His palms turned cold.

Castillo fired another shot at the boy. The ball ricocheted off his chest. Chepe Luis snatched it out of the air and ran toward Mariano.

Laughing, Castillo loped up and snaked out a foot that brought the small boy down. The ball rolled free and came to rest in front of Mariano. Castillo strutted up.

"Whose ball is this?" he demanded, his hawk nose inches from Mariano's forehead.

Mariano looked down and shrugged.

"I said, whose ball is this?"

"His," Mariano whispered.

"Wrong answer! Whose ball is this?" With a toss of his red hair, Castillo pushed Mariano in the chest.

"Whose ball is this? Whose ball is this?" The others chanted. Another shove, harder this time.

"Yours," Mariano finally said, his voice a whisper. He felt his chin tremble.

"Your little friend can't hear you. Louder."

"It's yours, IT'S YOURS."

"That's better." Castillo's voice changed to a soothing purr. He put an arm around Mariano's shoulder and turned him to face Chepe Luis. The younger boy's dirt-caked face was streaked by tears.

Anger seized Mariano. Bewilderingly, it was directed at Chepe Luis.

"Stop looking at me," he shouted. He ran to the boy, cuffed him on the ear. "Stop blubbering. Get home, go. GO."

Chepe Luis scrambled away and hobbled out of the pasture. Mariano couldn't meet his backward glances.

Castillo clapped a hand on Mariano's shoulder, flashed a smile.

"Oye, we need a fourth. Want to play?"

Mariano swallowed and nodded.

Castillo chose him for a teammate. Mariano scored several points for take-aways.

At the end of the game, Castillo said. "Oye, caballero, you belong with us."

Mariano, hating himself, nodded his head, knowing that he could never be part of them, that back in casa grande, as the valet's son, he would always have to tip his hat in their presence.

8

SLAP IN THE FACE

Standing there in the clearing at Bridger's Fort where the Indian boys had played their rough game, Medina tried to come up with a better ending to his memory. He could have stood up to Ricardo Castillo, shoved him back, grabbed the ball and run. But the real ending stayed with him. *Face it, I was afraid of getting beaten up, kicked, humiliated. I was a coward.* He kicked at a broken stick of sagebrush. *Stupid to remember such things.*

He glanced up. The sun was well past its zenith. Time to return to his tent, maybe ride Don Justino for an hour before joining Goodale and Jenny for supper and talk. He headed back through the willows toward the tall lodge with the gray gelding and two sorrels. From within growled a man's voice, rising to a shout.

He edged closer, screened by bushes.

Some twenty paces away, Takánsy stepped out of her lodge followed by a tall man dressed in buckskins, his gray-brown beard merging with the fur hat pulled over his ears, his face flushed. The man grabbed her arm, spun her around.

"For why you not race? You dishonor me!" His arms waved like windblown branches.

Takánsy's reply was too quiet to be heard. She appeared calm, standing straight as a post, dark braids cascading down the front of her buckskin dress. She turned slightly toward Medina, and once again he was struck by her beauty. But her gray eyes had that blank look he remembered from their first encounter at the creek.

"For you, the horse runs like the wind. Not for me," the man said, gesturing toward the gray gelding, which stared at him with pointed ears.

At Takánsy's softly spoken reply, the man shouted, "A stupid reason! Vow? Stupid!" He slapped her across the face.

Her head recoiled but her expression didn't change.

Another slap, harder this time. The horse jerked back. Medina winced. *Help her!* But he remained rooted in place. A memory of Señorita Filomena flashed through his mind.

The man turned away and stepped through the lodge opening into the tipi. Takánsy didn't move. Her eyes remained blank, almost indifferent. She touched her reddening cheek, then walked to the gray gelding and stroked his neck. The horse nosed her waist for a moment, then turned its head and pointed its ears at Medina. The woman followed the gelding's gaze, catching sight of Medina hiding behind the willow bush. Unlike Fili, no look of alarm appeared on her face, no plea for help. She simply took him in with wide, gray eyes.

Medina backed away and hurried toward his traveling lodge.

Later that afternoon, Medina walked to Jenny's lodge to find Goodale. He paused in front of the red buffalo painted next to the tipi opening, took a deep breath and cleared his throat.

"Mariano, that you? Get yourself in here."

Goodale sat against a willow backrest in his customary place at the rear of the lodge. Furs hung from the lodge poles to his left—wolf, badger, river otter—pots and cooking irons on the right. Sparse pickings, Medina thought. Jenny would be demanding better goods now that Goodale had some plunder. She was not one to accept low rank among the other women encamped there.

Goodale unfolded his long legs and raised a knobby hand in salute, flashing a gap-toothed smile.

"Just in time for some of Jenny's tea."

Jenny squatted beside a tiny cookfire in the center of the lodge. Short and plump, with an assertive jut to her jaw, she lifted a battered brass pot from the coals, poured tea into a tin cup and thrust it at Medina. He caught the steamy aroma: pine needle tea. He smiled a thank you and took a cautious sip.

Goodale cast a longing look at a jug at the side of the lodge. Tea, Medina knew, wasn't his favorite drink.

Jenny said, "Soon we get Fort Laramie tea, special, from beyond ocean. White women all have it. For now you drink this." She brandished her teapot like a weapon, daring Goodale to refuse.

Shadows played across his friend's hairy face. He took a swallow and set the cup down. "Time to go beavering again, as soon as cold weather hits."

Medina shook his head. Goodale couldn't stop pining for the fur trapping life, always hoping the pelt price would go back up.

"Forget about beaver," he said.

Medina wished they could return to the fur path. He liked working for himself instead of a *jéfe*, despite freezing in cold beaver ponds and twice nearly losing his hair to scalping knives. But there was no money in it now. "You hear anyone needing guides?"

"Jenny says they's news of a wagon train due in the next day or so," Goodale said. "Oregon travelers. Damn late in the season. Be lucky to make it to Fort Hall, let alone to Oregon."

"Crow raiders attacked them," Jenny said. "Stole cows, horses and mules. Their wagons, they are pulling them into camp by hand."

Medina immediately saw the opportunity before them.

"You can get replacement animals?" he asked Goodale.

"Reckon so," Goodale said. "Jenny's people got some horses. Jack Robinson, too. Mules, no. None here in camp. But they's plenty of horses if the price is right."

"You get the horses, do the bargain, yes?" Medina said. "I do the training, to pull wagons."

"Well hell, that's a good idea, damn good." Goodale slapped his knee. "Should be good coin out of that, for both of us." He poured the tea from his tin cup and reached for the whiskey jug. "This calls for a little celebration." He grinned and poured, then thrust the jug at Medina.

Medina swallowed the last of his tea and splashed some whiskey into his cup. "*Gracias.*"

Goodale drained his whiskey in one gulp. Medina sipped his.

Jenny stirred a cast iron pot on the cookfire.

"Venison," she said. "I am tired of venison, hungry for buffalo. You will get some?"

"Why sure. First thing tomorrow. Won't we, Mariano?"

Medina shrugged. They hadn't seen any buffalo at Bridger's place. Jenny ladled stew onto tin plates and handed them to the two men. No salt, no sage, but the food tasted good to Medina.

They ate in silence for a while, then Medina turned to Goodale and asked, "That gray gelding by the creek yesterday. You remember?"

"What about him?"

"I find out he is owned by a trader, Papín." Medina turned to Jenny. "You know him?"

Before she could answer, Goodale guffawed, a big grin spreading over his face. "Horse, my ass. It ain't horseflesh that's got you so curious."

Jenny's button eyes flitted from one man to the other.

"He done fell in love with an Indian gal on a gray horse," Goodale explained. "Tall woman, strange light-colored eyes. Had a gray gelding and two sorrel mares when we come up the creek. Maybe Flathead."

Jenny nodded. "She comes less than a moon ago. Trailing behind that man, Papín."

Medina said, "But the horse. It is a real..."

Goodale's laugh cut him off. Pointing a greasy finger at Medina, he rolled his head back and grinned through his moustache.

"Fess up, old hoss."

Medina surrendered. "Yes, yes. Tell me about the woman, Miss Jenny."

Jenny settled down like a prairie chicken onto a nest, her brow furrowed.

"Her name, Takánsy, something close to that." Jenny said the name with a funny little catch in her throat, trying to mimic the sound she had heard. "Papín is French trader from Saint Louis. I see them coming. First thing I notice is she... well, she is different. She is having a big silver cross around her neck. She is touching black beads in her hand, like the Blackrobes do, and she is doing the Blackrobe touching sign like her hands have minds of their own, flying up to her shoulders and forehead every now and then, without her seeming to notice."

Jenny mimicked the crossing motion with her hand. She reached for a puff on Goodale's pipe, which Goodale obligingly handed over.

"That woman keeps to herself. The other women talk. Some say she is possessed by a bad spirit and was driven out by her people. Others say she was won by Papín in gambling game. Who knows?"

"Tah-khán-see." Medina repeated the name as best he could, with the accent on the second syllable. "You talk to her? What does she say?"

"I talk to her only one time, sign language. She say she and Papín are married. Nothing else."

Medina rose from his squat, set the plate aside and stretched his legs. After witnessing Takánsy's strange ritual at the stream and the slap in the face, he felt certain the woman had been hurt. And those eyes, so haunted, so strangely compelling. Had she been driven out of her own village? Had she come willingly with Papín?

"What about this Papín?"

"He is trader." Jenny said. She raised the teapot. "This, I get from him, cheap. Honest man I think. A little too big in his own eyes, maybe."

"He hit her," Medina said. "Just saw him."

Jenny gave him a sharp look. "Beat her? With stick?"

"Slap in the face. Twice."

"Well...he only slaps her? Less than most men."

"Nothing wrong with that," Goodale grinned and took a swipe at Jenny, who ducked, then brandished the teapot at him.

Medina tensed. It wasn't funny, the woman getting hit. Maybe that explained her sad eyes. His next words came out more sternly than he intended.

"That Papín, he shouted something about horse race, about her not riding the gray gelding."

Jenny gave him a look, then nodded.

"Yes, the men, they race horses a few days before you come. She will not ride. People hear Papín yelling at her, calling her a..." She paused, averted her gaze. "A lazy whore."

"I'll bet she ain't lazy," Goodale said, grinning at his wife.

A little of Medina's stew spilled onto the ground.

"She is not whore either," he said, heat rising in his neck.

Goodale's grin disappeared. He wiped his mouth with his arm, adding another layer of grease to his leather sleeve.

"Well hell, you seem to know so much, maybe you can tell us more about her."

Embarrassed, Medina looked away.

Jenny said, "Some say she is witch. Bad medicine. We stay clear of her."

"Best to steer clear," Goodale said.

Medina looked from one to the other. Good people trying to keep him out of trouble. They were probably right, but he couldn't shake a resolve growing stubbornly inside him. He set his plate aside and stood to leave.

"Bad medicine for one may be good medicine for another."

His companions looked at each other, then back at him. Medina felt himself grinning and hoped he didn't look as foolish as he felt.

9

THE DEAL

Morning flared through frost-rimed aspen leaves beside Medina's tent. On the north side of Black's Fork, a circle of covered wagon tops glowed in the morning sun, floating above the fading yellow leaves of the willows. The Oregon travelers had limped in to Bridger's Fort yesterday. Now smoke rose from their camp, carrying the aroma of bacon and beans.

Goodale had wasted no time in replacing their lost livestock. The travelers had paid dearly—twenty-five dollars a horse. Twenty horses were waiting in a makeshift corral on the flats above the trading post for Medina to start their training.

After picketing Don Justino on a new patch of grass, Medina made his way to the corral where Goodale had arranged a meeting with two leaders of the wagon train. He stepped up to the fence and leaned against the top rail. The horses milled in a circle on the far side. Dust rose in a yellow-brown cloud smelling of horse sweat and dung.

He coughed, waved the cloud away and stepped back. A sorrel mare, ears flattened and teeth bared, cleared a path to one side. Medina eyed the mare. She would be his first challenge. He fingered the horsehair *reata* in his hand, imagined tossing it around the mare's neck, snubbing her down.

Goodale approached, followed by a tall man with white hair and a shorter, yellow-haired man with slightly bowed legs.

"This here is Captain Fields," Goodale said.

The tall man gave a curt nod but didn't tip his broad-brimmed felt hat. Tailored pants, black shiny boots, white shirt under a buttoned vest—an Eastern gentleman. Another captain.

"And this here's Mr. Curfew."

The shorter man had a scar across his chin parallel to his mouth. He wore homespun wool trousers and a stained cotton shirt. Perched on his head was the strangest hat Medina had ever seen—a short, black stovepipe rimmed by a narrow brim with two wool ear flaps sewn into it. He stared at Medina through bloodshot blue eyes enfolded in red-rimmed lids. Medina thought pig eyes looked good by comparison.

"Gents, meet my friend Mariano Medina here, the one I been telling you about."

Neither Fields nor Curfew extended a hand. Scar-chin tongued the bulge under his lip and let fly a brown tobacco stream into the dirt three feet from Medina's foot. Close enough to be an insult. Medina felt a trickle of sweat forming in his armpits, despite the morning chill. He averted his eyes to avoid Curfew's hard stare.

"Captain Fields is trying to get his pilgrims to Oregon country," Goodale said, waving toward the wagons. "Crows stole their horses and mules a week back and durn near lifted their hair. They bought this bunch of horses here to pull their wagons, but they's pretty rank. Need some work." Goodale winked at Medina. "The horses, that is."

Medina knew all this, of course, since the idea of training the travelers' horses had been his. He'd asked Goodale to negotiate the deal.

The sight of Curfew gave him second thoughts. Did he want to work for such a man? Curfew looked worse than the El Pueblo whiskey merchants who used to boss him around, cursing and calling him a dumb Mexican when anything went wrong, even when the fault lay with their own ignorance, their worn-out harnesses or their decrepit wagons. Most of them couldn't persuade a mule to eat, let alone perform the unnatural act of pulling a heavy wagon. To his own shame, Medina had put up with their insults, smiling and bowing like his father.

With Goodale and other free trappers you got respect. If you could shoot straight, work hard and stay cool, you had a place in the trappers' band. But the trapping days were gone. And here he was again, hiring out to an ugly man who nearly hit his feet with a gob of tobacco spit.

"How long?" Captain Field asked. "To get them ready, I mean?"

"About a month," Goodale said.

"A whole damn month? Shit!" Fields raised his hands to his hips, dark eyebrows knit in a frown. "Winter's going to catch us." He had the look of a man used to commanding other men, if not the weather.

"Shit," Curfew said. The short man kicked at a clump of buffalo grass and nearly lost his balance. His face turned pink. He cast a suspicious eye at Medina.

Medina looked away. Only a month, he told himself.

"These horses'll get you to Fort Hall," Goodale said, his tone soothing. "There you can probably get yourselves some more mules."

"The bastard that sold us the first ten said they were already broke," Fields said.

"The lyin' bastard," Curfew said. His hands clenched into fists, hammers on long arms.

"They is broke, after a fashion," Goodale said. "But they's Indian-broke, for buffler running and such. A few's probably pulled a travois a time or two. They'll pull your wagons just fine when Mariano here gets through with them."

The two men scowled at Medina. He forced a smile at Goodale.

"He don't look like much," Fields said, tilting his head toward Medina. "How do we know he'll do the job?"

"Like I told you, he's the best there is," Goodale said. "Besides, this here's beaver country. Folks ain't used to training horses for wagon work. He's the only one you got."

"Don't worry, Cap'n," Curfew said. "I'll make sure the little Mex works his ass off." His grin caused his scar to stretch into an ugly red line, like a second mouth.

Goodale put up a restraining hand and offered his most disarming laugh. "I'd be careful if I was you. He's liable to up his price to ten dollars a horse."

"Shit," Fields said.

"Shit," Curfew seconded.

Medina turned and walked away, slapping his *reata* against his leg. Acid roiled his stomach. Best get away. He thrust his chin out, raised his head, tried to look dignified. But the familiar clutch in his throat remained.

10

HORSE MAGIC

Medina jerked the *reata* and the horse toppled over in a billow of dust. This one was proving as difficult as the sorrel mare he'd subdued the day before. Wiping the sweat from his forehead, he stepped forward to give the rope some slack. The horse, a rangy buckskin with well-muscled hindquarters, struggled to its feet, panting. It lurched forward, head snubbed to its right hind foot by a short length of rope. It could walk, but the moment it tried to buck off the saddle he'd cinched to its back, it would fall on its side. Most horses learned not to buck after a few falls. This one was testing Medina's patience.

Nearly a week had gone by and he only had three trained horses to show for it. The September moon had passed. The bright October sun beat down, already past its zenith. He adjusted his hat, thankful for the wide brim's shade. This job was supposed to take a month. Twenty horses in thirty days. Not a lot of time, especially when you had horses like this one, not even green broke, let alone steady enough to pull a wagon. This buckskin, like the sorrel mare, would probably take three days.

A figure suddenly appeared on the other side of the rope fence he'd set up for his makeshift training corral. Takánsy. He hadn't seen her approach. Her gray eyes, intense, sought his. No vacant stare this time. He snapped his mouth shut when he realized it was hanging open.

She stepped closer, braids hanging like glossy black ropes on either side of a silver cross pendant. Frowning, face resolute, her hands flew into action.

"That horse," she said in sign language, "very afraid." "*Apeuré*," she added in French. "I work with him for a while?" It was not really a question.

Too surprised to say no, Medina nodded and stepped back.

Speaking low, soothing words in the Salish language she had used at the pool, the woman glided toward the quivering buckskin. She was all focused energy, a magnet drawing the fear out of the horse.

She reached out to stroke the animal's haunch, revealing a tawny forearm. Medina thought it was the most enchanting arm he'd ever seen.

With a low crooning sound, she unbuckled the cinch, lifted the saddle from the horse's back and set it off to the side. She returned to the horse and moved her hand down the gelding's hind leg. Squatting, she untied the *reata*, stood up, and backed away. After about ten paces, she turned to the side, looked away from the horse and stood still.

The horse, its heaving sides starting to calm, stared at the woman, ears pointing forward. It took a tentative step, then another and another. A neck stretch, a slow exhale of breath, and the horse's nose touched her shoulder, horse skin on buckskin.

Takánsy glanced sideways, walked forward ten paces, stopped and waited. The buckskin followed. After three such maneuvers, she murmured again and without looking directly at the horse, stroked its side, shoulders and neck. The horse tensed. She moved away, letting it approach her again. Then she repeated the stroking, each time reaching more and more of the horse's body. Eventually she moved behind the horse, lifted its black tail and patted its hindquarters.

That horse trusts her already.

After a pause, Takánsy moved to the side and placed her hands on the horse's back. Medina, standing on the opposite side, watched her face. She paid him no mind, as if he didn't exist. Her arms reached across the horse's back, and for a brief moment she hung there, suspended, lifting her feet from the ground. The horse sidestepped but didn't bolt. She resumed her stroking and crooning, alternating with more attempts to drape herself over the horse's back. Each time she hung on a little longer.

With a jump she pulled herself up and swung her leg over the animal's rump. Astride, she stroked the horse's neck. Instead of bucking, the horse just stood there, quivering a bit.

How is she doing this?

After sitting for a few moments, she slipped off and resumed stroking and patting. She mounted and dismounted a few more times, in no hurry, but making steady progress with the animal.

A shadow fell across Medina's face. He looked up, surprised to find the sun dipping behind one of the tall pines on the western side of the clearing. Takánsy's time with the horse had spanned a single afternoon. Yet the buckskin responded as if it had known her for weeks, no longer the wild-eyed creature he had started with that morning.

Medina recalled his work in Don Diego's stables, his tutoring by Omar, the Don's herd manager. He'd learned much from the old Turk, enough to earn a living in El Pueblo after he escaped from Taos. He had a good reputation as a trainer, a reputation embellished by Goodale. He might have broken this horse in two, maybe three days using Omar's methods. But to have a horse trust you, want to do what you ask, in a single afternoon? It was magic.

Takánsy led the buckskin toward him, hand on its neck, and stopped about five paces away. He liked the way the fringe on her sleeve brushed against the horse's buckskin hide. She slipped the *reata* over the horse's neck and handed it to him.

"Not afraid now," she signed.

Medina felt like applauding. He stepped back and made a short bow. She nodded, a slight tip of her head that sent a loose strand of hair across her eye, and turned to go.

Medina felt giddy.

"Takánsy." He spoke her name and moved to her side so she could see him sign. "I have many horses to train. You will help me?" He smiled. "Tomorrow, you will come here, yes?"

All he got was an undecided stare.

He pointed to the crucifix around her neck. "Catholic?" he said aloud. He made the sign of the cross.

She nodded.

"I am Catholic, too," he said, pointing at his chest then folding his hands as if in prayer.

She crossed herself.

He tried again. "You come here tomorrow and help me train horses? We make good Catholics out of them."

The corners of her mouth lifted slightly. A smile at his feeble joke?

She nodded, turned and walked to the edge of the clearing, steady strides, grace in motion, braids swinging in rhythm with the fringe on her skirt. Like the horse, he wanted to follow.

She stopped next to a fat ponderosa. A man stepped into view. Papin. The French trader smiled at her and extended his hand, palm up. She took it, paused, exchanged some words, then moved away with him through the trees, hand in hand. Just before they disappeared, the man stopped, turned to face Medina, swept his fur hat from his head and bowed low. His head, completely bald, bobbed up and down a few times as he walked backward.

"Papín," Medina said aloud.

11

TAKÁNSY'S LODGE

Medina stared after them. Holding hands! No sign of tension, as if the slap in the face had never happened. He was more troubled by the thought of her being beaten than she seemed to be. He'd imagined Papín as the source of her sadness. Now he wasn't so sure.

Cold air licked in from the east, whining through the corral ropes, a nagging prairie gust that put grit in his teeth and left him feeling edgy. He looped a *reata* coil into his hand and glanced around. Frost-bleached, the grass and willows were pale as bones, as if Takánsy's leaving had sucked the color out of the landscape. He hadn't felt so giddy about a woman since he had fantasized about Señorita Fili back in Taos.

"You foolish goat," he said aloud. *Stop thinking about her.* She's married, a Catholic, devout. Not the kind to break her marriage vows even if she were inclined to leave Papín.

He shrugged, turned his back to the wind and led the buckskin horse to where the rest of the herd was grazing. He had work to do. A month's worth, then it would be time to move on. No sense stirring up trouble.

He headed back to his lodge, moccasins whispering through the dead grass. Her sadness tugged at him. Those eyes. The image of Takánsy being hit by a cruel Papín returned in force. He was beginning to think of her as his woman. *Would I fight Papín for her?* He'd seen women change hands that way at rendezvous. Medina shook his head. In confrontations, his first impulse was to run away, as he had at Fili's pool.

What about a game of chance? Not likely with Papín, who according to Jenny was a savvy trader, not a reckless gambler. Contests of skill? Medina could probably win a knife-throwing contest, or a shooting match with his Hawken rifle. But as challenger, he would have to defer to Papín's choice—wrestling, perhaps a footrace. In those activities Medina's shortness would be a disadvantage. He settled on a shooting contest, imagined himself winning, imagined Papín handing the woman over, saw in his mind's eye her smile as he took her hand.

But what if Takánsy wouldn't go with him? She didn't seem to be afraid of her husband. She walked away with him holding hands. Why would she do that if Papín beat her? There was so much he didn't understand.

He exhaled a foggy breath into the gathering dark. Cooking fires glowed on either side of the path as he entered the encampment. He caught the scent of woodsmoke. Jenny's lodge, close at hand, glowed with cheer, laughter, warmth. His own small tent was dark as a cave. He stopped, bent to enter, then with sudden resolve, turned and set out for Takánsy's lodge.

He made his way around the edge of the camp and paused next to where the gray gelding and the two sorrels were picketed. The gray pricked up its ears and snorted. He stepped past the bundles of trade goods, wrapped up for the night, and stood outside the tipi entry. Throaty male laughter floated out. It sounded like a happy lodge, Medina thought gloomily.

The laughter stopped. His legs had no doubt been seen. He said, "Mariano Medina here. With your permission, may I enter?"

"*Bienvenue,*" came the reply, strong and confident, still hinting of laughter.

Medina ducked inside. A riot of valuables hung from lodge poles and lay in piles around the perimeter. A half-dozen trade guns. Three bolts of calico cloth. A small box of Green River knives. A keg of powder. Sacks. A wood box. Metal cans. Dark brown bottles with cork stoppers.

The owner of this wealth sat in the usual place of honor at the rear of the tipi, leaning against a willow backrest, a broad smile on his face. His moustache and beard were well-trimmed, dark brown with a few gray hairs showing. His hairless head bobbed a greeting. With a wave, Papín invited Medina forward, indicating with a theatrical flourish a spot on the buffalo robe next to him.

Takánsy knelt in front of the cookfire, unbraided hair spilling over her shoulders in lustrous waves, eyes fixed on the sizzling carcass of a cottontail rabbit. Its meaty aroma, spiced with herbs, set Medina's mouth watering. He circled to the left and sat down in the spot offered him.

"Coffee?" Papín asked.

At Medina's "*oui*," the woman rose and poured him a cup from a gray speckled pot of a kind Medina had never seen. He nodded his thanks.

"You speak French," the trader said. "And my wife, you have already met, no? She tells me about you training horses for those Oregon travelers. Her name is Takánsy in Salish"—his voice mangled the clicking sound—"but to say it is difficult, so I call her Marie." His laughter was infectious. "You understand?"

Medina nodded again. "The French, it is hard for me, but the English better," he said.

Papín switched to English. "You come from Mexico, I am guessing, no? Tell me, what brings you here to this new outpost of civilization?"

Medina told him of the Fremont expedition, his fur trapping life, his travels with Tim Goodale and other mountain men. He didn't speak about the whiskey trade.

"Good men, all of them," Papín said. "You are welcome here." A gust of wind flapped at the lodge opening. "This wind…it gets to a man after a while. Sure enough, those Oregon travelers are going to learn about wind, no?" Without waiting for an answer, he continued, "Very late to be moving on to Oregon, don't you think? Maybe it cannot be helped, though, with their loss of mules, cattle and horses to the Crow. Luckily, I am here to re-supply them." Papín laughed and slapped his chest. His large hands were free of grime.

"They are to winter at Fort Hall," Medina said.

"Sure enough. And when spring comes they will need flour, coffee, cloth, ball and powder. And cows." Papín took a sip of coffee and smiled. "Who do you think will be there with those things? Louis Papín, at your service." He leaned forward and made another sweeping gesture with his arm and hand.

Medina smiled, suspecting he would see a lot more of that particular gesture if he lingered long with Papín.

"And where do you think Papín will get cows?" The trader leaned closer, voice lowered. "The Crow. The Crow, *mon ami*! My friends in that tribe tell me they just happen to have about thirty of the beasts, acquired a short time ago from some prairie travelers, and those they don't butcher they would be pleased to trade for some of this."

This time Papín's hand swept in a grand circle.

"Of course, we will have to fatten up those cows before we deliver them to Fort Hall, no?" Laughter shook his lean body. He set his cup down.

Takánsy refilled it, kneeling before Papín and sweeping back the sleeve on her pouring arm to keep it out of the way. She looked at Medina, eyebrows raised. Medina held out his cup, mainly so he could watch her arm reach toward him. Smooth, tawny skin, long, supple fingers, well-defined muscles. Too thin to be considered pretty by most men. She sat down beside Papín.

The Frenchman drew his fingers through her glossy black hair. She didn't pull away.

"Beautiful, no? She only lets her hair down inside her lodge," Papín said. "When I ask her, that is. It reminds me of when we first met."

Medina didn't know what to say.

"It was up on the Bitterroot, winter last. She was sitting in a big crowd around my trade goods. Easy to pick out, the only one without braids. I find out later she called me 'upside-down face.'" He laughed again, big frame shaking.

Despite himself, Medina smiled.

At the sound of this nickname, Takánsy forced her husband's

head down so Medina could see it better. Completely bald. A slight upturn at the corners of her mouth was the closest thing to a smile he'd seen on her face. Whatever caused this woman's sadness didn't appear to be maltreatment from Papín.

Papín gently pushed her hand away.

"These Oregon travelers, what an opportunity, no? Monsieur Bridger says—not just him, but Vasquez and the others, too—they say next year will be big. Maybe ten times more of them. We must be ready, no?" Papín grabbed a beaver pelt and waved it at Medina. "The fur trade, she is finished. Poof! But the traveler trade, aahhh, my friend, that is the way to get rich. Especially if…well, you see how bumbling this Field bunch is. They leave with enough goods to fill a castle, then their wagons break, their livestock gets weak or gets stolen. But you know all this. You have been working with their replacement horses, no?"

Medina started to respond, but Papín kept talking.

"To train is fine—you get six, maybe eight dollars a horse. But my friend, you should sell them the horse as well. Think of it! You trade some powder and ball and geegaws to get a herd, or better, you find some wild horses and train them yourself. A hundred people in this wagon group alone. Imagine two thousand." Papín rocked forward, winked, and raised his hands in the air, spread wide. Then caught himself and settled against his backrest. "I am flapping my mouth too long, sure enough. But you haven't come here to listen to me. You have something to say, no?"

Medina swallowed hard and looked down. He'd come on impulse, putting aside his usual caution. His expectation of finding an abusive brute and a woman in distress were dashed. He had only the vaguest of plans. His words came out in disconnected little bursts.

"The training...the horses need...the horses are proving difficult, and well…. Time is short and…."

Papín cut in. "You need other horses, better ones?"

Medina drew in a deep breath, and plunged ahead.

"Señor Papín, I would like to hire your woman to help me train the horses."

12

PAPÍN

Papín's face went blank, as unreadable as his bald head. He pulled a twist of tobacco out of his possibles bag, tore off some shreds, stuffed them into a pipe and tapped them in with a long, yellow-stained finger.

Medina leaned in, muscles wound tight. Easy, he told himself. He took a deep breath and leaned against his backrest. Peripherally, he was aware of Takánsy looking at him. Was that interest in her eyes? He forced his gaze to remain on Papín.

The trader was still tapping tobacco into his pipe bowl, an ivory colored hawk's head.

At last he said, "For why you ask?"

"I pay her, of course," Medina said, then rushed ahead in a mixture of English and French, "I am a good trainer, and normally I do it myself. But the time, you see. Time is short and she...well, she worked with a horse today. You know, you saw her, and she is better with horses than anyone I have..."

"How much?" Papín cut in. He eyed Medina a moment, then fetched a stick from the fire and brought its lighted end to his pipe bowl. The tobacco flared, lighting his face. After the first puff, he offered a twist to Medina. The laugh wrinkles that fanned out of the corners of his eyes had disappeared.

Now it was Medina's turn to stall. He tore off a wad and tamped it into his own pipe. He would probably be willing to part with his entire pay, but thought it best to at least pretend to bargain, to avoid suspicion.

He lit the tobacco, took a puff, closed his eyes for a moment to take in the acrid taste and smell, then said, "Two dollars a horse, twenty horses. Forty dollars."

A smile spread across Papín's face, a well-honed charmer of a grin.

"But my friend Medina, she already brings in more than that here at the lodge. Look around. See? Here...and here." Papín pointed at two stacks of leather goods, shirts, mostly, plus some leggings and several beaded pouches. He dragged them closer to the firelight and handed a shirt to Medina. "Look at this beadwork. Have you seen anything, anywhere, to compare with this?"

Medina admitted he hadn't.

"This fetches two, maybe three horses, or eight pelts. In the short time we are together, a little more than a year, she has mastered the Crow and Snake patterns, in addition to her own people's, and she...you should see how the Crow chiefs' eyes grow big when they see a shirt like this." Papín's face morphed into an imitation of a vain warrior, mouth turned down, brows knotted to counteract the telltale delight in his widening eyes.

Despite himself, Medina smiled. Papín was not just bargaining. He was genuinely in awe of his wife's handiwork.

"Three dollars, then, and only a morning's work each day," Medina countered.

Papín eyed him, his face blank once again.

Was the offer too much? Had he tipped Papín off that he was willing to go unreasonably high?

"Five dollars," Papín said.

"But that's impossible! My own pay..." Medina stopped himself before revealing Goodale's bargain with Fields and Curfew.

Papín stroked his beard and looked at Takánsy, his dark brows arching into a silent question.

She rose and looked toward a dangle of wood spoons suspended from a lodge pole. Her expression gave no hint of her reaction. Did she fully understand what they were saying?

"You will do it?" Papín asked.

She shrugged. Her eyes had that faraway look, as if she cared not a bit whether she trained horses or not. She spoke a few words in her own language, then fetched a spoon and knelt beside the fire, loose hair curtaining her face.

Papín turned his palms up and looked at Medina with his charming grin. "Marie work with horses; we go four dollars, no?"

Medina swallowed, then nodded.

Papín grabbed his hand and pumped it. "This calls for food and drink. You will stay for dinner, no? We have plenty. Yes, and brandy. For you, my friend, the best." From behind him, Papín produced a brown bottle.

Medina needed a drink. He had just bargained away the better part of his future earnings for a chance to spend a few weeks with Papín's wife.

"*Salud*," he said. He tossed down a hefty gulp with a tip of his head. The brandy bit into his throat. He swiped his mouth with the back of his hand and passed the bottle back to Papín.

"*Salud*." Papín took a modest swig. "My friend, you have gotten yourself the finest horse woman I have ever seen. She and those animals..." Papín clasped his hands together in front of his chest. "They are like this. She has special powers. It sometimes makes the hair on my head stand up." Papín laughed at his own joke, then paused, his face falling. "It's too bad..." His voice trailed off.

"What?"

"It's too bad she refuses to run the races. Ahh, *mon Dieu*, if she would only do that for me, it would be a... Medina, I tell you something." Papín grasped Medina's arm and lowered his voice. "You persuade her to run the races, I will give you half your money back, no?"

"Why won't she race?"

"She doesn't say. I have asked, sure enough. My God, I have shouted, argued, cried...I even hit her once!" Papín paused. "I will never do that again, God help me. But she refuses. For why, I don't know. In everything else she obeys without question. For her father, she used to race horses. She was famous in her village. Her people made a song about her! Now she only rides to travel, or for work. I heard something about her once losing a race, something about a vow she took. Now, for me, she is no longer racing."

"Why does she..." Medina started to ask about her strange ritual with the obsidian blade, then thought better of it.

Takánsy handed a bowl to each of them, rabbit, braised in a stew of herbs and dried currants. It tasted delicious to Medina, more savory than the bland Indian food he was used to.

During the meal, Papín talked on and on about trading, the price of furs, his last trip to Fort Hall, opportunities along the Oregon Trail. His enthusiasm was infectious. Reluctantly, Medina decided that he rather liked Papín.

When the stew was gone, Medina stood to leave.

"We start tomorrow, then?"

"Yes," they both answered.

"At the corral, then, when the sun is rising over the trees." Medina stepped toward the lodge entry and put one foot through.

"One more thing." Papín's voice stopped him in mid-step. He turned to see the trader holding a rabbit liver on the point of his hunting knife.

"You touch her, and I'll eat your liver." Papín held his eye for a moment, then erupted into laughter that shook his lanky frame like an earthquake. "Good luck with the horses," he said, popping the liver into his mouth.

Medina gave him a weak smile, then walked out into the night.

"Mariano, you foolish goat," he said to the moon. It was as far out of reach as Takánsy.

13

THE SMILE

She sat cross-legged, facing him at the edge of the clearing next to the rope corral. The two horses they'd been training were picketed a few paces away in a shady patch of grass, sides sweating. The woman's own breath was cloudless in the still, noon air. The only sound was grass being cropped by horse teeth. The sun, a bright fire overhead, warmed his shoulders.

Papín had left the day before on a trading trip to Fort Hall. Medina leaned forward, breathed in a hint of her sage smell. His knees nearly touched hers, close enough to feel heat radiating off her body.

"Takánsy." He spoke her name carefully, trying to say it right.

"Takánsy." She pronounced the word slowly, twice. The tricky guttural click in the middle of the word flummoxed Medina, despite his gift for languages.

"Takánsy," he repeated.

She nodded at his effort. I am getting better, he thought.

Sign language and French sustained them at first, with Spanish and Salish increasing as they gradually learned each other's tongues. Medina never tired of listening to her Salish words, asking her to repeat phrases over and over until he could imitate them. She complied, not as eagerly as he wished, but enough so that he, in turn, could instruct her in Spanish and English.

They spoke of the training, about subtle changes in horse behavior as they adjusted to the unnatural act of pulling in harness as a team. Medina and Takánsy had also become a team. She would begin, helping horses accept the leadership of two-leggeds as safe, even agreeable. Then Medina would introduce the animals to leather straps and jingling harness metal, persuading them to pull increasingly heavy loads together.

Three weeks had passed since they started working together. Another week and the horses would be ready, a mixed blessing for Medina. Ridding himself of Curfew's annoying oversight would be a relief. But it hastened the day when he and Takánsy would have to part company.

Takánsy pinched some dried berries out of a pouch at her waist and lifted them to her lips. Medina watched her jaw muscles work, the swallowing motion of her slender throat. Shadows danced under her high cheekbones, highlighting the creases that bracketed the corners of her mouth. He forced his gaze away from her, toward the trees. Wouldn't it be a grand thing to see a smile on that somber face?

"You make magic with the horses. What is your secret?" he asked

"No secret," she said, brushing her hands in the desiccated grass. "Horse four-leggeds like doing what Takánsy asks because..." With each hand she grasped her opposite wrist and held them there, locked in place.

"Trust." Medina supplied the missing word.

"Yes, trust, and not afraid."

He caught himself staring at her face again and shifted his gaze to her clothing. Men's leggings and breechcloth covered by a short leather skirt of a kind he'd never seen.

"Your skirt," he said, pointing. "Your doing?"

"Make easy, the riding."

Medina liked the way her words came out in inverted phrases.

They finished eating. Takánsy's eyes shifted away, vacant, drifting into that far-away place where Medina couldn't follow. He wished he could make the ghost stare go away.

"You are sad?" he said.

Startled, she looked up. "Working with horses, not sad."

He waited for more, but nothing came.

"But just now, your eyes. Sad. Like at the creek." He pointed to her upper arm where she'd cut herself.

She swallowed, averted her eyes.

"What happened?"

"Takánsy leave the people."

"But why?"

"Takánsy go with Papín."

"I know that, but..." He searched for a new opening. "You race horses, yes? When you were with your people?"

She nodded.

"You don't race now. Why?"

She shrugged. "New life. No race." She plucked at a clump of grass.

"So sorry, I didn't mean to..."

She turned and met his gaze. "A vow. I make a vow to Jésu to race never. To thank him."

"To thank Jesus Christ?"

"Yes. For me, new life. For forget old life." She moved her head once to each side, as if to shake off an unpleasant memory. "Medina race?" she asked.

"Yes, sometimes I race. My horse Don Justino. He runs very fast. But only when I feed him before I drink my coffee in the morning." He laughed, back in comfortable territory.

"Maybe you race Papín horse," she said.

"Maybe...if the prize is big enough." He gave her what he intended as a meaningful look, but it didn't seem to register.

"Not race against Papín horse. Ride Papín horse. He is away now. Return soon. You race his gray gelding?"

She's trying to help her husband, Medina realized.

"Perhaps," he said. Then he risked a touch on her arm. "Will you take that chestnut mare for a run? Not race, just run a little, to see how fast she is. Part of her training."

She looked at him for a long moment, her face hard to read. Then she nodded, rose and approached the mare. A nuzzled greeting, an effortless leap onto the horse's bare back, and she guided the mare with her knees and hands, from the holding pen onto the sage flats beyond the corral.

Medina scrambled to saddle and bridle the other mount.

On the flat, Takánsy warmed up her horse, trotting a bit, then easing into a slow lope. The chestnut wove through sagebrush, changing leads at every turn without a break in stride.

A shining thing, their bonding. He caught up to her.

"To that pine." He pointed to a tree about a thousand paces away.

She nodded and loosed her braids, hair spilling like black gold onto her shoulders and back. Leaning low over the chestnut's neck, she murmured a few words, squeezed her legs, and the chestnut leaped ahead. Medina followed, heels pounding his horse's sides, stirrups holding him above his mount's rocking frame. How the woman rode bareback was a marvel.

Takánsy was already circling the pine by the time Medina drew near. His horse felt like a slow-moving ox compared to the chestnut. He hailed her with a wave, wheeled his mount before reaching the tree and galloped back toward the training corral. She soon caught and passed him. By the time he arrived, she had dismounted. Medina unsaddled his horse, released it into the holding pen, and walked with Takánsy back to their lunch spot.

"Fast," he said. "As I thought."

"Yes. She is like a horse I used to ride." Takánsy's face was flushed, animated. Gone was the ghost stare.

"What horse was that?"

"Shy Bird." Takánsy made the bird sign, thumbs locked together, hands spread to the side. "A black mare."

"Did you race her?"

"Yes. Shy Bird won many races for my father, Ironhand."

"Your best race. How was it?"

Her words flowed slowly at first, then came in a torrent of Spanish, English and Salish punctuated by hand signs.

She had outraced three challengers from some tribe—Medina

couldn't quite catch which one—in front of a crowd of cheering people who, at the celebration afterward, had made up a song about her. She sang the song for him, her voice low, accompanied by beats of her hand on her thigh.

He asked her to repeat the song three times. Then he jumped up and, in an exaggerated imitation of a warrior dance, repeated her song in a quavering voice. He was rewarded by a clasping of hands and a smile—the first he had ever seen on the woman's face. He stopped his antics, laughed out loud, raised his arms to the sky and let out a Spanish yip-yip-yip of victory. Horses looked up, startled.

Takánsy rose, smile fading like a cloud blotting out the sun. She drew a rosary from her waist pouch and fingered the black beads into clicking aliveness. The ghost stare returned.

"I going now." She hurried toward the edge of the clearing clutching the rosary as if it might try to escape.

Medina stared after her, stunned by her sudden change in mood. In the beam of that first smile, Medina's heart had leapt. Now it thudded dully against his ribs. He'd crossed into new territory with her today, then just as swiftly was forced to backtrack.

What had changed? Papín? He thought of the bald trader smacking his lips on rabbit liver speared on a knife point.

14

CURFEW

On the following day she arrived late, the sun already streaming above the thinning cottonwood leaves on the east side of the clearing. He searched for any hint of yesterday's smile. *Nothing.* She gave him a brief nod, her eyes sliding past his to focus on the horses. She picked out a light-colored palomino with two front socks and began her sideways approach, her spell-casting.

Medina willed her to look at him, but she was all business. He gave up and turned back to his own work. To a small wagon he harnessed two geldings, a black and a chestnut, to see if they would partner well. For the next few minutes he drove them around the small corral, then out on the rutted wagon track that ran along the stream toward the fort. The black was lazy, wouldn't pull his weight despite frequent flicks of Medina's whip. Not a good match. He turned back toward the corral, removed their harnesses and tied them to a post. He glanced at the sky. A little too early for lunch. He called for Takánsy anyway.

She came willingly enough. They sat in their usual spot in the dry grass next to the west edge of the corral. He drew out a stringy length of buffalo jerky, she a flat cake of seeds and berries.

He said, "That looks good."

She broke off a pinch and handed it to him.

"Those berries, where do you find them?"

She shrugged. "Along the creek. Farther up, last moon."

They chewed in silence for a while, then Medina said, "That chestnut mare you rode yesterday. Very fast. A shining thing to watch."

She stopped chewing and stared at the cake in her hand.

"Your smile. At the end. It was so...nice." He couldn't think of a better word.

No reply. No smile.

Medina felt his spirits fall.

A raspy voice sounded from the edge of the corral.

"These two ready yet?" Curfew stood there, long-armed and bow-legged, earflaps dangling from his strange black hat.

Medina rose and walked up to the rope fence.

"One day more," he said. He sensed Takánsy moving in behind him.

A drool of brown tobacco juice trickled down from Curfew's mouth, ran through the stubble of his beard and pooled above the scar on his chin. He spat and wiped his mouth with the back of his tattered sleeve.

"They say a big storm's coming. You got to finish this business so we can get our wagons moving."

Medina felt his body tense. This yellow-haired *cabrón* came every day, stood around for half an hour giving useless advice, and threatened to reduce Medina's pay if he didn't speed up the training.

"But *Señor*, only ten horses are left. I am sure...soon they will be ready. A few more days."

Medina hated his own halting speech, the way his voice thinned when speaking to this man. He looked at the scar to avoid Curfew's red-rimmed eyes and breathed through his mouth to avoid the man's reek.

A grin spread across Curfew's face like slow poison.

"You got the help of this purty Injun gal...should be done twice as fast. Or is she slowing you down? Maybe I'll take her into the bushes for a while so's you can get back to work."

He grabbed Takánsy's wrist, pulled her toward the ropes.

She pulled back at first, then her arm went slack. She let him draw her close, waited as he pushed the corral rope down. Her face was blank, eyes vacant. Curfew's gap-tooth smile turned into a laugh.

Medina felt as if roots had grown out of his feet into the ground. *Why is she not resisting? Why am I not stopping him?* But he knew why. The icy spine, the falling stomach. "Run, get away," the voice said. He watched, transfixed, as Takánsy hefted a leg, prepared to climb over the rope.

Then, without thinking, he lurched forward, pulled her back, lifted his knife from his belt and thrust it toward Curfew's leering face. He stopped short of a lethal stab, the knife point drawing a bead of blood from the end of Curfew's veined, bulbous nose.

Curfew jerked back. "You crazy sonofabitch." He let go of Takánsy and wiped his nose with a sleeve.

Medina lowered the knife and stepped back, hand shaking.

Takánsy turned toward him, eyes wide.

"Fuck a cactus. You cut my damn nose!" Curfew, his voice an outraged roar, lifted his leg to climb over the corral rope, then pulled back. Retreating a step, he clenched his fist. "You little bastard."

He glanced at Medina's knife and backed away two more steps. A strand of stringy blond hair fell over his brow. His eyes narrowed as his lips twitched into a smile.

"Enjoy her while she's still around." His voice oozed venom. He moved sideways toward the trees. Just before he disappeared from view, a ponderosa limb poked him in the shoulder.

"Fuck a cactus," he muttered. Turning, he slithered into the trees.

The knife fell from Medina's hand. Takánsy knelt to retrieve it and looked up at him, wide-eyed.

"Medina big angry."

"Yes." But anger was not what he felt. Hands still shaking, he thrust the knife into his belt.

"Why?"

"He has...no respect."

She touched his arm.

He pulled away, not wanting her to sense his fear. "And you. Why did you not resist?"

She shrugged. "Not important. It is in Jesu's hands." Once again, the ghost stare. "To Papín, we will not speak of this."

"No," he agreed. Nor to each other, it seemed.

She picked up her bag, stepped over the corral rope and walked out of the clearing into the trees.

He stared after her for a long moment, then busied himself harnessing and unharnessing horses, pairing different ones to find the best match, occupying his mind for the rest of the afternoon.

Later that evening, lying under the canvas fold of his traveling lodge, he thought about how easily he had switched from fear to anger, then back again. About what might result from his rash act.

He awoke early, threw off his blanket, jammed his feet into moccasins and pushed out through the canvas tent opening into the cold darkness of the aspen grove. Pulling aside his loincloth, he urinated into the bushes. The memory of Curfew's hairy hand on Takánsy's arm clung like bad breath. He chewed some mint, rinsed out his mouth and spat, then set out for Jenny's lodge. To make up for his early arrival, he took along an offering of venison.

Dawn glowed faintly above the horizon when he reached the tipi. He paced around the outside of the dark lodge for a while, hunching his shoulders against the cold. He cleared his throat. Stirrings sounded from within, a soft whump of a robe being thrown aside, a click of flint against steel.

Goodale poked his head out, squinted at Medina, then stepped out and stretched off sleep.

"Mariano, you cussed little hoss. Fields called me out yesterday. I durn near had to promise to carry him to Fort Hall on my back to make up for that fight you picked with Curfew." Goodale wasn't smiling, which meant things were serious. "Come on in. Jenny can use that meat."

Medina stooped through the opening. Jenny was blowing into

a nest of dry grass held in her palm. When it ignited, she shoved it under the sticks on the cookfire.

"Fields. What did he say?"

"Said you cut up his assistant."

Jenny gave Medina a quizzical look.

"It was only a tiny cut. His nose got in the way of my knife." Medina tried to smile, but it felt more like his face cracked.

"What the hell was he doing, sniffing at your waist?"

"No...but he has a big nose."

Goodale was not amused. "And you got a big problem: an overly sensitive nature. Fields claims his man can scarcely cross your path without you getting into a durn fight." Goodale's eyes hardened into little pebbles. "The woman. It was about her, wasn't it?"

Medina's face flushed. He tried to return his friend's stare.

"He's a *cabrón*."

"Dammit. Who'll it be next? Papín? One of these days I ain't going to be around to smooth things over." Goodale turned away. "Food will be ready when sun's full up. Come back then."

Later, as they squatted to eat, Goodale's mood softened.

"The sooner that bunch gets them horses out of here, the better off we'll be." He spooned some venison stew into his mouth and took a sip of black coffee. "Then maybe we can go catch us some beaver this winter. I heard they's plenty just south of here, up in the Unitas. Uncle Jack's hunters say they seen plenty of beaver lodges right here on Black's Fork, maybe twenty miles upstream. You game?"

"Might as well," Medina said. He was glad for the change in subject. "We use them for pillows if they don't sell."

"The trade'll come back. You'll see."

To Medina, Goodale looked a little like a lost boy.

After breakfast, as Medina rose to leave, Goodale said, "Something to keep in mind. Fields will be all right. He's annoyed, but he knows you're turning out some fine animals. I'd watch out for that damn scar-chin, though. He ain't the kind to let things be. They say he near kilt a man back in Ft. Laramie. Now he runs on about how he'll set you straight."

"I'll be ready," Medina said, with a confidence he didn't feel.

15

MISSING

Medina walked back to his shelter, grabbed his whip, rifle and *reata* and set out for the training corral. Takánsy would be waiting for him. He was anxious to see her after yesterday's encounter with Curfew. What was it the man had said? "Enjoy her while you can?" Or "while she's still around?" Something like that. Medina quickened his pace.

Ten more horses to go. She would already have a couple of them in the holding pen. She never seemed to have trouble catching them, even though they were allowed to range out beyond the pen into the surrounding sage flats, where two or three boys from the Oregon caravan kept night watch.

The corral was empty when he arrived, the frost on the grass undisturbed. *Strange.* He leaned his Hawken against a tree and settled down to wait. Juncos flitted along the ground, chirping and fighting over fallen seeds. A snarl of wind blew through the willows, chilling him as pale sunlight spilled onto the far edge of the clearing, filtered by rare haze.

Where was she? He rose from his squat and walked through the gate toward the holding pen. The frost on the path was undisturbed by footprints. The pen stood empty. He called out her name. No answer. Beyond the trees, the bushes demon-danced in the gusting wind. No horses in sight. No one from the wagon train either. Where could they be?

Turning, he retraced his route. Maybe Papín had kept her busy in her lodge for some reason. Then he remembered: Papín was still at Fort Hall. He picked up his pace.

Halfway to the encampment the path crossed a low sandstone outcrop some twenty paces wide. He hurried across, then stopped. There in the sandy path were two sets of footprints: his own, and underneath, some smaller moccasin prints, toes turned slightly inward.

He hadn't noticed her tracks on his way to the corral, but then, he hadn't been paying attention. She'd been there ahead of him, had stepped onto the rock but not continued past it. As if the wind had whisked her away. Had she turned and walked across the hard surface in a different direction? The stone slab stretched about fifty paces in both directions. He looked one way, then the other. Which way?

He chose the northern edge of the slab. Torn between the need for speed and the need for scrutiny of the adjacent ground, he moved in fits and starts through scattered clumps of skunk brush and an occasional stunted juniper growing from a crack in the rocks. A small scrap of torn cloth caught his eye. Gray with dark stains, it clung to a bush. Medina rubbed it between his fingers and lifted it to his nose. Tobacco juice. Curfew!

Heart pounding, Medina sprinted toward the camp, Hawken rifle swinging at his side. He caught a glimpse of Jenny's startled eyes as he ran past her lodge. Breathing hard, he reached Takánsy's lodge and ducked inside. The coals from her breakfast fire were barely warm.

An image of tobacco juice drool on Takánsy's arm spurred him toward the Oregon camp. Behind him, Goodale's shout vaguely registered through the pounding in his head. The Oregoners were bunched around a Conestoga wagon, some sitting, others standing.

Field's head was easy to spot above the circle of hats. Beside him, like a dog at heel, hovered Curfew. They turned as Medina pulled up to face the scar-chinned man.

"The Indian woman. Where is she?" Medina's tongue felt dry.

Curfew's mouth curled up in a humorless smile. He shot a stream of brown juice at Medina's feet.

"That purty Indian gal? She's still asleep. Spent the night with a real man, and she's done in." He laughed. The others seemed more nervous than amused.

"Where is she?" Medina scarcely recognized his own voice.

A few of the wagoners stepped back, leaving Medina and Curfew inside a semi-circle of onlookers.

"Where?" Medina repeated, louder. He leaned in, Curfew's scabbed nose mere inches away.

Curfew's smile vanished. He nodded at two men who stepped up to flank him, a bony red-haired youth with big, dangling hands and a squat but powerful-looking older man in red suspenders.

"Ain't no cause to yell," Curfew said, his own voice a low roar. "She ain't here. Now back off." He shoved his hairy paw into Medina's chest.

As if jolted awake from a dream, Medina suddenly realized what he faced. Three powerful men advanced toward him. He felt his stomach seize up, his throat fill with acid. Staggering back, he swiveled around seeking escape. Reflexively, he raised the Hawken.

"Look out!"

"The gun!"

"Back off..."

Shouts. Hands gripped his shoulders and yanked him back. Someone wrenched the rifle from his hands. Curfew's fist glanced off his jaw. Medina went down. A boot narrowly missed his head. Another caught his arm, numbing it. His mouth tasted grit. Hands and someone's knee pinned him to the ground. Boots milled around, surrounding him.

Through the forest of legs he caught a glimpse of Goodale running toward them. The mountain man pointed his rifle into the air and pulled the trigger.

The blast, followed by Goodale's shouted "Hold on," froze everyone in place. "Back off. Keep clear."

The knee lifted off Medina's back. Arms and hands jerked him to his feet. A few paces away, Curfew struggled against other restraining hands, his fists hairy hammers, his face twisted.

Two more mountain men rushed up beside Goodale. He gave Medina a piercing look.

"What's going on?"

Medina swabbed the dust from his mouth with his tongue.

"This man." He nodded toward Curfew. "He took her. Takánsy, Papín's woman." His voice quavered. He tried unsuccessfully to shrug off the hands that held him.

Goodale faced Curfew. "That right?"

His voice was quiet, but his eyes caused the scar-chinned man to look away. All eyes shifted toward Curfew.

"No, goddam it. No! I don't know what the hell he's talking about. Where he gets that shit." He wrenched free of his handlers, knocking his strange stovepipe hat to the ground. He picked it up by its earflaps and yanked it back onto his head. "Fuck a cactus! I been here the whole damn time."

Fields stepped forward.

"It's true. He hasn't left my side all morning. Been helping us repair that wagon over there." The wagon boss nodded toward the Conestoga. Its axel rested on a stump; a broken wheel leaned against its side.

Medina said, "Earlier. When it was still dark." He forced his muscles to relax, but his voice still had a shaky, high pitch. He spotted the Hawken lying on the ground two steps away.

"I was in my..." Curfew began.

Goodale cut him off. "Anyone see this man afore first light?"

A small woman, wisps of graying hair straying from under her bonnet, stepped forward.

"He was with me," she said. "Asleep. He didn't go nowhere." She spoke with a wince that deepened the furrows in her ravaged landscape of a face, "I was up most all night."

Goodale looked hard at Medina.

Medina scanned the wagons, the tents, the smoldering campfires for a sign, anything to prove Curfew wrong, but there was nothing. The verdict was in. He bowed his head.

"Very sorry. He threatened her, yesterday. I thought he...A

thousand pardons." The subservient tone of his own voice repelled him. He felt his shoulders sag. The grip of hands relaxed.

"Being sorry ain't good enough," Curfew said, his face a snarl. He stepped forward. "No fucking little Mexican is going to..."

Goodale intercepted him. "I'm sure Mr. Medina will make things right." His voice was soothing.

But Medina had no time for peacemaking. He jerked free, darted past the startled men on his left, scooped up his Hawken and ran back toward his tent. If not Curfew, then who? Or what? The possibilities flitted through his mind like black shadows.

16

PURSUIT

Medina tore through the wagoners' camp and raced toward his own. Out of the din rose Curfew's enraged squeal, "Git'em!" followed by Goodale's command, "Hold on, you eedjits. Just hold up there."

He stepped on a sharp rock but it scarcely registered as he sprinted past his tent toward Don Justino. The big roan pulled against his picket rope, snorting, side-stepping and rolling his eyes.

Medina slowed, tried to sound calm. "Get ready to run, *caballo*." He slipped a hackamore over the horse's nose, swung his saddle blanket and saddle into place and tightened the cinch with a single yank. Don Justino huffed his displeasure.

At least two hours had passed since Takánsy vanished. He dismissed the idea that she might have gone to the pool where he'd witnessed her cutting ritual, or that she forgot something and returned to her tipi, or stopped to talk or got sidetracked. No, something was wrong, something worse than abduction by Curfew. The strange silence of the horse pasture nagged at him. He would need to search the area on horseback. And if his intuition was right, he would need provisions.

Ducking into his tent, he grabbed a skin of water and slung it over his shoulder. He stuffed some jerky into his possibles bag, emptied a ration of oats and corn into a saddlebag and ran outside to tie it into place behind the cantle. He snatched up his Hawken and thrust it into its scabbard. He reached for his knife, only to realize it must have been lost in the scuffle with Curfew. Cursing, he ran back into his tent, dumped the contents of a *parfleche* onto the floor, grabbed a replacement blade and thrust it into his belt. Rushing back to Don Justino, he leapt aboard in one swift motion and reined onto the trail toward the training corral.

At the point where her footprints ended beside the sandstone outcrop, he reined to the right, eyes sweeping from side to side. He paused to look into a clump of junipers, found nothing, and continued his search along the edge of the rock to where it disappeared under the sage-covered landscape. There in the sandy soil he found her tracks. They pointed southeast toward the sage flats where the horses were pastured. As he rode, the distance between her prints lengthened. Running strides.

Why did she go this way? Had she seen something wrong? Had she heard the boys from the wagon train sounding an alarm? He fought the urge to rush ahead, remembering how much time he'd already wasted on Curfew. Her tracks wove through the sand and patches of frosty grass. Wind brushed through the tall sage. No sound of stamping hooves, no welcoming snorts. Unnaturally quiet. He pulled the Hawken from its scabbard.

Don Justino stopped suddenly, ears pointed toward a large sagebrush. Beneath it, a boot stuck out, toe pointing up. Medina circled the bush. The boot was attached to the sprawled body of a youth, no more than fifteen years old, his homespun wool shirt pinned to his chest by two arrows. His head was crowned in a bloody halo with a white dome of skull where his hair used to be.

Medina dismounted for a closer look. The fletching on the arrows indicated Utes. Ants clambered over the boy's head. Medina fought back an urge to heave. He crossed himself, imagining the other boys out there sprawled in gore. Imagining Takánsy's shining hair hanging from a Ute's belt.

He recalled stories of Ute savagery in Taos: decimated flocks, children sold as slaves, boys and men slaughtered. He prayed Takánsy had arrived after the Ute's murder of the guards. He dredged his memory for snatches of the Ute language he had learned from Negrito, the Ute slave boy in Don Diego's big house. He soon might have need of those words.

A scramble of moccasin prints surrounded the boy's body. Impossible to tell if any were hers. He led his horse in a widening spiral, casting for sign. Time was his enemy, tormenting him with visions of finding her too late. Finding her like the scalped guard. He fought against panic, to make sure he didn't overlook some clue.

A hundred paces from the corpse he found a churned patch of soil where many horses had been gathered, then driven away heading southeast. On one edge of the trampled area he spotted her moccasin prints, overlaying the horses' hoof marks.

A sign of hope. It meant she'd arrived there after the killing, after the roundup. But then where? Had she possibly gone after them on her own? Run back to fetch her gray gelding to chase them down? Crazy thought. No, there wouldn't have been time, and surely she would have alerted him.

He urged Don Justino into a circling lope around the flats. If she were lying among the sparse sagebrush, he would find her sooner by looking rather than tracking. And if she wasn't there? Taken captive? He gritted his teeth. He'd seen what happens to captives.

He continued his search and found two more scalped Oregon travelers. One was stripped naked, his bloody penis stuffed into his mouth. He'd seen enough. The raiders had to be hunted down, and quickly. He turned back toward the camp to get help, then pulled up. Surely Goodale would figure out what happened and follow him. Better to start now and save time. He reined Don Justino back to the captured herd's exit trail and set out on his own.

The prints continued southeast toward the labyrinth of shallow canyons that fringed the Green River just before it plunged into Flaming Gorge. Following the tracks was as easy as following a wagon road. He urged the big roan into a ground-eating trot.

He squinted at the sage flats stretching before him in a cold shimmer. It was now midmorning. The raiders had at least a two or three-hour head start. But with Don Justino's long stride, Medina reckoned he would close the gap by nightfall. Then what? He didn't know how many raiders there were, but judging from the jumble of tracks in places where the horses had spread out to water at a creek crossing, there might be a dozen. He would have to slow when he caught up with them, watch for sentries, creep closer, try to get a count of people and weapons, then backtrack to intercept Goodale and plan a rescue.

Good luck with that. More likely they would spot him first, treat him to some Ute torture. Copper hands holding knives. *Run, get away!* There was that voice in his head again.

With a soft curse, he urged Don Justino forward.

17

THE WOODPECKER

Around mid-afternoon the flats gave way to low ridges sprouting juniper and pine. After passing a divide, he dropped into a shallow draw that wound its way south and east toward Green River. He paused beside a spring. The raiders had stopped there too, judging from the trampled bank. They were making no attempt to hide their trail. Confident. Moving fast.

While Don Justino drank his fill, Medina bit off a piece of jerky, refilled his water bag and fed Don Justino some grain. He relieved himself on a sagebrush, mounted up and started off again. Recharged, the horse moved quickly down the draw as it deepened into a shallow canyon. Medina scanned the ridges on either side for raider sentries. Nothing. Too soon for them to stop for the night.

By the time shadows pushed their way into the creek bottom

he was nearing the Green. But before the big river came into view, the raiders' trail turned sharply to the southwest, heading upstream into a smaller tributary canyon. Medina stopped and scanned the slopes ahead.

Not much farther, he guessed. The raiders would be setting up camp for the night. Sentries would be posted to watch the back trail. If he followed along the canyon floor he would surely be discovered. The safest approach would be to ride back the way he'd come, cross over the divide between the two creeks, and come down on them from above. But it would take three, maybe four, hours.

The thought of what might happen to Takánsy forced a different strategy. The canyon walls were not steep, and along them ran several terraced ledges that looked passable. The middle terrace on the north-facing slope had some scraggly tree cover. Sneaking along it might be possible, but any sound would carry, and there was no way of knowing whether a sentry might be posted on that same ledge.

After peering at every conceivable hiding place for sentries, Medina dropped down to the grassy point of land where the two streams merged. He picketed his horse, and with rifle in hand, climbed the opposite side toward the middle terrace. When he reached it he stopped to breathe in the chill evening air. By morning there would be frost on the grass and ice crusting the edges of the slower creek runs. Behind him Don Justino tore off clumps of dry grass. Even Goodale will know how to find me after seeing my horse, he thought.

The ledge was about ten paces wide where he stood. Farther along it narrowed to a few feet; at other spots it widened to more than twenty. He set out at a trot, staying close to the rocky wall. On the wider stretches he was able to run, keeping well back from the edge out of view. At the narrow points he slowed to an armadillo crawl, peering down and ahead, scarcely breathing, searching for sentries he knew must be there. The light was fading, but his night vision was better than most. In the moonlight he might gain the advantage of spotting the raiders before they saw him.

The farther he advanced, the closer he came to the creek bottom as it sloped upward. A quarter mile farther and the ledge and creek would intersect. *Why haven't I seen a sentry by now?* Had he misjudged their intent? Would he be forced to retrace his steps, retrieve his horse, and resume pursuit after yet another delay?

A prickling sensation brought him to a sudden halt. It was nothing he had heard or seen, just a heightened awareness, like he sometimes got while hunting. He inched forward to peer over the edge of the rock. About fifty paces below, the creek twisted like a rattler, coiling first to one side, then the other. Two twists farther upstream, across from where the creek ran close to the cliffs, a shoulder of ground rose gently from the water up to a flat area bordered by an overhanging cliff about a hundred feet high. Along the cliff base fallen slabs of rock the size of wagons were scattered like dice on a gaming table. On the side of one of those boulders a faint glow flickered. A tiny campfire.

In another ten minutes he crawled to a point on the ledge directly across from the flames. A horse snorted, dangerously close. Below he saw the stolen animals grazing along the creek bank, but his attention quickly returned to the flickering orange of the fire.

Five figures squatted around it, their forms turning into silhouettes as darkness advanced. One reached out to twist a stake leaning over the coals. On it, a chunk of impaled meat sizzled and dripped. A long-barreled muzzle-loader leaned against the boulder in easy reach. It was the only gun Medina could see, but that didn't mean there weren't more. There was no shortage of bows and arrow-filled quivers among them.

Something stirred about ten paces down slope from the fire. A figure, legs spread, stood pissing against another boulder. He was too far away for his features to show, but Medina was able to make out the feathered outline of a Ute warrior in full raiding array. He was squat and heavyset, almost bear-like. Three feathers sloped back from his headband like a woodpecker's crest.

That would explain their direction of retreat, returning south through the rugged canyons leading up into the Uintas, the range of mountains that marked the northern limit of their territory. He recalled the old Ute chief Lechat, a relentless enemy of the Cheyenne and Arapaho who he had met at Fort St. Vrain. The man shaking drops from his *pene* did not appear old enough to be a chief, but he might be the leader of the raiding party.

Medina probed the surroundings. He scanned from left to right, starting at the top of the overhang then returning to a spot lower down, working his way back and forth in systematic strips of vision that took in everything. He saw no sentries. No prisoners. No Takánsy.

The moon rose above the eastern horizon, gradually dispelling the gathering gloom.

A clack of hoof on rock sounded from below, near the base of the steep ledge where he lay. His missing horses, mixed with the raiders' mounts, were grazing there, ravenous after their day-long journey. A Ute stood guard beside the creek bank, outlined in the moonlight reflecting off the water. From his slight build Medina judged him to be no more than fifteen or sixteen winters. Probably on his first raid. The youngster waved to Woodpecker standing upslope, who lifted a hand after he replaced his breechcloth. The chunky man turned and started up the slope toward the fire, feather crest bobbing.

The raiders had chosen a good campsite. From the grassy saddle they commanded excellent views upstream as well as downstream. No attack was possible from the cliff above, as their fire was tucked under its protective overhang. From his vantage point on the ledge, Medina might be able to shoot one of them, but the boulders would provide plenty of cover for a counterattack while he reloaded. There could only be one outcome—he would be killed. Or worse, captured. He glanced back along the ledge. Escape beckoned.

Voices. The braves around the fire bobbed their heads as Woodpecker rejoined their circle. He said something to them and got a laugh in response. The firelight revealed his dark skin, red paint streaks under his eyes, glints of yellow beads on his shirt, a yellow breechcloth. One of his head feathers was red.

Woodpecker walked to the far end of the circle beyond the rim of firelight. With his foot, he nudged a bundle on the ground. The bundle moved. He bent down and hauled up a figure. Medina nearly jumped from his hiding place. Takánsy.

18

CAPTIVE

Medina groaned. He hadn't seen her there behind the circle of Utes, lying prone and still. She didn't appear to be bound. Her hands and feet moved freely as her captor grabbed her hand and jerked her toward the fire. He fumbled at her side and pulled her right legging down. Her bare leg glowed softly in the firelight. An appreciative hoot rose from the circle.

A hint of nausea seeped into Medina's gut. He hoisted the Hawken and aimed at the feather-crested form. The figure wavered over the sight at the end of the barrel like an elusive ghost. Medina tried to steady the gun by wedging his elbow against a stone. *Think. Think!* A shot might hit Takánsy and, even if it didn't, killing her tormentor wouldn't save her—or him—from the others.

Feathers bobbing, the stocky Ute circled behind Takánsy

and cut the strap holding her other legging. More hoots as the soft buckskin telescoped down around her foot. Then he sliced through the leather thong that held her orange breechcloth. It fluttered to the ground like a wounded butterfly, leaving her clothed only in her shirt and short riding skirt. The circle of men erupted in cheers. Below him, the young brave at the river bend left the horses and ran up the slope for a better look.

Takánsy stood in front of the fire, legs slightly apart, arms at her side, head erect. Medina wiped a sleeve across his face to clear a sudden wetness in his eyes.

The Ute leader grabbed her elbow, jerked her away from the fire and propelled her down the hill. At the same boulder where he'd pissed, he forced her to the ground, pressed her shoulders back onto the grass, and with his back to Medina, forced her legs apart.

Medina watched, hands shaking, throat in a cold strangle, as the Ute pulled his breechcloth aside and rubbed at his crotch. Medina watched as the feathered form moved into position over Takánsy's prone figure. He watched as the Woodpecker knelt between her splayed thighs and lowered himself into position. He watched until a combination of helpless rage and abject fear welled up like a tidal wave, joined to his horror by something dark and shameful. A hot, swelling arousal in his groin pushed its way into his consciousness and perched there, unwanted, like a hungry vulture.

He bit his tongue hard. He imagined fear on her face, haunted eyes, a scream for help. A familiar voice in his own head screamed, *"Run! Get away!"* He leapt to his feet, backed away from the terrace edge, turned to flee, then jerked to a halt.

With a hoarse cry, he spun around and launched himself down the slope in a shower of pine needles and gravel toward the startled horses, shouting in Ute, "Greetings in Peace, Greetings in Peace. From Chief Lechat. Greetings in Peace."

19

PARLEY

Medina's shout bounced off the cliff and ricocheted among the boulders. He splashed through the creek and charged through the horses as they snorted, side-stepped and strained at their picket ropes. He yanked a cloth out of his possibles bag and jammed it into the bore of his rifle barrel. Thrust aloft and waving gray-white in the spreading moonlight, it signaled a request to parley, the universal flag of truce. Or so he hoped.

The raiders scrambled to their feet, grabbed bows, knives and tomahawks and fanned out into a line facing downslope. Woodpecker got up, adjusted his breechcloth, ran back to the campfire and jumped into the middle of the line. He snatched the rifle leaning against the boulder and pointed it at Medina's chest. Two other rifles materialized and were leveled at him.

Medina stopped, hoisted the cloth aloft and repeated, absurdly,

"Greetings in Peace, from Chief Lechat." Then in sign language, the motions exaggerated to bridge the distance between them, he signaled for permission to approach and talk.

Woodpecker signed for Medina to drop his rifle. As soon as it was lowered to the grass, the Ute leader barked out an order, and one of the youths ran to pick it up. He prodded Medina up the hill and handed the Hawken over to Woodpecker, who pulled the cloth out of the barrel and examined the rifle. Smiling, he handed the other rifle to the youth.

Glancing sideways, Medina saw Takánsy turn onto her hands and knees. *Run! Get away!* His silent shout had no effect. Instead of running to a horse, she crawled to the boulder and leaned against it. Medina forced himself to look away, locking eyes with the Ute leader and putting his hands to work.

"We smoke, talk trade?"

The Ute gave an abrupt shake of his head that set his feathers wagging. Up close, he looked to be about thirty winters old, with surprisingly soft features that contrasted with his snake-sharp eyes. His arms and torso were pudgy, his movements abrupt, as if to compensate for flabbiness.

"No smoke." He turned to two other raiders and fired off a staccato order punctuated with hand chops. The two nodded and ran off in opposite directions, one upstream and one down.

Making contact with the sentries, Medina supposed.

Woodpecker watched them go, then scanned the surrounding terrain with quick cocks of his head.

Medina positioned himself between the Ute and Takánsy.

In an impulse born of desperation, he said, "I have guns." He pointed to himself with exaggerated emphasis, to hold the leader's attention. "You have horses. We trade. Chief Lechat wants rifles to fight Cheyenne and Arapahoe."

A sneer slowly worked its way into the plump folds of Woodpecker's face.

"No one comes to trade at nightfall."

Medina's smile felt tight on his face. He could smell fear wafting up from his armpits. With a flurry of hand motions and halting Ute words he admitted that he was the trainer of the captured horses.

"You took those horses from Bridger's camp. I hurry to catch you, for trade. I need horses back, to save face. I pay plenty to get them back."

The Indian stared hard at him, black eyes glittering. Medina blathered on.

"Chief Lechat has many horses. He needs guns. You go back with horses, you have small celebration. You go back with guns, you have big celebration. You will be remembered in the songs of your people. All of you." Medina swept the circle of faces with his eyes. He got two nods of comprehension and, he hoped, approval.

Woodpecker's face did not change. "The guns,where are they?"

The question made Medina feel he might have bluffed his way across a threshold. But how to answer?

"The guns are close by—a short walk. But first, we smoke, we talk trade."

Without waiting for a response, he stepped between two braves and walked toward the campfire, now nearly out. His shoulders tightened, anticipating an arrow in his back. Instead, the raiders let him pass and followed him to the campfire. He took a deep breath.

As they hunkered down, the rising moon, nearly full, bathed the camp in its pallor. Faces around the fire glowed with the warm tones of the coals. Medina risked a glance downslope. Takánsy still sat against the rock. *Run*, he willed. *Run!* She didn't stir.

Squatting, Medina frantically searched for his next move. To stall, he pulled his pipe from his bag and began tapping in a shred of tobacco. He wished he had brought more to share.

Woodpecker pushed the pipe aside and signed, "No Smoke. How many guns? How much?"

This wasn't going to be a normal, drawn out trading session. Not surprising, considering how Medina had entered their camp.

Medina shrugged, made a show of putting his pipe away. He might drag out the bargaining for a while, but if they eventually agreed, he would be expected to produce some guns. He could gain time by pretending to be confused about where he had stashed the weapons, but at some point they would catch on. *Then what?* He might take his chances with a surprise knife attack using the blade hidden in the top of his moccasin. But if Takánsy wasn't going to try to escape, what use his sacrifice?

Sacrifice. Whatever had possessed him to get into this situation?

And what of Goodale and the mountain men? How many would there be, and how soon would they arrive, if they came at all? If they did, could they prevail in a firefight? Among these boulders, the raiders could hold off twenty men. And even if they couldn't, his own survival, and Takánsy's, was about as likely as ice in summer.

Woodpecker poked him in the arm, hard. The Ute's stone black eyes bored into him. Medina signed into existence five weapons in his imaginary inventory. More than enough to compensate for the horses, which, he pointed out, were trained for wagon pulling, not buffalo running, making them less valuable to Lechat's band.

All Medina got in reply was a grunt, an emphatic shake of the head and a hard stare. Just his luck to get a man of minimal expression when what he needed was someone talkative. Someone he could read.

Medina launched into another one-sided haggle, extolling the virtues of the weapons, detailing the honors that awaited the raiders for delivering them, and denigrating the quality of the horses. At the end he got another grunt and head shake. Exasperated, Medina added one more weapon to the bargain. That, too, was rejected.

Medina felt the noose tighten. He couldn't keep upping his offer without losing credibility. They would begin to wonder why these horses were so valuable to him.

He signed, "You want how many guns?"

Woodpecker looked at him for a long moment then raised both hands with fingers extended.

"Ten. One for each." He nodded around the circle. Each brave nodded back.

Now it was Medina's turn to shake his head no.

"Those horses are not worth ten guns," he signed. At least he now knew how many raiders there were: Seven here in camp, three sentries out there somewhere.

A slow movement beside the rock where Takánsy sat caused him to look in her direction. Woodpecker's eyes followed. With a quick nod the Ute leader sent a brave with unusually wide shoulders to fetch the captive. She came willingly, complying with an order to kneel beside the smoldering fire. An ugly bruise darkened her right cheek. A three-pronged scratch, dark in the moonlight, disfigured her leg from just below the knee to the ankle. Her shirt barely covered her

David M. Jessup

hips. Below that, the short riding skirt extended her leg protection only to mid-thigh.

Her stare passed through them all, including Medina. Without looking down she retrieved her breechcloth and tied the severed belt around her waist.

"Woman-who-dresses-like-man," one raider signed to some appreciative chuckles. Medina allowed his own laugh to mingle with the others. Then he leaned close to the feathered head of the leader.

"That woman," he signed, "is cursed by the spirit of the dead."

Woodpecker's expression became that of a man learning something which confirmed what he already suspected.

Medina pressed on. "You have seen her eyes. If you take her or kill her she will bring bad luck. Leave her here. Take the rifles. I will trade you seven, no more. A better bargain you will never have." Medina folded his arms, trying to appear resolute.

Woodpecker cocked his head at the woman, then at Medina, then at the circle of raiders. Brow furrowed, he nodded his assent.

"Agreed," he signaled.

"Agreed," Medina replied.

Papín would be proud of him, except for the fact that he had no way to fulfill the bargain he'd just reached.

20

EXCHANGE

The Ute leader brushed off his leggings and heaved himself up from his squat, knees popping, gun leveled.

"We get guns now."

Medina got up slowly, mind jumping from one risky tactic to another.

He said, "First, we take the horses and the woman down the canyon. We leave them there, then I show you the guns." He nodded toward the Hawken. "After I get mine back."

Suspicion glittered in the Ute's eyes like black beetles scuttling between fat eyelids.

"You lie. You have no guns." He leveled the Hawken at Medina's face.

Medina forced himself to smile into the black barrel hole.

"If no guns, you still have horses, my rifle, and…" He patted his head. "…my hair. Now we go." He turned, stepped out of the circle of raiders and headed downslope, once again expecting an arrow, or a shot, in the back.

To his amazement, the raiders did his bidding. Woodpecker followed him down the hill. The big-shouldered brave pulled Takánsy away from the campfire and propelled her along behind. Medina glanced back to see her breechcloth secured around her waist, leggings hanging over one arm, eyes fixed straight ahead. The other five raiders ran to gather the stolen horses. Each brave led three mounts by their picket ropes while the remaining horses followed, a ghostly parade in the moonlight, marching in silence broken by snorts, clacking hooves and splashy creek crossings.

Medina's mind churned with dangerous possibilities. If he led them clear to the confluence where his horse was picketed, the game would be up. He mentally rehearsed the only option he could think of: drop to one knee in a feigned stumble, retrieve the knife in his moccasin, stab Woodpecker, take the Hawken and shoot Big Shoulders, get Takánsy onto a horse and gallop off with her before the others could react. Probably get them both shot. Yet it was the only chance he had. He crossed himself.

As they emerged into a straight section of stream that cut through a meadow on either side, a raider burst into view and ran toward them with arms upraised. A sentry. The Ute leader brought the procession to a halt. Soft cursing came from behind them—a horse stepping on someone?—then silence. The runner, sweat dripping from his face, breath coming in gasps, began jabbering in a low whisper.

Medina heard enough to understand what had spooked the sentry. Goodale and the others had arrived. He whirled on Woodpecker.

"No fight! Trade guns! No Fight! My friends bring the guns. We trade guns for horses. I must parley with them. No shooting!"

The Ute leader's mouth twisted into a murderous snarl, eyes narrowing into slits. He raised the rifle to Medina's head. Behind him, Big Shoulders shoved Takánsy forward and raised his own weapon to her head. Before either could fire, they were distracted by a commotion downstream. Into the far end of the clearing galloped a group of riders—eight, ten, sixteen.

Goodale on his black mare was in the lead, a tall figure behind him, Fields probably, with a shorter man—it had to be Curfew—close beside him.

A piercing whinny rang out from one of the captive horses. Medina whirled to face Woodpecker, his words and hands working together in urgent frenzy.

"No shoot. They will kill you. You shoot, you die; they kill you all. I go, talk to them now, get your guns."

Without waiting for a reply, Medina turned and for a third time walked away from the raiders, his life hanging in the balance.

"Holaaaaa!" Medina's voice carried down the draw. He walked forward, arms waving. *"Holaaaaaa!"*

The riders pulled up in a snarl of dust, curses, grunts, and snorts. They formed a line across the meadow. Moonlight glinted on their weapons.

"Parley," Medina shouted. "Goodale."

No one moved. A buzz of argument rose from among them. Medina sweated in the cold, shifted from one foot to another.

"Goodale," he shouted again, his voice hoarse.

Finally, Goodale rode forward and dismounted.

"I need seven rifles," Medina said.

"You what?" Goodale's bushy brows hunched high.

"We're in a tight spot here." Medina explained the situation and outlined the terms of his bargain with Woodpecker: guns for horses.

Goodale shook his head. "It ain't going to happen. The boys'll never hand over their..."

"I will replace their guns. The other way will not work. No attack."

Goodale inclined his chin toward the cluster of raiders and horses standing upstream.

"How many?" he asked.

"Not sure," Medina lied. "But they have a fortress up there. No way to attack them without a lot of killing."

"The woman?"

"Behind me. They will kill her for sure. How many trappers with you?"

"Ten."

"They will follow your lead."

"Hell, Fields is here, too. And Curfew, and three more from the wagon train. They ain't going to agree..."

"They will get their horses back and their guns as well. What is wrong with..."

"Mariano, you damn fool. They's three boys gone under back there. Scalped. They ain't going to back down. There's a score to settle."

"Yes, I saw those poor boys. But...look, tell the wagoners they will have their revenge. They can go after the Utes in the morning, after they leave the stronghold. That way they will get their horses and revenge, too."

"But by then those Utes will have guns. Better to attack now."

"Guns, yes, but no balls, no powder. Not part of our bargain. Those raiders, they will be easier to attack once they leave this canyon."

Goodale gave him a searching look. "And you'll get the woman back."

"Her, too."

"You risked your hair for her."

Medina looked away, avoiding Goodale's stare.

"Please go. Persuade them."

Goodale shook his head in wonder.

"I'll do it. Damn me if I won't."

Medina grabbed his arm. "You come alone. Bring the rifles, only you. No one else. Bring them here."

The Hawken's barrel was still pointed at Medina's head as he walked twenty paces back to where Woodpecker stood. Big Shoulders' rifle remained leveled at Takánsy's head. She hadn't moved, and from the expression on her face—vacant and far away—Medina wondered whether he was more desperate to save her life than she was.

"The trade is agreed," Medina signed.

The Ute leader's eyes jumped from Medina to Goodale to the surrounding canyon sides and back again.

Medina explained the arrangements. All seven rifles would be brought by one man to a point half-way between the two groups. Woodpecker would have the horses and the woman brought to the same spot. Then Medina and the woman and Goodale would walk the horses downstream while the raiders carried the guns back to their stronghold.

"Ball and powder?" Woodpecker signed.

"No." Medina chopped the air with his hand. "You take guns and leave. Tonight. The wagon travelers are many. They will take your scalps if you stay."

Woodpecker stepped close to Medina and looked hard at him.

"You lied. You had no guns. One day," his hand made a chopping motion at his hairline, "I will come for your scalp."

At the far end of the meadow, sounds of argument drifted back to them, hot and angry. A rider emerged from the group and was immediately surrounded by two others. "Fuck a cactus," came a familiar shout. More curses. A scuffle. After a few minutes the commotion ceased and Goodale walked out, arms laden, to the point of rendezvous. He stacked seven rifles in a pile.

Woodpecker gave Medina a shove and signaled his followers to lead the horses forward.

Medina pointed at Takánsy. "The woman, too. And the Hawken." Woodpecker gave him a long look, as if memorizing his face. His fleshy lips contorted into an imitation smile. Finally, he handed the Hawken to Big Shoulders and snarled an order.

The brave pushed Takánsy ahead of him down the creek to where Goodale stood. He shoved her to her knees at Goodale's feet, threw the Hawken into a patch of bushes, scooped up the weapons and waited until the horses were picketed close by. Then he turned and padded back upstream.The other raiders followed. The horses snorted and cast white-eyed glances at the line of riders below.

Woodpecker's band faded back into the willows and disappeared up the creek. Medina glanced at Takánsy, who had risen and was pulling on her leggings. Then he bolted to the edge of the clearing, fell to his knees and heaved up what remained of the jerky he had eaten.

After the exchange, while they were walking the captured horses downstream through the meadow, Medina felt Takánsy's touch on his arm. For the first time that evening, her eyes were focused, luminous in the moonlight, aimed directly at him.

"You risk much," she said.

So he had. He stared at the moon shadows under her cheekbones, darker on the bruised right side. He had overcome the urge to flee, stood his ground with the Utes, nearly forfeited his life. The memory of her near rape flashed through his mind.

"Why didn't you run?" He was surprised at the harsh edge to his voice.

Takánsy shrugged.

Medina bored into her with his eyes.

"I want you to live." It came out in a fierce whisper.

As they arrived at the line of waiting men, she faced him, eyes holding his for a long moment. Then someone jostled her, and they lost contact in the onrush of movement and sounds, men demanding explanations, Goodale urging calm, horses snorting and pawing, Curfew whining and cursing at cactuses.

Medina, energy draining out of him like water from a breached dam, grabbed hold of a nearby saddlehorn to keep himself upright.

21

SECRETS

It took them the rest of the night to maneuver the stolen horses back to Fort Bridger. They removed the picket ropes and enlisted the help of four mountain men to herd the animals along. Takánsy rode the same chestnut mare she'd tested for speed at Medina's urging only a few days ago. Medina rode Don Justino, flanking the stolen animals on the opposite side. With low crooning and adroit positioning of their mounts, they calmed the horses and kept them moving with minimal disturbance, despite some of the wagon train members' clumsy efforts to help. They arrived at the fort just as the sun bulged up over the eastern horizon.

Medina marveled at Takánsy's indifference to the ordeal she'd suffered. In the light of morning, as they watered the horses in Black's Fork before securing them on pickets to graze, he worried over the darkening bruise on her right cheekbone. He told her he would send Jenny to her with medicine.

"No need," she said, and set off for her lodge.

Medina asked Jenny to go anyway. Later, he learned from her that Papín had not yet returned from Fort Hall.

Later that day, while devouring a meal of venison prepared by Jenny, Goodale asked Medina how he planned to replace the weapons.

"I will have money," Medina replied. But as he turned the numbers over in his head, he realized that between the cost of replacement guns and paying Papín for Takánsy's help, he probably wouldn't have enough.

Fields had wasted no time in gathering twenty wagoners to pursue the Utes. Two mountain men were paid to guide them. Fields voiced no thanks for Medina's rescue of their horses. Instead, he focused considerable ire on the loss of their seven rifles. Ever his boss's echo, Curfew warned Goodale that if replacement guns weren't waiting for them when they returned from chastising the savages, there would be "holy hell to pay."

Goodale remarked that whatever hell the scar-faced man might have in mind, it wouldn't be holy.

They set off on fresh horses a few hours after returning to Fort Bridger, Curfew in the lead, riding one of the buckskins that Medina had trained. Listening to their noisy departure, saddle leather squeaking, bits and bridles jangling, horses snorting, men cursing and shouting, Medina guessed they wouldn't get within two miles of the Utes. The mountain men's faces registered no enthusiasm for the job ahead.

Two days later, Medina and Takánsy sat together in the grass beside their rope corral, their noon meal of jerky and pemmican spread before them on a swatch of faded calico. The dried meat never tasted so good; the noon sun never felt so comforting. A shower of light splashed through the still-clinging canopy of cottonwood leaves. He savored the moment, resisting the knowledge that it wouldn't last.

Takánsy's hair, unbraided on that morning, framed her face in two lustrous cascades. She winced as she wrestled a legging up over her left knee. Red spots marred the skin of her calf. With her thumb and forefinger she plucked at near invisible spines that stuck out from the center of each spot.

She shot him a sideways glance.

"Cactus is no *fiesta*." Crinkles fanned out from the corners of her eyes.

He smiled. He didn't have to ask how the spines had got into her leg. There were plenty of cacti beside the boulder where Woodpecker had forced her down.

"Prickly pear," he said. He pulled a pair of tweezers from his possibles bag. "This will help. From St. Vrain's fort."

She examined the shiny pincers, then plucked out a cactus spine. She held the tiny prize to the light, her mouth lifting in the faintest of smiles.

Using tweezers behind her knee proved awkard. Medina reclaimed the tool and signaled her to lie on her stomach. He knelt beside her and bent close, pulling out the hairlike spikes one by one. Her skin was lighter there, fawn colored. It tempted his touch, but the spines stood guard. Her scent, fresh-washed, with a hint of sage, threatened his concentration.

To distract himself he told her about his search for her, his suspicion of Curfew, his discovery of the missing horses and the dead youths, his careful approach to the raider camp. He said nothing about his fear-filled paralysis when witnessing Woodpecker's assault.

"Done," he said, the last spine removed. "The curse of the Woodpecker." He flicked the cactus needle into the air.

She rolled to her side, propped her head on her hand, and regarded him with searching eyes. Her right cheekbone glowed purple-green in the sunlight.

"You are very brave," she said.

His eyes slid away from hers. All he could muster was a shake of his head.

"Why you come into raider camp?"

"I am one *loco* Spaniard." His laugh failed to deflect her

expectant gaze. After a pause, he ventured, "I am always rescuing the *señoritas*. There was a girl once..." He trailed off.

She waited.

"I only had fifteen years. She was daughter of the *patrón*. You understand *patrón*?"

She shook her head no.

"Like chief, but bigger, more powerful. He owned land, far as here to those mountains." He pointed to the Uintas, where the raiders had fled.

"Owned?"

"Controlled. On *patrón's* land, you can do nothing if he says no."

"Not hunt?"

"Not even that."

She thought about that for a moment, frowning, then said, "The girl. Beautiful?"

"Yes. Slender, high cheek bones, long hair...like you."

If this compliment registered, Takánsy gave no sign. She waited for him to continue.

Medina said, "She often rode alone. The horses of her father. Beautiful, strong fine animals. One day she rode into a canyon, to a pool. She liked sitting on a rock and cooling her feet in water."

He paused, wondering why he'd started this story, a trail leading into a thicket of thorns.

She prompted, "You rescue her. From what?"

"Some boys. Friends of her half-brother. They were...bothering her. I yell at them. They run away. I didn't do anything, really. Just get there at the right time." The memory of what really happened sent a wave of heat into his face.

She reached out, touched his cheek. "Your face, red. You are gone away. Tell me what troubles you." She leaned closer, her face intent, eyes gray probes.

He pulled away, embarrassed.

"I did not... Truth is, I..." He couldn't continue. He didn't want her to know how he'd run away, how he'd almost done the same thing two days ago and left her with the Utes. He wanted her to admire him, to think him brave. *Besides, in her case, in the end, he'd acted with courage, hadn't he?*

He said, "I was thinking of that Ute, what he was about to... do to you. That Ute..."

"I am unharmed. Except for bruises and cactus." She shrugged and placed her hand over her heart. "You have brave heart. I thank you. My husband will thank you when he returns."

Papín. Had he risked his hair only to reunite her with the Frenchman? He sighed, searching for something to say. Instinct told him that if he was to have a chance with this woman, he would have to understand her past.

"You married Papín to escape your old life. What happened? Why did you leave your people?"

She pulled back, familiar dullness clouding her eyes.

"Best forget," she said. "No go back, even here." She tapped her head with her finger.

A dead end. But could he blame her? Hadn't he just lied about his own past? Perhaps she was right. Leave such things behind. Bury them like garbage and walk away.

Her eyes softened.

"You have a place in my heart. Large, like mountain."

He looked at her a long moment. Then he smiled, winked, and stood up.

"Not big enough for me," he said, trying to sound playful. "Come, we finish the training. It will not hurt so much with those cactus spines gone."

She rose and walked with him toward the holding pen, a slight lift at the corners of her mouth.

At least, he thought, I can get her to smile now and then. *I can enjoy this moment.*

A sudden breeze dislodged a shower of cottonwood leaves that added another layer to the yellow carpet underfoot. The ground smelled faintly of winter decay.

Late that afternoon, after they returned to their separate lodges, Medina got word that Papín had returned from Fort Hall laden with trade goods, and Curfew had returned from chasing the Utes, empty-handed.

22

REPLACEMENT GUNS

"I owe you, *mon ami*, I owe you big, sure enough." Papín's long arms wrapped Medina in a bear hug.

"Easy, my friend, or you do more damage than those Utes," Medina said.

Papín laughed and released his grip long enough to pull Takánsy into the circle and embrace them both. Her body pressed into Medina's side.

They stood outside Takánsy's lodge next to a pile of new trade goods from Fort Hall. Medina had hoped Papín would be delayed. He'd trudged over to Takánsy's lodge that morning with the wind nipping at his heels, his mood falling with the last of the leaves.

Papín lifted the lodge flap and waved them inside.

"My Marie has told me how she found those raiders after they kill the wagon train boys. *Mon Dieu*, she is brave, no? My Papín brain is split apart, one part feeling proud and another feeling angry that she does such a thing." He butted his two fists together, knuckle to knuckle, miming the war between his two brains.

"But they catch her, beat her, the sons of whores. Then she tells how you come running down the hill yelling like a madman. Well, she didn't say 'madman,' that is just me thinking how it must have seemed to those Utes, no?" Papín laughed and put his hand on Medina's shoulder.

"Tell me how you tricked that raider chief," he said as he maneuvered the three of them into a sitting position around the lodge fire. Takánsy picked up a shirt and began beading it, her fingers flitting over the leather like dancing spirits. Her hair was once again loose around her shoulders.

Papín will be running his fingers through it tonight, Medina thought. He forced his gaze away from her toward the French trader. He retold the rescue story as he'd done for Goodale and a dozen others. It was beginning to sound like one of those campfire tales that live on the border between fact and fiction. Only Medina tried not to exaggerate his own role. He wasn't that proud of it. Of the near rape and his reaction to it, he never spoke.

Papín said, "That Ute, he is short, a little fat?"

"Yes. Dark skinned. Flighty mean eyes."

"Sounds like one the Americans call Captain Jack. A bad one. Carries grudges. Does not forget." Papín rubbed his bald head. "They say he once hunted down a man who had cheated him in the stick contest. Or at least Captain Jack claimed he cheated. A French trapper, Labonte, I think." He pulled a brown jug from somewhere behind him and began loosening the stopper. "Years later that Indian tied Labonte to a tree and peeled off his skin. Three days for him to die."

Takánsy crossed herself. The two men did the same.

Papín said, "You bargained away seven rifles for how many? Twenty horses? Not such a good deal, no?"

"It was not just for the horses," Medina said, nodding toward Takánsy.

"In that case..." Papín's hands swept out to the side to showcase his wife. "A thousand rifles would not be enough." He laughed his infectious laugh.

Takánsy looked up from her work, a faint smile on her lips.

Medina said, "The hard thing was making that Ute believe I had rifles."

"I would not have believed you either, my friend, coming in at night like you did, all shouting and breathing hard." Papín wiped his mouth and thrust the jug toward Medina. "So, how did you convince him?"

Medina took a small swallow, handed the jug back and patted his head. "I told him he would have my hair if I was lying, and still have the horses. What could he lose?"

Papín set the jug down and turned both palms up, imitating a weighing scale. "Let us compare...your sorry scalp..." He lowered one palm an inch. "Seven rifles..." His other hand dropped a foot as the first rose. "An easy choice." He slapped his knee and grinned. Then his face turned serious. "You risked much. Why?"

Medina felt Takánsy's eyes on him. He hoped Papín couldn't see the flush he felt creeping up his neck.

"I could not leave those horses. Too much hard work. If the Utes steal them, Curfew and Fields not pay me." He rubbed his thumb against his fingers.

Papín gave him an appraising look.

"So now they pay you, and you use your money to buy new rifles. Not such a bargain, no?"

Medina shifted position. No, it didn't make much sense.

"Speaking of replacement rifles, can you...do you have...?"

Papín smiled his trader's smile, shrugged and raised his hands.

"My friend, my friend, of course I can help. I manage to get new rifles at Fort Hall." He looked at Takánsy. "And out of gratitude for rescuing my wife, I am prepared to offer them at a special low price..."

Takánsy interrupted him with a hard look and a wave of her hand. "My pay for the horse training. How much?"

They both looked at her. Medina thought, at four dollars a horse, for twenty horses, that would be...

"Eighty dollars," Papín said.

"I buy guns," she said, her voice sharp.

Papín's eyebrows arched like twin caterpillars.

"But that is my..."

She fixed him with an icy stare.

His face shifted as if he'd been slapped.

Finally he said, "Seven rifles. Maybe seventy dollars. But of course, Marie is right. Seven rifles. Horse training fee, eighty dollars. An even trade. We owe you that." He swallowed another swig from the jug, a little too quickly, Medina thought.

Medina said, "But I want to pay her, too. She deserves..."

Takánsy silenced him with a shake of her head.

Papín sighed. "It is settled then, no?"

He offered his hand to Medina and they pulled each other up.

"Come. We will have a look. I cannot match every gun the wagoners lost. But I will convince them...no, you will convince them that the replacements are better, no? You are good trader now, sure enough."

Medina didn't know if it was a compliment or a joke.

Papín's trade goods were piled around the outside of the lodge, bundles covered in buffalo hides. He walked with Medina from one to another, regaling him with stories of how he'd bargained for them, who had parted with them. Each bundle held a story, told with such fondness that Medina had the impression he was meeting Papín's children.

"Clyman," Papin said, pointing to a bulging skin that looked newer then the rest. "Last week I get from Jake Clyman tools, axes, knives, hammers, shovels, pole skinners." He pulled Medina closer and continued in a conspiratorial voice. "Clyman does not know the value of what he has. These cost me twenty beaver plews. Twenty! I will get four times that from the Oregon travelers next year."

Papín squatted down beside a long, narrow bundle and untied its leather straps.

"One thing about Clyman, though...one good idea he has. He is thinking about running a ferry across the Green."

"A 'ferry'?" Medina didn't recognize the word.

"You know, a flat-bottom wood boat, big enough for a wagon. He will pull it across on a rope attached to both banks. He may get rich despite himself. The wagon trains will pay him plenty."

"I would like to see that." Medina imagined owning a ferry. He imagined Captain Fremont asking him politely for a crossing. He imagined Fields and Curfew standing hats in hand. He would tell them to wait their turn.

Papín tugged open the buffalo skin to reveal twenty flintlock rifles, mostly fifty caliber, some fifty-four caliber, for trade with Indians. He rummaged through the weapons, setting aside seven.

"These should do," he said.

Medina pictured Fields and Curfew's reaction. Better that Goodale be present, he thought. He gathered the weapons and nodded his thanks to Papín.

"What are your plans, now that the training is finished?" Papin asked.

"Bent's Fort, maybe. But first, Goodale wants to trap up there this winter." Medina pointed to the Uintas with his chin. "I will go with him. I do not want him to get lost."

"Those Utes. Be careful up there."

"Captain Jack, he is by now far south. Curfew tried to catch him. With twenty men and much noise, he left one day after we get the horses back. Came back with only frowns on faces."

Papín smiled. "Not much danger to those Utes."

"No." Medina turned to leave.

Takánsy stepped out from her lodge, hand shielding her eyes. Papín moved to her side.

Medina glanced at the guns, then at the two of them.

"Thank you."

"To you, our thanks," Takánsy said.

Medina didn't like her saying "our." He said, "Until tomorrow, then. The money, I will bring to you."

She reached for him then, took his hand in hers and squeezed it, while Papín looked on, beaming.

23

PAY DISPUTE

Medina stood still as stone, his face and hands under strict control. *Best to let Goodale handle this. Best not to get involved.*

"We're not going to pay the full amount." Field's finger jabbed the air in front of Goodale's face. "Not unless we get back the same kind of guns this damn Mexican gave to those thieving savages."

"Thieving bastards," Curfew said.

The Wagon Boss and his scar-faced shadow stood facing Goodale in the center of the wagon train camp. Medina waited a few paces off to the side. Around them, men loaded bundles onto wagons, strapped down gear, oiled harnesses, took down tents. Here and there women packed cooking equipment or scolded squalling children as they buttoned them into warmer clothes.

A north wind gusted through, threatening to lift Field's

broad-brim hat and blow Curfew's tobacco juice back into his face if he spit in the wrong direction. Medina pushed his hands deeper into the pockets of the worn army jacket he sometimes wore over his skins.

Big storm on the way, Medina thought, snow, probably. The Oregon-bound outfit would be getting out just ahead of it.

A gust rippled through Goodale's moustache and lifted the leather fringe of his shirt. His face, normally a crinkly collection of smiles, radiated irritation. He folded his arms across his chest, looked down and nudged a stone with the toe of his moccasin.

"Captain Fields." The words came out strained, as if harnessed to a heavy wagon. "Mr. Medina here risked his hair..."

"Been through all that." Field's interruption brought his finger even closer to Goodale's face. "We thanked him twice, but that don't change the fact that the two of you took our rifles against our better judgment..."

"...risked his hair to get them horses back..." Goodale was suddenly shouting, "...and by God, if he hadn't, you wouldn't be leaving this afternoon. You'd be stuck here for the winter with no horses and by God you would be missing a lot more than a few guns if you'd tried to fight them Utes like you wanted and we hadn't held you back."

Medina stared at his friend's blazing eyes and quivering beard. He'd never seen Goodale so agitated. He felt his own muscles tense. Sucking in a cold draught of air, he concentrated on remaining still, willing his feet to stay planted, stifling the impulse to get the hell out of there.

Fields lowered his finger and backed up a step.

Curfew had to jerk his foot out of the way to avoid the wagon master's boot heel. He glared at Medina and shot a glop of brown spit into the dirt between them.

Something hot and unfamiliar surged through Medina's body. Instead of looking away, trying to be invisible, he raised his gaze to bore directly into Curfew's watery blue eyes. A mistake. Before he quite realized what was happening, Curfew was advancing on him, knife in hand, its honed edge facing up.

It took two shouts, one from Goodale and one from Fields, to bring the scar-chinned man to a halt. Curfew's jaw went slack, loosing a trickle of drool.

"Fuck a cactus if I don't even the score with you summbitch Mexican." Curfew's voice rasped low, more steely than angry.

It was Medina who broke eye contact.

The four men stood for a moment as men do when they stumble onto the brink of a chasm. Fields finally broke the silence. He reached into his coat, a knee-length affair with an enormous collar, and pulled out a fat leather pouch.

"Here's eighty," he said. "We'll keep the other eighty to buy replacement guns at Fort Hall."

Goodale kept his eyes fixed on Fields and his hands tucked under his arms. The pouch hung there for a long moment, suspended from Field's fingers. Then, released, it fell with a plop into the dust. Fields said, "Suit yourself," and turned to leave.

"Captain." Goodale's voice, once again under edgy control, brought Fields to a halt. "Without the full one sixty, them horses of yours ain't never going to make it to Fort Hall."

Fields and Curfew turned back in one motion.

"What?" Fields said.

"What?" Curfew said.

"You heard me."

"You can't stop us...how would you..." Fields said, his voice spluttering.

Goodale cut in. "Them horses got stole once. No reason they won't disappear again. Or they could fall sick on the way. Lotsa dangers out there on the trail. Lead poisoning, for one."

Fields' face paled, his jaw fell open, no words came out.

"Fuck a cactus, Captain, I can take care of this if you give...." Curfew's words trailed off as Goodale pinned him with a look.

It dawned on Medina that Curfew was all bluster. Revulsion welled in his gut toward the vile man. And something else, a kind of swelling in his heart. Instead of averting his eyes, he found himself smiling at Curfew.

"Think about it, Captain." Goodale's affability returned, his smile crinkled, his hands waved, his voice soothed. "Ain't it worth eighty more dollars to be on your way, ahead of this storm, teams rarin' to go? You don't want to spend any more time stuck here, do you? Think about it."

He turned, beckoned to Medina and marched away. Medina

had to trot to keep up. They crossed the stream into the mountain man camp. Goodale shouted a few names loud enough for Fields and Curfew to hear.

"Uncle Jack. Pegleg. Hungry John." They came, rifles in hand, curiosity on their faces. Two more heads popped out of nearby lodges.

"You are not planning to shoot those horses, are you?" Medina asked Goodale as the mountain men gathered.

Goodale grinned. "Don't think it'll be necessary. I was just adding a little weight to our side of the argument. Something to help Fields make up his mind."

"You were angry."

"Naw, I just wanted to look mad. Sure got Field's finger out of my face, didn't it?"

Medina felt a new admiration for his friend. *How does he manage to control such anger, use it like an arrow in his quiver? There is a lesson for me here.*

"You need us for something, Tim?" Uncle Jack Robinson asked.

"We just had ourselves a little disagreement with Captain Fields over there. He owes us a hundred sixty dollars, and I'm figuring he'll pay up sometime soon. All I need you boys to do is to stand over there on the creek bank for a little while and look mean while you watch those wagon folks pack up." Goodale peered around the circle of expectant faces and laughed. "In other words, just look natural."

All but Uncle Jack grinned. "Hell, I ain't mean," he said, frowning and curling his lips into a snarl.

Goodale turned to Medina. "Come on, *amigo*, let's head over to Jenny's lodge to wait."

Medina padded along behind him, through more gusts of wind. Jenny greeted them with cups of hot coffee and corn cakes.

About an hour later a whispered warning from Uncle Jack hissed in from just outside the back wall of the lodge.

"Curfew's coming."

They heard a hacking spit, then saw Curfew's boots shuffle up just outside the lodge opening. Instead of inviting him in, Medina and Goodale ducked outside into the sunlight.

Curfew proffered the leather pouch, avoiding their eyes.

"One-sixty." His words were barely audible through the gob of tobacco that lumped in his cheek.

Goodale took the pouch and counted the coins. Two of them required testing with his teeth.

Satisfied, he said in his most polite voice, "Why thank you, Mr. Curfew. That evens things up."

Curfew looked hard at Medina, his eyes red-rimmed under stringy yellow hair, his stench clouding the air between them.

"Even? Things sure as hell ain't even between me and this fucking Mexican." He spit a gob at Medina's feet, then immediately backed up a step, spun half-way around and crabbed away.

Medina felt Goodale's restraining hand.

"Let him have the last word, *amigo*. We got our plunder."

Medina sighed and nodded. "I think Oregon is a place I will not visit."

Goodale grinned and counted out $150 in coins. "I sure as hell had to earn my ten," he said. "Keeping you and Curfew apart, chasing after you and them Utes…" He shook his head and winked.

"Señor Tim, your tongue alone is worth ten. *Grácias*." He carried the handful of coins to a flat rock and counted eighty dollars into a separate pile. "Of course, my assistant is worth a lot more."

"You and that woman…more trouble on the way, I'm figuring." Goodale's face turned serious. "*Amigo*, I've never seen you take such a shine to a skirt. Am I going to have to settle things between you and Papín next?"

Medina shrugged and shook his head. No, there would be no need for Goodale's intervention. As soon as he paid Takánsy he would have to bid her goodbye. There would be no further reason to be with her. He would leave tomorrow with Goodale to trap beaver as agreed and would probably never see her again.

How many times during the past month had he imagined an encounter where he would ask her to leave Papín and go with him? He'd think of her lying with him in his buffalo robes, whispering secrets in his ear. He'd even imagine finding a priest to marry them. But never had the distance between desire and reality felt so great.

No, he would have to leave. He would continue being Goodale's sidekick, giving him ideas, letting him "lead." They would return to Bent's fort, do some guiding, hire on for some mule training, continue their lives. That was reality. That was what he had to accept.

"Señor Tim. The beaver, they are waiting. I go pay Papín's

woman tomorrow, wish them well, and then we pack up. Next day, first light, we go." He gave Goodale a weak smile. "I will keep you from getting lost up there."

Goodale stroked his moustache. "And I'll keep you away from them Utes. Come on, let's see what Jenny has cooked up." He disappeared into the lodge.

Medina followed, but he couldn't work up any appetite.

24

NIGHT ATTACK

Sleep eluded Medina that night. The wind squalled and tugged at his canvas shelter. His mind replayed his visit to Papín and Takánsy. The sensation of her handshake wouldn't leave him. Hadn't she held his hand longer than necessary? It made the hairs on the back of his hand stand up.

Papín hadn't seemed to notice. He was his usual expansive self, head bobbing, hands waving, smile gleaming. "You are always welcome in this lodge, my friend," he'd said.

Medina turned over one more time, then gave up on sleep. He stretched, pulled on his jacket and moccasins, and stepped out into the night chill. Dawn was still hours away. The expected storm had stalled somewhere to the north, leaving only the accursed wind and a low mantle of clouds that cloaked the earth, blotting out stars and moon and infusing the normally dry air with a heavy dampness.

The wagon camp had departed, leaving behind a field of trash, discarded items, and eerie silence. What would this land look like if more of these people came? It disgusted him. His own campsite was immaculate, gear packed in two bundles ready for departure, coins stashed away in his money pouch under a bush, waiting for him to deliver his payment to Takánsy in the morning.

A rustling sound issued from a nearby patch of sage. Medina turned to look, but his eyes couldn't penetrate the darkness. Coyote, he guessed. Maybe skunk. When silence returned, his attention drifted back to Takánsy and their original meeting when she was watering her horses.

A desire to re-visit that place suddenly seized him. He hefted his Hawken and headed down to the streamside trail, barely visible in the darkness. After about twenty minutes he reached the spot. His muscles relaxed, his lungs feasted on the chill, moist air. Maybe he would be able to sleep when he returned. From where he stood on the streambank, he could just make out the place where he had first seen Takánsy and the three horses. He squatted beside the gurgling water.

The ghost stare came back to him, along with the memory of her striking beauty. In the two months he'd known her, that stare had become less frequent. Partly his doing—not that it mattered anymore.

Another rustle, faint as a whisper, came from somewhere behind him. Why would a coyote follow him here? Or maybe it was just a stray dog left behind by the Fields bunch. He started to turn.

A familiar voice rasped, "Don't turn around you little shit or you'll have a hole in you big enough to ride a horse through."

Medina froze. The Hawken rested in his hand. He fingered the trigger. He might be able to duck sideways and get off a shot. But in this blackness, how would he aim? And how many were there? He couldn't believe Curfew would come by himself. He would have to shoot and keep moving, maybe make it to that willow clump about ten paces to the left. It seemed more like a mile when he thought about the time it would take to get that far.

Then he remembered. When he left his tent, he hadn't tamped ball and powder into the Hawken's muzzle. The weapon was useless, except as a club. He inched his hand toward the knife in his belt and chanced a slow turn of his head to the right.

Curfew's hissed "Go ahead" froze him in place. The voice was closer. Several pairs of boots crunched on gravel.

Medina, his mind scrambling, said, "The money pouch, it is not here with me. Cached."

"And I'm the Prince of Wales," Curfew cut in, close now.

"Captain Fields will not want you..." Medina never finished. He sensed rather than saw the descending rifle butt as he twisted to the side. His skull exploded in a shower of pinpoint lights as hardwood crashed behind his right ear. He felt himself falling as consciousness flicked off like a doused candle flame.

25

MIND HAZE

"They was lucky. Stupid, but lucky." Goodale's voice sounded to Medina as if his friend was talking with a blanket over his head. Or maybe his own head was covered with something.

"Saved by an ice dam. It is not right," Papín answered.

His voice also sounded muffled, far away. Something was odd about all this, but Medina couldn't figure out what it was. He felt confused, disoriented.

Goodale's voice again—"No way for us to chase them across the Bear with all that ice sweeping down. Made a roar louder than anything I ever heared before, or likely to again. Me and the other boys just stood there with our mouths flapping."

"While that son of a whore Curfew escaped and ran to catch

up with his wagon train. With Medina's money. My God!" Outrage thickened Papín's voice.

"Not sure they got his money, though," Goodale said. "Three of them. Left a trail even I could follow. They scampered across the Bear without hardly getting their feet wet. Strange to get that much ice on the upper Bear, especially this early."

"Cold or not, we must catch them, no?" Papín said. This time I will go with you, sure enough. You must not leave without me."

"They'll be safe in Fort Hall in a few days," Goodale said. "We can't fight a whole wagon train."

"Fight? There are other ways," Papín said.

"Not likely to be able to sneak up on them either, once they get in camp. We'd have to spend too much time just setting and waiting. And as I said, my guess is they couldn't find Medina's money cache. Not for lack of trying. His fixins are scattered all over the place." Goodale made a sound in his throat, an expression of disgust.

"They took his finger. His finger! Cut the end of it off. They are shit. Shit!" In Papín's version of English it came out "sheet," spit out fast and hard.

"It's probably dangling on a string around Curfew's neck, collecting tobacco drool," Goodale said. "Revenge trophy."

They fell silent for a moment, with the stirring of spoons against tin cups the only sound. Medina caught the aroma of coffee filling the air, mixing with a smoky scent.

"If Medina lives and ain't too stove up, we'll get him his finger back one of these first days, I'll wager," Goodale said. "If it's still around Curfew's neck when we cotch him, I wouldn't bet on his head staying attached to his body."

"If he lives...If he lives..." Papín repeated the phrase like an incantation. "Whether he lives or goes under, we must go after the scar-face soon, no?"

"Iffen we can get ourselves across the Bear," Goodale said.

What do they mean, 'if he lives'? Mariano opened his eyes, but saw only blurs. He tried to push himself up, but the effort sent a sharp pain through his head.

He strained to hear more, but his mind drifted to memories of the Taos plaza, to slogging through beaver ponds. It transported him into the lap of his long-dead mother, her smiling face peering down at him, her forgotten features suddenly appearing and disappearing under a blood-red flow. At one point his mind conjured up the Virgin Mary, beckoning him with smiling eyes and a giant rosary. Or was it an angel, with dark hair and gray eyes?

Then blackness overtook him.

Black lightened to gray. Medina wiggled his left hand. Something soft, a cloth maybe, was wrapped around his fourth finger. It hurt when he touched it. The flash of pain chased more of the blackness away. He saw a blur of movement then felt the touch of a hand on his forehead.

"Takánsy?" He heard her name come out like a croak.

"Mariano. You are coming back, as I told them."

Her voice made him want to claw his way out of the blackness. He reached out with his good hand and found hers, its warmth radiating up his arm. He tried to lift his head, only to feel an ax blow of pain that threatened to raise a slug of vomit into his throat. Her hands enveloped his head, holding it still.

"No, no, not yet, my Mariano. Not yet."

He let the blackness take him again, rescuing him from pain. He would be back. He wanted to hear her say "my Mariano" again.

Light and dark shapes played in his vision. One shape became her head. Dark hair flowing down around her face, still indistinct. Her hand cupped his head, raising it. More pain, but not so great this time. He felt the rim of a tin cup pressing against his lower lip.

"Drink," she said.

A vile-tasting warm liquid slid past his tongue. Some sort of bitter root. He swallowed.

"What happened to me?"

"Your head. They hit you many times. Kick you, too. Your leg, it is broken. But your head, that is the worst." She stroked his cheek. "Your face, it is not hurt."

He raised his bandaged hand. "My finger?"

She grasped her own fourth finger at the last joint and held it in front of his face. "Only to here. Just the tip. Curfew cut it off."

"Where was I?"

"By the creek. The place where I first see you."

"How long...?"

"When they are still hitting you. Papín, he chase them away."

"How did you know...?"

"Something, a spirit maybe, comes to me, making me awake. I touch the cross of Jésu. I make Papín get up. The spirit guides me to the place where they are...trying to kill you. Papín shoots at them, *pah!*, with pistol. They run away."

She paused to rub some warm goo on his chest. It tingled on his skin and smelled of mint. Her voice fell to a near whisper.

"You not moving. I am big afraid you are...dead."

Maybe he was dead. Everything seemed unreal, a dream. Wind moaned through the tipi smoke hole.

She paused before saying, "I help you breathe. I...blowing my breath into your mouth."

He tried to smile. "Too bad I was not awake when you did that."

She made no reply. He hoped she was smiling.

"Your body, very cold. We put blanket on you, bring you here on a *travois*. Your friend of the long moustache and Jenny, they help. Your head, I have to tie it down to keep it still when we move you."

He tried to make out his surroundings.

"We are in your lodge?"

Flickers of light danced on what he presumed was the tipi wall. Could be fire, or maybe sunlight filtering through moving branches. Just below was a shape he remembered, her beaded shirts hanging from a lodge pole. To the right, lower down, he saw the shape of her wooden cross. Details were becoming clearer.

"Yes. You are here now six nights. Yesterday you speak. First time."

With his good hand he gingerly touched his head, felt the bandage. He moved on to his face, nose and mouth, then slowly explored down his arm and torso, then below. He realized he was naked, uncovered.

"Your clothes. I cut them off."

"I have missed out on all the good times."

He had never known her to blush, but wondered if she was blushing now.

"Your tongue wags in your head." She gave his chest one last rub and drew a heavy buffalo robe over him. "Better you sleep now."

26

TOUCHES

"Curfew wasn't so lucky the second time around. Ice flow must of caught him after it swept 'round the big bend of the Bear farther down."

Goodale squatted on a blanket just inside the tipi opening, across from where Medina sat against a willow backrest. "That river was growling like an old she-bear."

Two weeks had passed since the attack. Medina's head had cleared. Goodale was visible in all detail down to the brown stains on his buckskin shirt. Medina's leg was mending, a clean break, no complications. Next to him lay the crutch that Takánsy had fashioned out of an ash sapling.

He had yet to use it. Pain still cleaved his head whenever he tried to rise to his feet. His right leg stuck straight out, bound by wood staves and leather strips. The skin on his back and rump felt sore, chafed from lying on it. He drew his left leg up with his arms, shifting position to seek relief from the ache of the mending limb. He adjusted his loincloth to cover the exposed skin above the splint.

Goodale brushed a light coating of snow off his sleeves and pulled Curfew's black hat out of a pouch he'd carried into Takánsy's lodge. The stovepipe crown was crumpled; the earflaps hung down like banners.

"We found him with his head stove in; probably a rock. Too bad...I'da liked to stove it in myself."

He tossed the hat across the fire to where Medina sat. A dark stain could be seen on one of the ear flaps.

"The hat's not all we found." Goodale said. He signaled to Papín, who stood beaming at his side.

"Behold," said the Frenchman, stepping aside to reveal Medina's Hawken rifle hidden behind his back. Papín bowed from the waist as if introducing the President of the United States.

"She was a little rusty and scratched by rocks, but we have applied the magic of my finest buffers and oils, and *voilà*, she is as ready as a beautiful dove from the finest San Francisco bordello, no?

Medina glanced at Takánsy, kneeling at the cookfire, and saw her frown at the comparison of his Hawken to a whore. He smiled at Papín and Goodale.

"A thousand thanks to both of you. Lucky my shooting finger is not damaged." He wiggled it at them. "Too bad the river got him instead of me."

The news of Curfew's death left Medina with a confusing mix of regret and relief. He savored revenge, had fantasized smashing the butt of his Hawken into the scar-chinned man's terrified face, brown juice flowing into his beard stubble. But part of him didn't want to put his courage to the test again. He had surprised himself with Captain Jack, stood his ground, bluffed his way through and found favor in gray eyes. It was enough. Best to keep his relief to himself.

Papín stood beaming, holding the Hawken, firelight dancing on his bald head.

Medina reached up to shake his hand. "To you, my friend, I owe my life. My Old Lady Hawken also thanks you. And, thanks to Takánsy my eyes see again. I am able to shoot Curfew's finger off at fifty paces. I'm sad to hear he can no longer hold up his finger."

The two men laughed, but Takánsy did not. Her eyes shifted toward her wooden cross glowing in the light of a stubby candle burning at its base.

Medina added, "And thanks be to God for His healing power." She gave him a quick look that deepened the creases on the corners of her mouth.

He felt Papín's alert eyes slide from him toward Takánsy and back again.

"My wife and Jésu, they make good team, take good care of you." He curled a smile at them, but the laugh seemed to have gone out of it.

Goodale shifted on his feet. "I best be going. Jenny'll chew on me if I don't report in." He bent to retrieve Curfew's hat. "I'll bury this with the rest of the trash." He nodded and slipped toward the lodge opening. "Oh, I almost forgot. We didn't find your money pouch."

"It is safe," Medina said. He was glad he'd taken the time to cache it, and that he now remembered where.

"Figured as much. See you tomorrow." Goodale cocked his head and ducked out through the lodge opening. A triangle of late afternoon light spilled in, illuminating the cross, then disappeared as the flap fell back into place.

Papín leaned the Hawken against a lodge pole, sat down across from Medina and began sorting through a sack of trade goods, small items like needles and knives and cooking utensils—things of use to travelers on the Oregon trail.

Takánsy turned away to stir another of her poultices. This one smelled more like skunkbrush than mint. The clack of wood spoon against tin cup was the only sound. Medina watched her shoulders sway as she stirred, a dark braid swinging in rhythm.

Papín was watching her, too. "When will we eat?"

She paused. "I finishing soon with this."

Papín frowned, rose and stepped out into the crisp air. The lodge flap whapped down behind him, leaving Medina alone again with Takánsy.

During the past two weeks of his recovery, her ghost stare had mostly vanished. In its place arose looks of such focused caring that Medina sometimes felt like a one of those shirts she beaded with time-consuming attention. Had he felt this way as a child under his mother's touch? He couldn't remember.

During this healing time, Takánsy would leave the lodge and return with sprigs and twigs, berries, sometimes roots. Whenever she found something new or rare, her eyes flashed and her words flowed as she set to work on a new concoction.

The poultices were the ones he liked best, as they required her touching his body. He could not tell her this, of course. He feigned complaint or indifference, all the while reveling in the acts of healing she lavished on him.

He watched her now, stirring the skunkbrush mixture. She pinched a bit of powder from her waist pouch, dropped it in the cup, warmed it over the fire, sniffed it and stirred some more. He guessed it would soon be applied to his leg.

At first, Papín showed an interest in her excited talk about herbs and medicines. More recently his eyes wandered, his replies grew perfunctory, his smiles faded. He spent more time outside the lodge. If a meal were delayed, he would empty his pipe bowl after a couple of puffs, then refill it, his finger tapping fast and hard.

In the meantime, the stack of leather shirts awaiting her beadwork sat abandoned to one side. Papín never spoke of them, but sometimes his eyes lingered on the shirts, shifted to her, then focused on his pipe, which came in for an unusually vigorous tapping.

Medina knew he was in danger of overextending his stay. Papín never said anything about it, in fact, his good cheer flowed unabated. But to Medina's ear, Papín's words of encouragement were beginning to sound forced. So he exercised his limbs till they hurt and vowed to be on his way soon. Then Takánsy would loose her braids in a glorious cascade, and Medina's resolve would melt away.

Every evening, Takánsy lit a candle at the base of her wooden cross, knelt before it and prayed in Salish. Medina would join in silently, repeating from memory the Spanish catechisms he had learned during his childhood. One day he asked her what she was saying.

"I make vow to Jésu that I am lighting candle every day for one winter if He lets you live," she said. "Every night I thank Him."

Medina's reply caught in his throat. He stared into the gray depths of her eyes then looked quickly away.

Vows. What about marriage vows? He turned to face her.

"You and Papín..." he hesitated for a moment until her expectant gaze called for him to continue. "You and Papín, a priest married you?"

She shook her head. "We leaving my people before that can happen. But Padre de Smet, the Blackrobe, is giving me this." She gestured toward the cross with the candle burning at its base. "With this I make my own marriage vow."

Medina searched her face. He found no hint such a vow might be easily broken.

Medina had heard of Father Pierre-Jean de Smet but had never met him. He thought of his own priest in Taos, whose round, self-satisfied face signaled his ties to the area's rich *patrones*. Medina's own faith was a mixture of a daily ritual—signing the cross when rising in the morning—along with a healthy respect for the power of a whimsical God. No point in alienating the Almighty, he reasoned.

His faith paled next to hers. Yet under her care his piety had increased. He silently mouthed his prayers twice a day, asked for a candle to place beside hers, told her of his own upbringing in the Taos parish, agreed with her that by God's miracle, his life had been spared. Her pleasure at such moments gratified him. And, he had to admit, left him feeling a little guilty, knowing that the closeness he sought was less to God than to her.

Physically there was more closeness than he thought possible. Almost every day she undressed him, bathed him and rubbed his body with one of her ointments. Lately he had to struggle to repress an arousal. He would think of Curfew, or freezing in some beaver pond, or of driving mules for Captain Fremont, to keep himself under control. Or of Papín returning at the wrong moment.

She turned to him now, cup in hand, and motioned for him to lie down. He eased himself away from the backrest and stretched out on the buffalo robe that had been his place of rest for the past two weeks. He took in the furs dangling from the lodge poles and the wisps of smoke disappearing through the tipi top.

Her hands brushed against his skin as she unfastened the leather strips that held his splint in place and moved his loincloth aside to expose his leg. She dipped her fingers into the cup and rubbed liquid between her palms, blowing on it to cool it. The liquid burned when she slathered it on his bare leg. He winced, then settled as the pungent ointment began its healing work.

He forced his mind away from her touching, toward Goodale and Jenny, toward Curfew, toward Papín pacing somewhere outside, awaiting his dinner. It was no use. As her hands kneaded his inner thigh, his member lurched to attention, rising like a willful tent pole under his loincloth. He coughed and tugged at the edge of the buffalo robe to cover the evidence.

She paused, fingers resting on his knee. He chanced a glance at her face. The corners of her mouth were curled up into that subtle, private smile he fantasized was meant for him.

She said in French, "So. you are very much alive."

He laughed and reached for her, his fingers tracing the curved creases at the corners of her mouth. She clasped his hand in hers and pressed it to her cheek. Her eyes sought his and held, gray pools inviting him to plunge in.

Medina's universe shifted. In that moment he resolved he would have her, ask her to go with him, to leave Papín and become his woman. He knew with sudden certainty, as bodies sometimes know such things, that she would say yes.

There was a sudden stirring at the lodge opening. Medina jerked his hand away as if from a campfire coal.

Papín stepped in, his face beaming and a steaming copper pot in his hand.

"From Jenny. Buffalo liver. Just the thing for our patient, no?" His eyes swept past Takánsy and settled on Medina. "You look better, my friend. The color, she is returning to your face, sure enough."

27

DILEMMA

Medina struggled out of the canvas tent that was once again his home after leaving Takánsy's comfortable lodge. The splint was off, but his stiff leg wasn't yet ready to bear his full weight. He pulled himself up to a standing position next to where his gear was piled, using the crutch Takánsy fashioned for him. The smooth ash wood felt reassuring after a week of practice. A few more days and he would use it for firewood.

Yesterday he'd retrieved his money cache and delivered eighty dollars to Papín for Takánsy's help with the horses. That done, there was no reason to stay at Bridger's. He dropped his remaining coins—seventy dollars—into the hidden carrying pouch on the inside of his belt.

He glanced at his tent. Frayed on its edges, smudged dirty

gray by campfire smoke, it looked forlorn, despite being lit by the morning sun. In a few more days he would roll it up, tie it to a pack horse and head off for a last fling at beaver trapping.

The question was, would he leave with Takánsy or without her?

Ever since that promise-filled touch of her hand on his, he'd grappled with possible ways to make this happen. He'd have to find the right moment to ask her. Would she agree? After three long days in his old surroundings, doubt nibbled at him like termites tunneling through wood. What if that touch, the way she'd held his hand to her cheek, that caress of her eyes, had been a momentary impulse? What if he'd only imagined it? Even if he hadn't, what if their mutual attraction was outweighed by her loyalty to Papín and her marriage vow?

Maybe he could pretend to have a vision. God could appear to him in a burning bush or a cloud of smoke, like in the Bible. Jésu could approve of what he was urging her to do.

He rehearsed the telling of it, but envisioned her eyes boring through the falsehood.

What about Papín? Should he wait for him to leave on one of his trading trips? What would be the look on his friend's face when he returned to find his wife gone? Would Papín seek revenge, or would he accept fate and go on about his business?

Sneaking off with Takánsy would be the coward's way, like a coyote slinking through the underbrush. It wouldn't be honorable, if one could speak of honor when stealing his friend's wife. He would have to speak to Papín directly. Could he propose a simple trade, appeal to Papín's instinct for a bargain? How much money could he offer? The idea of treating Takánsy like an item for barter soured his stomach.

Papín's wealth overshadowed his. She'd be less well off if she left him. Medina wanted her and their children to have good things, not scarcity. He thought about the river ferry idea, or a toll bridge on an Oregon Trail river crossing, a trading post perhaps. He imagined growing rich, outfitting her future lodge with fine things. He vowed she'd never regret going with him.

He nudged his saddlebag with his toe, bent down to pull out a dried mint leaf, popped it in his mouth and began to chew. He spat out the green froth and wiped his mouth with the back of his hand.

At times during the past few days he'd tried to forget his obsession with Takánsy. Go with Goodale, find another woman, get on with life. Yet he couldn't shake her. Two nights ago he'd spent an evening in Jenny's lodge, Goodale talking, him drinking. At one point Goodale set the bottle aside.

"You carrying on like this be the last hooch for a thousand miles. What you trying to do, pickle your insides?"

"Killing the pain," Medina said, pointing to his leg. What he was really trying to kill was his obsession. It hadn't worked.

Now, standing beside his tent, he recalled seeing Takánsy's ghost stare for the first time, witnessing the sadness of her cutting ritual. Her marriage to Papín had not lifted her melancholy. Only he, Medina, had been able to that. He'd lifted her spirits, brought a smile to her lips, put the spark back into those gray eyes. More was at stake than his own selfish desire. Her future happiness depended on him.

Armed with this thought, he rinsed his mouth with water, tucked the crutch under his arm and limped out through the sagebrush toward Takánsy's lodge. The day was bright with promise; no leaves were left to filter the sun, no clouds hinted of November snows. Medina took this as a good sign.

He stopped in front of her lodge opening. There was no sign of Papín. Sunlight poured through the open flap onto her legs crossed on a buffalo robe. She was sewing tiny red beads onto one of the neglected leather shirts. Her slender fingers left a trail of red bumps straight and true as an arrow shaft.

Her hands paused as his shadow darkened her knee.

"Mariano."

She set the shirt aside, rose and stepped out into the sunlight. She raised a hand to shade her eyes then moved around him to put the sun at her back.

She was dressed in her working clothes: fringed shirt, leggings, and that trademark riding skirt. Her braids curtained over the gentle curve of her breasts. He caught a whiff of sage as he turned to face her.

Her eyes roved over him. She cupped his chin in her hand and peered into his eyes.

"Eyes like eyes should be," she said. "Head healed." She stepped back and pointed to his leg.

"Better. Almost ready." He leaned the crutch against the

sloping wall of the tipi and circled around her, causing her to turn in place to watch his progress. His limp was almost gone.

She nodded, appearing satisfied, then fixed him with her gaze. "You are leaving soon?"

Her voice, he convinced himself, hinted of sadness.

"Takánsy." The word came out softly, almost reverently. He regarded her for a long moment, groping for what to say next. "Is Papín...where is he?"

She shrugged. "Horses, maybe. He goes and comes. You wanting to see him?"

"No. You will walk with me to the stream, yes?"

She cocked her head and smiled. Without hesitation she lowered the lodge flap and reached out to retrieve his crutch.

"No. Leave it."

He led them away, trying hard not to limp. They passed through the sage into the willows along the stream. He led her upstream to the place he had bathed, where she had performed her ritual. He patted the rock ledge. They sat down, side by side, turned toward each other, his right knee touching her left.

"Takánsy. There is something I must ask you."

That elusive smile appeared on her mouth. "You are saying my name better now. Like one of my people."

He nodded. God knew he had practiced it long enough, in dreams as well as when awake.

"Takánsy, my wounds, they are almost healed now. Thanks to you, I am ready for the new life. I think much about it, what I am to do. I will build a crossing, a river bridge along the trail the Oregon travelers use. There is fortune there. I know it." He said this fiercely, willing it true. "The horse trading, it will be a big part. I plan to have big herd, the finest animals, worth much, yes?"

She gave him a slight nod, eyes alert, waiting.

He swallowed to moisten his dry mouth.

"The horses will need training. You are...I need you for the horses. We are a good team in our work with the horses, and I..."

He paused, annoyed that his words sounded like a business deal. Then he took in a deep breath and plunged ahead.

"The truth is, I ask more than that, more than the horse training. The last time we were together, I touched you, here."

With his fingers he traced the lines at the sides of her mouth. She turned her face into his open hand and brushed his palm with her lips. A current traveled all the way to his toes, nearly lifting him off the rock.

"To leave alone, to go without you, it is not possible. I am asking you to come with me."

He stopped breathing.

She held his gaze for a long moment, then cast a glance toward the camp.

"Papín."

There it was. Spoken as a statement, but raised as a question. Frowning, she turned back to face him.

He drew in a quick breath. She hadn't said no, but the Papín question might turn into a no.

He said, "I will speak with Papín. He knows that between you and me, there is…heart." He closed his hands and crossed his arms at the wrist in front of his chest, the sign for love. "I will offer him much. More than..." he started to say, more than you are worth, but changed to, "more than he will think possible. More than he can resist."

Doubt clouded her face.

He rushed ahead. "Your marriage to Papín, your vow, it is strong for you, I know. But a priest can fix it. For us, we find a priest, do a Blackrobe marriage. Jésu will bless us."

She reached into her belt pouch to finger her rosary beads.

"It is a big thing I ask. A hard choice. Your answer, it needs time. Maybe you can tell me later?"

Her expression didn't change.

He rummaged for more words, but none came. He placed a hand over his heart to calm the thudding in his ribs.

She pulled his hand away and held it against her cheek. A smile worked its way onto her face, that understated, elusive smile he'd so often strived to coax from her. A smile that said yes.

In return, his smile stretched into a grin wide as Green River. He stood, pulled her to her feet, and buried his face into her neck, drinking in the scent of her. Laughter seized him. He grasped her shoulders, pushed away and let out a wolf howl into the warming air. He turned, pulled her into line behind him and set off in the direction of her lodge to look for Papín.

28

THE CHOICE

Papín was standing in front of the lodge when they returned, Medina's crutch in his hand. The sun gleamed on his hairless pate, freshly oiled that morning, and bounced off a new brass compass suspended on a chain around his neck. His spotless shirt and leggings, decorated with Takánsy's beadwork, hugged his frame as if they'd been sewn on. Medina felt a familiar tug of admiration for the trader, which didn't make it easier to do what he was about to do.

Papín stepped forward, hoisting the crutch aloft.

"Aha, my friend, I see you are walking again, almost without the limp, no?" He set the crutch back against the tipi, stepped to one side and with his showman's flourish, gestured toward the carved wood staff. "This, you can throw away now. I sell him to a traveler."

Medina forced out a chuckle.

Papín drew Takánsy into a quick embrace, then held her at arm's length so his eyes could rove over her face.

"So, for why you two are walking together? Testing the leg, maybe? Looking for the plant medicines?"

He winked at Medina. Takánsy looked down.

Medina bobbed his head in what might be taken as a yes, and tried to smile. He searched Papín's face for any sign of suspicion, but found only friendliness. He swallowed hard.

Papín released Takánsy and laid a hand on Medina's shoulder.

"You are soon traveling with Tim Goodale to the beaver country, no? For you, I have something." He ducked inside the lodge, knelt down and began rummaging through a pile of trade goods.

Medina glanced at Takánsy, but her eyes were cast down. She would not meet his gaze.

Papín popped back out of the lodge holding a cloth bag. He emptied its contents into his hand: an elegant ivory pipe carved in the form of a fox head, along with a silver pipe cleaner and tobacco tamper stamped with the image of a fox.

"With those Utes, you are smart like the fox," he said. "For those long nights beside the beaver ponds, I give you this to remind you what I tell you about the Oregon trade. You have the knack, my Spanish friend, to become a trader first class. That is where riches lie, not in beaver skin. If you ever decide to take up the trading, you must join me. We will become famous, like Chouteau, no?"

His smile enveloped them like a warm blanket. Papín stepped forward to embrace Medina and in the French fashion, implanted kisses on either side of his face.

"We will miss you, my friend. You are always welcome in our lodge, no?"

Medina gaped at the trader's smiling face. Where was the Frenchman's canny scrutiny, his shrewdness in reading other men's motives? Instead of suspicion, Medina saw appreciation, friendship, admiration. It was the kind of trusting look Chepe Luis had given him on that dusty play field long ago.

Medina blinked and tried to smile. The words he'd been rehearsing skittered away like field mice scurrying for cover.

"What is it?" Papín asked, cocking his head. "Your tongue, she is tied up at the grandness of my gift to you?"

"Yes, yes. Thank you. It is more than I...deserve." Medina's voice squeaked like a rusty hinge. "I owe you my life. My thanks to you. A thousand thanks." He clapped Papín on the back, Spanish-style. That way he wouldn't have to look him in the eye.

On his right, Takánsy regarded him gravely. He stared at her and tried to muster the will to finish what he'd decided to do. Resolve eluded him. In its place rose the specter of betrayal, the look on Papín's face that would appear if he carried through with his plan. The same look that had devastated the face of Chepe Luis when Medina had abandoned him to the bullies. Whatever else happened, he didn't want to be the cause of such a look on the face of Papín. The shame of it would undo him.

But what about Takánsy? Was he averting one betrayal only to commit another? Would he now abandon her after persuading her to go with him? He pulled away from Papín and looked up at the sky, hoping for a sign. A golden eagle circled overhead. He wished he could grab its talons and be carried away, far from the impossible choice he'd set for himself.

The moment stretched into an awkward pause. Their eyes, Papín's and Takánsy's, went from soft to questioning to verging on alarm. Medina stepped back, tried to force a smile.

"It is time to go pack my gear. Señor Tim will chew off his moustache if we do not get to those beaver. Tomorrow I will come back for a goodbye, before we leave."

He turned. Takánsy was staring at him. He squared his shoulders, sucked in a big breath and limped away. Inside his chest, his heart nearly failed him.

29

THE LEAVING

Morning dawned like a shroud, cold and gray. Medina fastened the second pannier to the horse's packsaddle, balancing its weight with the one hanging on the other side. Beaver traps and chains thudded against each other, their sound muffled by their leather wraps. Traveling into the Uintas should be silent as possible. The other pannier held his canvas traveling lodge, blanket and cook gear.

Jenny Goodale stepped out of her lodge waving a wood spoon.

"You come in, eat," she said. A tiny cloud of vapor puffed from her mouth into the frosty air.

Medina caught the scent of meat cooking.

"Thank you, but this morning I have no hunger." He forced a smile and got a frown in response. "Tell Señor Tim we leave soon. I must tell my goodbye to Papín."

Jenny cocked her head, gave him a knowing smile.

"The leaving, it is sometimes hard to do."

The rising sun poked above the eastern horizon as he arrived at Takánsy's lodge. She stepped out to greet him, followed by Papín. Medina could scarcely look at her.

She handed him a leather pouch.

"Use these," she said. "You must promise."

He nodded and accepted the medicine as he managed an abrupt "Thank you."

He turned to Papín.

"For you, it is hard to find a gift you don't already have. But this, you may not see before." He pulled a small Spanish dagger with an ivory handle from his belt. "This once belonged to my father. You carry it here, in special holder." He pulled up his legging to reveal the leather scabbard he had sewn into the top of his moccasin. "Takánsy can make the holder for you, yes?"

Papín accepted the dagger, turned it over in his hand. "This… she is beautiful. Such craft."

"That hiding knife will keep you safe when Captain Jack comes to take your rifle," Medina said, trying to sound light-hearted.

Papín laughed, clapped him on the shoulder. "Then you will need it more than Papín."

"I have another. A replacement."

"You do, sure enough. Thank you, my friend." Papín stepped away, gave his courtly bow. "Travel safe, and come back when you tire of the beaver."

Medina forced a smile. "Perhaps some day."

He turned to Takánsy. The beads on her doeskin dress flashed blue, red and white in the dawn's pale light. A breeze lifted a strand of hair over her cheekbone. Her face betrayed no emotion, but her eyes pinned him like bayonets.

He drew from his possibles bag the tiny cross he had spent much of the night carving from a juniper branch. It was threaded onto a thin leather thong. He draped it over her head.

"For you. Jésu protect you always."

She touched the cross with her hand.

He spun away to leave before the constriction in his throat choked him.

PART III

David M. Jessup

30

GAMBLING

El Pueblo, March 1844

Mariano Medina glanced at the card he drew and tried to keep his face from twitching. No help for the two pairs he held in his hand. Fives and sevens. He resisted the urge to bite down on his pipe stem.

A year and a half had passed since he said goodbye to Takánsy and Papín at Bridger's Fort. Now he sat on the hard floor of an adobe room in the scruffy new trading post of El Pueblo, five hundred miles to the south, risking his remaining coins in a poker game.

Four pairs of eyes stared at him, probing for his reaction. The men sat in a circle on rolled-up blankets and buffalo robes, elbows resting on knees. Acrid tobacco smoke hung close above them, trapped by the ceiling of *vigas* supporting the *latillas* that made the base of the mud roof. Their poker game occupied nearly half the dirt floor in the kitchen room of Robert Fisher's squat adobe house.

Medina leaned back against the rough wall and glanced at the crude cottonwood plank door, already beginning to warp and crack. Eleven other hovels surrounded the El Pueblo plaza, which was not much bigger than a courtyard. Medina's room was two doors down. Like all the others, its back wall formed part of the fort wall that surrounded the entire settlement, while its front door opened onto the plaza.

Medina wished he were in his own room.

He plucked up his last coin and tossed it into the center of the rough gray blanket lying on the floor in front of them.

"Raise one dollar," he said. He tried to sound confident, but knew he'd hesitated too long.

To his left, David Spaulding folded his cards and tossed them on the blanket. But Ed Conn, with a crooked smile Medina didn't like, tossed in a dollar and said, "I call, you banty rooster."

"Me, too," said Robert Fisher, next to him.

Charlie Autobees, last man in the circle, folded.

They showed their hands. Medina's two pairs lost to Conn's three queens. Conn raked in his coins with a hairy hand.

"Another round?" he said. "I'll spot you another five."

"No, grácias," Medina answered. He hooked his finger through the handle of the brown jug that Charlie handed him and took a long swallow. Simeon Turley's Taos Lightning hadn't lost its bite. He stood up and moved toward the door. He staggered, recovered, straightened his shoulders.

"Need some help?" Conn asked, his voice a sneer.

Medina shrugged, smiled, and backed out the door. Of the faces that watched him leave, only Charlie's showed any sympathy.

Outside, March cold hit him in the face. It was dark, probably close to midnight. He stared around the small plaza. The only light came from a candle flame glowing through the cracks in the door he'd just closed behind him. He hugged his arms to his chest and stepped unsteadily toward the room that Charlie Autobees had lent him. He pushed in through the door, slumped down onto the buffalo robe in the corner, covered himself with a rough wool blanket and closed his eyes to shut out the view of the ceiling, which seemed to swirl in circles.

Strange to have linked up again with Charlie Autobees. Here he was, back on the north bank of the Arkansas across the border from

Mexico, close to where he'd landed after leaving Taos. What was it now…seventeen years ago? Once again helping Charlie. Once again hauling trade goods for a living. His hopes for a new kind of life hadn't "panned out," as the gold prospectors might say.

Why hadn't he followed through with his plan to leave with Takánsy? His sense of honor felt hollow now. Instead of betraying Papín, he'd betrayed her. She would have come with him, and Papín would have regained his footing quickly. He tried to recall her face at their parting. Had there been a look of disappointment in her eyes? In truth, her reaction had been unreadable. There had even been a trace of that smile. Had she felt betrayed? Relieved? Or nothing at all?

After leaving Bridger's Fort, he'd set off with Goodale for a last fling of beaver trapping. They'd survived that first winter in the Uintas, dodging Captain Jack's band of Utes. In the spring they packed a skimpy trove of beaver plews down to Bent's Fort on the Arkansas, only to discover that the pittance offered for them was not worth the taking. Goodale decided to haul the furs all the way down the Santa Fe Trail to St. Louis for a better price.

Left on his own, Medina signed on as muleskinner to a party bound for St. Vrain's Fort on the Platte. From there, he swallowed his pride and took up with Fremont's second expedition in July of 1843. Before the hawk-nosed captain could reach Bridger's Fort, Medina asked for his pay and headed back south. He couldn't face seeing Takánsy again. It would be like losing another finger.

After returning to Bent's Fort, Medina gambled away his remaining Fremont earnings and hired himself out to a trading party on its way to El Pueblo farther up the Arkansas. He accepted a room in Charlie Autobee's house in return for doing odd jobs—caring for mules and sheep, patching holes in the roof, hauling wood. So far he'd resisted Charlie's requests to haul whiskey north. At this point, April 1844, El Pueblo had been his home for three months. Three cold, gray, wintery months. Not even the Mexican women's determined efforts to celebrate Christmas had cheered him.

El Pueblo was not where Medina wanted to be. It was a new border town full of men with borderline occupations. Mountain men trying to survive rock-bottom beaver prices, traders without licenses, illegal whiskey runners, buffalo skinners, men with shadowy pasts.

A low adobe wall as shabby as their occupations surrounded

the settlement. Inside they kept their Indian and Mexican wives in crude adobe huts. Outside, they grazed their cattle and sheep herds along the river bottom. They hauled St. Louis trade goods down to Taos and brought back Simeon Turley's whiskey to the Indians to swap for buffalo robes and skins, which they hauled to St. Louis in exchange for more goods. They passed back and forth over the border with Mexico like phantoms. Through the long nights, they drank, told lies, and gambled away their meager earnings.

A rough equality reigned in El Pueblo. As a trapper, hunter, guide and muleskinner, Medina was accepted. But it was a hardscrabble equality, a leavening at the lowest level. What was he doing there? He used to think he was made for better things, a life of prosperity as the owner of a ferry or a toll bridge. Now he'd just gambled away most of his money stash. At thirty-two winters he had nothing to show for his life. He wiped his mouth with the back of his hand. How had he fallen into such a state?

His eyelids grew heavy. He shivered into his blanket and drifted off into a drunken sleep.

31

A FAVOR FOR CHARLIE

When Medina crawled out from under his blanket the next morning and groped his way out onto the plaza, his head was pounding and his eyes bleary. He proped himself up against the rough adobe wall and squinted into the light.

The first thing he saw was Sycamore, Charlie Autobees' Arapahoe wife. She was his "out-of-door-wife-in-a-tent," Charlie's companion and workhorse on his trading trips. In Taos, Charlie had another wife, the daughter of a Mexican trader, who raised his three children. Both wives were well connected among their own people, a boon to Charlie's trading business.

Big as a tree, Sycamore loomed over Medina, silver ear ornaments flashing in the sun.

"Charlie want to see you," she said.

Her voice seemed unusually loud, grating on Medina's ears like the squawk of a magpie. Her fat cheeks heaved upward into a smile, nearly closing her eyes. She waddled off toward the Pueblo gate to fetch water from the river in a huge clay jug. It looked like a toy tucked under her arm.

Medina found Charlie in his room, sitting behind a rough plank table, poring over a ledger book. A thin man of slight build, he glanced up as Medina pushed through the door.

Charlie was a year younger than Medina, but looked ten years older. This was mostly due, Medina thought, to two deep parallel lines that angled down each side of Charlie's face, one starting from the side of his wide nose and the other from the corner of his mouth, like twin ruts running through a stubble field. His face seemed locked in a perpetual scowl, lips pursed, narrow eyes squinting. When he smiled, his face lit up in toothy friendliness, like night turning into day. Trouble was, he almost never smiled.

"Counting up the plunder you stole from me last night?" Medina said, forcing a heartiness he didn't feel. He winked at his old boss, which also served to clear his vision.

Charlie obliged him with a grin. He tipped the broad brim of his hat—which was folded up in front instead of on the sides—back over his brown curls.

"Stole, my ass. You was so drunk you was giving it away." He pushed back from the table, stood and grabbed his coat off a wall peg. "I got a way for you to get your money back. Come on, look sharp. Got some gents you need to meet."

Medina followed him outside to the corner of the compound where the horses and mules were corralled. There were three men waiting there. Thin and lanky, each taller than the next, like stair steps. All three of them held Kentucky long rifles in the crook of their arms. Wool pants, dark boots, heavy coats buttoned against the cold. Their fur hats had no brims—a badger and two skunks. Medina was struck by how alike they were. Long, thin noses, jutting jaws, scraggly beards over hollow cheeks.

"Meet the Strong brothers, Lew, Lem and Lester," Charlie said. He pointed to each as he said their names, starting with Lew, the shortest.

"This is Mariano, the guide I was telling you about. He's

been all over creation. He can get you to Taos the back way, like we talked about."

Medina froze. *Taos?* That was the last place on earth he wanted to go. He swallowed a protest and managed to nod and smile at the three men. Somehow he knew not to extend a hand. It was obvious the Strong brothers wouldn't have taken it. They stared at him like slave traders assessing a new arrival.

He glanced at Charlie with a look that asked what in hell this was all about

Lester, the tallest, gave a slow nod. His badger hat matched the color of his beard.

"We're traders. Missouri. Goods in those bundles over there, some fine trade items." He pointed toward three canvas-covered mounds in front of an adobe house nearby. His voice was surprisingly rich and cultivated.

"Mr. Autobees here says the main road is blocked by that governor, Armijo, from Santa Fe. Says you know a different trail to Taos."

"Mosca Pass," Charlie said helpfully.

Medina glared. He had no intention of going to Taos.

"Once we get there we'll have some fine gifts for the Governor," Lester added. "He won't mind us slipping past his border guards." He smiled, a fine row of white teeth appearing through the underbrush of his hairy face. Lew and Lem smiled in unison.

The smiles weren't friendly, Medina thought. More like wolves grinning over a kill.

Charlie grabbed Medina by the elbow.

"Boys, now that you've met, I'll take Mariano here and help him get outfitted for the haul. Be ready to ride first thing tomorrow."

He steered Medina back toward his room.

"Don't have a conniption," he whispered in Medina's ear. "You're going to get some real plunder from that bunch."

Medina jerked his arm out of Charlie's grasp and stalked ahead. Memories of Taos still robbed him of sleep now and then, even after seventeen years. His betrayal of Chepe Luis, his cowardice in the face of Ricardo Castillo, his failure to help Señorita Fili, the death of his mother, the life of humiliation with his humble *peón* of a father.

He wondered if his father was still alive, but had no wish

to see him. He had no other relatives there, no friends, no reason to return. Every reason to avoid the place.

Charlie caught up with him. "Hear me out," he said.

Medina turned to face him.

"Mariano, you and me, we go back a long ways. I helped you out when you needed it. Now I need your help."

Medina sighed. It was true. Considering all the man had done for him, he owed Charlie big.

"Look around," Charlie said. "Most of the Pueblo boys is gone, out on trading trips. I'm leaving myself, tomorrow, soon as Sycamore gets my gear packed. Fisher and Conn, who picked you clean last night, ain't taking those Missouri boys nowhere. You're the only one who can guide them three brothers over Mosca Pass. And they'll pay plenty. Make it worth your while."

"Yours, too, I am thinking," Medina said. "Who are they? Don't look like traders."

Charlie leaned in, voice lowered. "You got that right. Don't really know what they's all about. Only a guess, mind you, but I suspect they work for the United States government. Spies for Tyler, I reckon."

Medina nodded. He'd heard talk of a possible war between Mexico and the United States. Ever since Sam Houston ran Santa Ana out of Texas, more and more Americans were traipsing into Santa Fe and other parts of northern Mexico, clamoring for what they called annexation.

"They say President Tyler wants to bring Texas into the United States, and iffen he does, there'll be war for sure." Charlie said. "Heard that at Bent's fort, direct from William Bent hisself."

"That is why Governor Armijo shuts down the border?"

"Yep. And because some fool Texans marched on Santa Fe last year and killed old Chavez on the Cimarron branch of the Trail. A good man, Chavez." Charlie stroked his chin and shot a thoughtful glance back toward the three men at the corral. "But the Governor done made things worse. Closing the border has got everyone riled. Feelings is runnin' high against Mexicans. Can't blame the Strong brothers for that."

"They think I'm a Mexican," Medina reminded him.

Charlie looked surprised. "Well hell, I guess you are."

Medina sometimes wondered who he was. He'd been born in Arroyo Hondo when it was a part of New Spain, before Mexico won its independence in 1821. He didn't feel much like a Mexican citizen. Or an American. Mostly just mountain man who happened to be Spanish.

Charlie tipped back his hat and scratched the curls that spilled out.

"They's plenty of Mexicans mad at Armijo, too. Folks in Taos and Santa Fe depend on the Saint Louis trade. They sure as hell can't get the things they need from Mexico City."

"Armijo probably gets everything he needs," Medina said.

"Yep. The Governor gets his take at the border and the custom house. Makes sure his cronies get their share, too. It's the common folk that suffers."

Medina nodded. He imagined Ricardo Castillo outfitting his hacienda with luxuries from St. Louis. That red-top bully was probably a patrón now, in place of old Don Diego. Probably making the servants bow and scrape. Medina swallowed, mouth suddenly dry.

"Another thing," Charlie said. "Mexicans, rich and poor, depend on the Americans to fight the Comanches. Those bloody bastards are raiding clear down to Chihuahua, Nuevo Leon, even Tamualipas. Killing men, raping women, stealing children and selling them as slaves. Their own damn Mexican government don't do nothin' to stop it. Or can't. Least the Texans fight the Comanches. 'Bout the only thing they's good for."

Medina's throat tightened at Charlie's mention of Comanches. It triggered that damned knife image of blood waterfalling over a copper colored hand.

"You sick?" Charlie asked. "You just turned into a white man."

Medina shook his head and tried to laugh. He needed a drink. He turned and walked away. What had come over him? Must have been his unease over the prospect of running into red-top Castillo.

"Mariano." Charlie caught up with him, put a hand on his arm.

Medina drew a deep breath. "Charlie, you are good friend. But Taos, it is not possible. What I can do—will do—is take them to Arroyo Hondo. It is only twelve miles from Taos. The road from there, it is easy."

"Arroyo Hondo, then. Sure. That'll do. That'll do just fine. You can talk to Simeon Turley while you're there. Find out when we can expect the next shipment of whiskey. This border business has slowed things down. Up north, Arapahos and Cheyennes are getting impatient."

"How much? For the guiding."

Charlie eyed him. "They offered eighty, but I can probably..."

"You keep the money. What I am wanting is horses. Say, five horses. Good ones."

Charlie nodded. "I'll agree to four. You seen my animals. Take your pick of the four best. But why horses?"

"Not so likely to gamble them away. Charlie, I must leave this place. Start over. Up north. A river crossing somewhere, along one of the trails."

"Sure, Mariano. Wish you'd stay here. There's plunder to be made, hauling. But if you, well, you know..."

"Deal, then?"

"Deal. Much obliged." They shook hands.

Medina walked back to his room to get some water and gather his gear. Arroyo Hondo. Going there would not be so bad. Not likely he would run into Ricardo Castillo. Or Chepe Luis. And even if he did, maybe they wouldn't recognize him. It was all so long ago.

Fili? Well, he had to admit to some curiosity about the Señorita Filomena. What had become of her? She would be what, thirty-four, thirty-five years now, a couple winters older than he? Would she still be as beautiful as he remembered? No matter. Seeing her would be about as likely as finding gold in the Arkansas River.

One thing he could do in Arroyo Hondo is visit his mother's grave, if he could find it. He would leave a memento on it, a bouquet of dried flowers perhaps, maybe some red berries. She'd died of sudden heart failure while Medina was asleep, according to his father, and was buried behind their house. Medina remembered the grave, a pile of stones with a cross, but he couldn't remember seeing her body. Strange, now that he thought about it. In other funerals he'd attended as a boy, they displayed the body so you could lay a flower on it before nailing the casket shut.

He shook his head to clear it and stepped into his room to prepare for the trip ahead.

32

ARROYO HONDO

Six days later, on April first, Medina left the Strong brothers at the Arroyo Hondo turnoff on the road to Taos. The trip had been easy. Mosca Pass still had snow, but it was not deep. From the summit they'd descended past the great sand dunes into the treeless San Luis Valley. He'd kept away from the main road and avoided settlements. One small band of Utes had watched them from a hillock in the distance, but no Navajo or Comanche had appeared.

Most importantly, they hadn't encountered any of Governor Armijo's border patrols. The customs house still awaited the brothers when they entered Taos. But the Strongs were prepared. Bribes would be paid. The governor and his cronies would get their *mordidas*. Medina wondered if Ricardo Castillo would be one of them.

David M. Jessup

Despite their pack mules laden with trade goods, Lew, Lem and Lester never asked about prices, exchange rates, or the availability of items in Taos. Whatever their true purpose, they'd been close mouthed about it. In their eyes, no doubt, he was a goddam Mexican, no more to be trusted than a coyote skulking around camp at the far edge of firelight.

At the fork in the road to Arroyo Hondo, Medina pointed them toward Taos, explained that it was just a few hours away. They gave him a hard stare, a curt nod, and rode off without a word, pack mules in tow. They carried their Kentucky long rifles in the crooks of their arms, like men spoiling for a fight. Medina was glad to be rid of them.

He reined Don Justino around and into the village of Arroyo Hondo to find Turley's Mill so he could report to Charlie about whiskey supplies. It was getting on toward supper time. The sky was stark blue and cloudless, the temperature early-spring warm. The lowering sun set the surrounding hills aglow, turning washed out sand into a rich brown color, faded junipers into squat bunches of deep green. Something about that slanting, late afternoon light nagged at his memory.

The road ran along the back side of an *acéquia* that channeled water to scores of narrow strips of land running down to the Rio Hondo, a water-starved stream flowing out of the mountains to the east. Each small plot hosted an adobe hut, a tiny corral with a goat or two, a few bedraggled chickens, a burro, sometimes a pig. None of the houses seemed familiar.

Close to the river a man planted seeds in an open furrow. Children played outside some homes, barefoot boys rolling hoops or whacking at each other with sticks, girls with dusty knees playing jumping games or fussing with corn husk dolls. Their squeals and laughter heralded the end of winter, the exuberance of coming spring. Had he played like that as a child?

Next to the road, a short, round woman drew a stack of steaming *empanadas* out of a round adobe oven. She stared at him as he pulled up beside the fence. The onion-meaty smell set his mouth watering.

"Turley's Mill?" he said. "Which way?"

She pointed with her chin in the direction he was already headed. She didn't move or speak; just stood there like a stump as he rode past. Her dark, unblinking eyes radiated mistrust.

He rounded a curve and followed the road down toward the creek. A barn-like building with vertical wood plank siding and a stone foundation stood there, mill wheel turning slowly in the flowing water. Several big freight wagons were parked at its side. Mules milled around in a nearby corral. Two men pushed through a door, walked over to one of the wagons and pulled out some wood crates. Medina rode up to a hitching post, dismounted, looped Don Justino's halter rope over the rail and stretched his saddle-stiffened legs.

"Hola," he said, as the taller man hefted a crate out of the wagon and carried it back toward the mill. The other one turned to face him.

"Buenos días," The short man wore a small *sombrero*, a frayed wool shirt, grimy canvas pants, and sandals. His hand rested on a machete stuck in his rope belt. He didn't smile.

"Mariano Medina, at your service. Charlie Autobees sent me to speak with Señor Turley. He is here?"

The man's jaw dropped. He grasped the corner of the wagon to steady himself and thrust his head closer to peer at Medina's face. His eyes were a little bloodshot, as if seeing clearly was a strain, but there was no smell of liquor on him. His skin was smooth, face round and bland, except for the look of surprise on it.

"Mariano Medina? From Taos?"

"Well, yes, long ago, but..."

The man's face broke into a wide grin. He clapped his hands together in a gesture that Medina recognized. Now it was his turn to go slack-jawed.

"Chepe Luis?"

"Yes, yes, my God, how many years has it been? *Dios Mío,* we were just boys." He stepped forward and grabbed Medina in a back-slapping embrace. *"Un abrazo, mi amigo.* Welcome home!"

Medina stiffened, then did his best to respond, but words failed him. Chepe Luis didn't seem to notice.

"You can stay for a while? We can talk? Señor Turley is not here, gone to Taos for supplies, so we can wait at my house for him to return. We can take a cup or two together. Señor Turley, he gives us a pint of whiskey each week, part of pay. You come. Meet my wife, children. We will speak of the old days."

Medina stared at Chepe Luis.

"But of course," he finally said, his voice strained. Then, at a loss for better words, he said, "Here, allow me to help you unload these boxes."

Two hours later, as the sun's flaming rim dipped below the horizon and triggered the release of the desert's cold, Medina sat smoking inside his childhood friend's modest home. Chepe Luis had cleverly crafted two chairs out of twisted juniper and two canvas cushions stuffed with straw. On these they sat talking as Chepe Luis's wife, Candelaria, cleared away the wooden bowls with the remains of their dinner of tortillas, beans, and chicken, which Chepe Luis had insisted be cooked in Medina's honor.

Candelaria was a pretty woman, small and graceful, with a quick smile that enlivened her dark eyes. She bobbed her hair short, exposing her neck above a white blouse and collar embroidered with blue thread. Two small children clung to the dark folds in her full length skirt. They peered at Medina with wide, curious eyes. He smiled and winked at each in turn, causing them to bury their faces in the fabric.

Candelaria lit two candles and set them on the table. With a *"Con su permiso,"* she bowed to the men and tugged the children toward a thick curtain that closed off one end of the room.

"To bed," she said to the little ones, who showed no signs of being tired.

Medina stood and bowed. "A thousand thanks, Señora. The meal, it was delicious."

Teeth flashed, and she disappeared behind the curtain.

Medina settled back into his chair. He took a deep breath, taking in the scent of the meal and a hint of juniper that permeated the room. The dirt floor was swept clean, the table top washed, the sparse utensils in their place, a vase with dried flowers set in an arched alcove in the adobe wall. Beside it hung a wooden crucifix.

Medina felt tears brimming. Surprised, he looked away from Chepe Luis and wiped his eyes. He reached for the cup of whiskey that Chepe Luis set before him and emptied it in one swallow.

Medina was grateful their discussion focused on current issues: the whiskey business, tense relations between the provincial government in Santa Fe and its central government in Mexico City, the slowdown in trade on the Santa Fe trail, the ever present threat of Indian raids by Navajo, Ute, and lately, from the east by Comanche.

As they talked, Medina felt his own tongue loosen. It had been a long time since he could carry on a conversation entirely in Spanish, with no groping for words.

Chepe Luis raged about *los ricos cojudos*, the rich assholes who dominated the area. "Their *haciendas* grow ever larger from stealing all we have. They sell seed and tools to *campesinos* at high prices, then take their land when they can't pay it back with interest. Sometimes they just muscle in, take more land, force the people to work for them. No better than slaves. They squeeze down trade with the Americans, charge high tariffs and make them pay bribes, so everything costs more. When the Indian barbarians attack, the *ricos* force us into their army to fight for them while our own homes and wives and children go unprotected. The central government rules us through Armijo, takes taxes from us, gives us nothing in return. No protection from the *salvajes*. Nothing!"

Chepe Luis paused in his tirade for another swig of whiskey. The muscles in his short forearms bunched into hard cords. Sweat beaded his forehead despite the evening chill.

"Those white Spanish bastards!" If words had been fists, his would have felled a man.

Medina swallowed hard. They were coming close to the topic he wanted to avoid.

33

CHILDHOOD HOME

"You remember Ricardo Castillo, the *patrón*'s son?" Chepe Luis's eyes bored into Medina's, hot and steady.

Medina nodded, averted his eyes.

"He is one of them, one of the worst. He forced us out of Taos after his father died. He took over as *patrón*. He is much worse than Don Diego. He has a mean streak like that lock of red hair on his head. We lost everything. Had to move here. "

"Yes, I remember him." Medina swigged some courage from his cup and risked a glance at his friend. "And there is something I must say. What I did, when we were boys, it is something that gives me much shame."

A smile spread over Chepe Luis's round face revealing a row of uneven teeth.

"We were just boys. Better to feel shame than be without shame." He took another drink, his smile fading. "For me, the shame was when Castillo and his gang came on their high horses to throw us off our land because we couldn't pay our debts. My brother stood to face them. I ran out the back door and hid in a juniper bush."

"What happened?"

"They threw a rope over him, dragged him through the cactus."

"Did he...?"

"He is alive. Crippled. Has a hard time with his leg now. But he has his honor." He looked toward the curtain where Candelaria crooned softly to his children. "I am blessed with a beautiful wife, two children. But the shame of hiding from them, it is still with me."

They both stared at a candle. Somber shadows flickered across their faces. They lifted their cups in a wordless toast, drank, set them down, lost in thought.

Medina broke the silence. "You have news of my father?"

"You don't know?"

"What?"

"Dead. Comanche arrow. A few months ago. He got snared in one of Governor Armijo's conscript roundups. They force us into the army. No pay. Mexico City gives them no troops and no money to pay for troops, so they round us up like stray cattle, put some old muskets into our hands, powder and ball sometimes lacking, and send us out to protect the sheep and cattle of the *hacendados*. Meanwhile our own families are unprotected. The savages come for us instead, and leave the *ricos* alone."

Medina felt hollow in his stomach. He hadn't missed his father all these years, had tried to be as unlike him as possible. But...dead?

"What happened to his body?"

Chepe Luis looked at the floor. "You don't want to know. The Comanche raiders, they do terrible things."

A chill spiked up Medina's spine.

"At least the militia brought his body back here," Chepe Luis continued. "Usually they leave them for the wolves."

"Why did they bring him here? Wasn't he living at the *hacienda* of Don Diego?"

"No. He was living here, in his old house. He was forced out of the *hacienda* after Don Diego died. Forced out of Taos, just like us.

Another victim of Ricardo Castillo." Chepe Luis screwed up his face as if to spit, then swallowed instead. "You don't know any of this?"

"No. I have avoided this place since I...had to leave."

"They accused you of raping Don Diego's daughter. I never believed it."

Medina shot him a grateful glance. "Ricardo and his two bully friends attacked her. They blamed me. They would have killed me."

"No one else believed it either," Chepe Luis said.

"What happened to her?"

"Thrown out of the big house as soon as Don Diego died. Another act of spite by her half-brother, the new Don. I haven't heard where she went, or what happened to her."

"Poor Fili. I wish I..." Medina sighed. "My father. Where is he buried?"

"Behind his house. The one at the far end of Arroyo Hondo. It is the only one up there with a stone foundation. You will see it when you ride east through the village, a good way past the other houses. There is a woman living there now. I have not met her. She moved in a week or so ago."

"I think it might be the same house where I was born. Where my mother died." I will go there tomorrow, Medina thought.

Chepe Luis nodded. "Strange," he said, giving Medina a look. "Both your father and your mother. Killed by the Comanche."

Medina felt as if a mule had kicked him in the stomach. His hand began shaking so hard he had to set his cup down.

"What? My mother?"

Chepe Luis stared at him. "Yes, but why...? Are you all right?"

"My mother was killed by the Comanche?"

"Yes, in that very house. You don't know?"

Medina shook his head, dazed. "My father told me she died of a heart attack. He took me away from there right after. To Taos. He never.... Are you sure?"

Chepe Luis's eyes softened. He grasped Medina's arm.

"I'm sorry. Yes, the story comes to me from two old-timers, Enrique Casteneda who keeps ledgers at the mill, and old Eusebio, the mule owner, who used to live out that way. The Comanche came in the early morning, before light. Three of them only, not a big raiding party. Your house was hit when your father was not there. They took your father's horse, all of Eusebio's mules, and…well…murdered your mother. I'm not sure why but she was the only one killed. You were lucky they didn't kill you. They usually kill all the *niños* they find. Asleep. Probably you were asleep."

Medina stared at his hands. They shook like aspen leaves. He clenched them into fists and stuck them between his thighs.

"My father never told me. Why would he not tell me this? No one else in Taos told me. I do not…" He paused, his voice catching.

"Your father would not speak of it. Why, I can't say. When he came back here a few years ago, after being kicked out of Don Diego's *hacienca*, the old-timers warned me not to say anything to him. They said he…" Chepe Luis pointed a finger at his own head and twirled it. "It would make him crazy."

Medina slumped back into his chair.

"I am sorry to be the one to tell you this. I thought you knew."

Medina nodded, took another drink. Mother and father, both killed by Comanches.

Candelaria emerged from behind the blanket. Eyes averted, she explained that the children were asleep and excused herself to step outside.

She'd heard it all, Medina supposed. He rose from his chair.

"Would it be possible to sleep in my tent, outside your home?"

"But my friend, our home is your home, there is no need to sleep outside. Here you are more than welcome."

"Tonight it is better for me outside. Alone."

"Yes, of course. But at least allow me to feed your horse, rub him down, yes?"

"Thank you. You are a true friend."

They parted with a warm *abrazo*.

Medina stumbled on his way out, kept himself from falling by bracing his hands against the door frame. Once outside, he spread his blanket and raised his canvas shelter on the west side of Chepe Luis's home, where he would be shaded from the morning sun.

He fell into an alcohol-induced sleep, but awoke a few hours later, his mind in tumult. What Chepe Luis had told him turned over and over in his head, even as he turned over and over in his blanket. Resigned to wakefulness, he arose just before dawn, retrieved Don Justino from the corral, saddled up, packed his gear on the cantle, bade goodbye to Chepe Luis and rode away to find the home of his birth. A cock's jarring crow marked his departure.

He found the house just as Chepe Luis had described it, at the far end of the village where a branch of the Rio Hondo flowed through a ravine in the piñon and juniper hills. His eyes roamed over the dilapidated structure, searching for something familiar. Some of the rocks that formed the foundation had fallen away, giving the house a gap-toothed look. He recognized the rough stone step where he had played as a child, but not much else. The flat roof was supported by *vigas* that extended a short distance beyond the front wall. There were cracks in the adobe next to a single window covered by wooden shutters. One corner of the roof was patched with a piece of tin that flapped slowly in the morning breeze, like a hand waving him away. A current of unease prickled his neck.

He tethered Don Justino to a juniper and stepped up to the front door. He rapped on it just as the sun topped the mountains to the east. A stirring inside.

Then a woman's sleep laden voice asked, "Who is it?"

"Mariano Medina. I used to live here. As a child."

Silence. He heard a faint brushing sound on the other side of the door, then a pause. He imagined an eye scrutinizing him through a crack between the boards.

The door swung open to reveal a sleep-lined face. But all Mariano saw was a flare of brown hair with auburn streaks that used to be lustrous, and a pair of baffled blue-green eyes that used to sparkle.

Medina gaped. "Señorita Fili?"

34

THE GRAVE

She stared at him blank-faced.

"Who are you? How do you know me?" Her left hand clutched a worn gray blanket around her shoulders. Her right held an old musket pointed at his middle. Her fingers twitched. The scent of soap-scrubbed skin and yesterday's tortillas wafted toward him.

Medina stepped back and doffed his hat.

He stammered, "Señorita Filomena, I used to work with your father's horses. Mariano, the stable boy."

Her eyebrows knotted up. "Mariano. At the stable?" She peered at him, appearing to search her mind as if plodding through a cemetery looking for a lost marker.

His eyes did their own search, looking past her into the room, but it was too dark to see much more than a pallet on the floor against

David M. Jessup

the far wall. He focused again on her, astounded at finding her here, an older version of the beauty he'd once adored from afar. And despite some lines in her skin, some padding where none used to be, she was still beautiful, even in her just-now-awakened state.

Recognition finally flickered on her face as her eyes regained their old sparkle.

"Mariano, at the stable. Yes, I used to ride my father's horses. You helped me. Mariano." She repeated his name as if trying to memorize it.

"A thousand pardons. I had no idea you lived here. My father used to own this house. His grave, I am told, is somewhere in back. I was born here, lived here until I was five, then we left, and...well, I have never returned until now."

Her eyes narrowed. "You have come to take this house away from me."

"No, no, not at all. I'm not staying. Just passing through. Trying to remember."

She nodded, face softening. "Your father. Antonio Medina. You know what happened to him?"

"I just heard."

"Killed. He was a good man. He knew my mother. He told her I could live here if...anything happened to him. Or her."

"And now it has."

"Yes."

"Did you...see him after he was killed?"

"No, they buried him before I got here. His grave is behind the house. I will show you. But first I will dress. Make something to eat." She frowned. "I have no coffee. But some juniper berry tea. You would like some?" She spoke in short bursts broken by pauses that seemed a bit too long.

"Yes. I would like that. I can go to see the grave on my own while you..."

She backed into the room before he could finish and closed the door.

Medina stepped away and examined his surroundings in the growing light of morning. His headache had dwindled to tolerable levels. His drinking must stop, he told himself.

A round adobe *horno* squatted near the corner of the house, cold ashes spilling out of its arched opening. Next to it was a fire pit, also full of ashes. Instead of searching for the grave, he busied himself by laying a fire, postponing his encounter with his past.

He found a shovel with a broken handle leaning against a wooden outhouse. He scooped out the ashes and tossed them into the opening in the outhouse seat. From a shuck of dry corn stalks he gathered some cobs and husks and laid them in the fire pit. The area around the house had been well gleaned of wood, but he found a few dry sticks and laid them over the corn husks and backed off a step. The oven and fire pit stirred nothing in his memory. Maybe they weren't there when he was a child.

He left the fire pit and walked around the north side of the house. The pole fence that formed a small corral there seemed more familiar. He recalled sitting next to it, wedging small stones and bits of cloth into the spaces between the skinny fence poles, hiding places for child treasures. The fence was broken in places and the dung piles inside were gray and crumbling. It had been a while since any burros had called it home.

He continued around the back corner of the house where he discovered a single, faded skirt and blouse hanging from a rope stretched between two mesquite trees. Just beyond that, two earthen mounds were visible, one fresh, covered with rocks guarded by a wood cross, the other a mere bump in the landscape with a few tufts of grass sprouting from its surface. His mother and father, side by side. He walked over and knelt before the older mound. He reached out and picked up an egg-sized clod of dirt from its surface. Dried hard, it wouldn't yield to the squeeze of his thumb and fingers. His memory, equally unyielding, refused him a glimpse of his mother's face.

Murdered by savages. She hadn't been a victim of heart sickness after all. The hairs on the back of his neck rose. He dropped the clod and jumped back from the mound, his eyes sweeping the piñons and junipers upslope from the house. No painted faces appeared there, no rustling in the bushes. Only the normal sounds of morning, a piñon jay's squawk, a ground squirrel rummaging through dried leaves. How had she died? How exactly had it happened? Morbid questions. He took a deep breath and unclenched his hands.

He stepped away from his mother's grave and knelt beside the fresher mound with the cross. With his finger he traced the words carved into the horizontal arm: his father's name, plus the numbers 10-10-1843, surely the date of his death. His mind whirled back in time, turning toward thoughts of his father. He crossed himself and tried to feel sad. Early memories of his father were few, and none of them came from this place.

He repositioned himself and rested his back against the cross, stretched his legs in front of him and settled in to wait for Fili.

His mind drifted back over his childhood. His earliest recollection came after he'd had left this place and gone to live with his aunt Esperanza. He remembered lying on a pallet, sick with fever. Above him loomed the face of his father and another man, a white-haired *curandero* with an enormous mole on his nose. The mole man was doing something to Mariano's chest. It hurt, and Mariano was trying to push his hands away, but his own arms were pinned to his sides, maybe tied or wrapped in a blanket or something, and he was yelling at his father to make the man stop, but his father just looked away and didn't do anything. Helpless. That was Father. When something bad happened, there was nothing to be done.

Aunt Esperanza had three children of her own, two boys and a girl, all older than him. The boys, especially Hugo, the oldest, never let him forget he didn't belong in their family. Hugo would force him to save part of his tortilla and beans at meals and give it to him afterward, or face a beating. Sometimes Hugo beat him anyway, just for the sport of it. When Aunt Esperanza saw this, she would blame Mariano and give him a cuff on the ear. But mostly she never saw it, and Mariano didn't dare tell her lest he get an even bigger beating afterward. He learned to be silent and hide when Hugo was around.

In that family, the only kind one was Hugo's sister, Maria Elena. She would sometimes save treats and slip them to Mariano when no one was looking. She was the one who liked to put poultices on his bruises and fuss around playing nurse. He wondered if she ever became a *curandera*.

He never told his father about Hugo's beatings. No use. Father rarely visited Aunt Esperanza's house, so Mariano didn't see him that often, anyway. He came more frequently after Mariano turned ten and started stealing things from his aunt, like a chicken egg now and then, or a pinch of bread dough while it was rising. She complained to his father, who gave Mariano a stern warning and threatened to swat him, but he never did. He was weak. Didn't follow through on what he said he would do.

Still, Mariano wanted to be with his father, and came to realize that misbehavior brought Papá to him more often than good deeds. He escalated his thievery until one day Espernaza caught him filching a coin out of her bag. That was the end of it. She called his father and said he must take his son and good riddance. Medina smiled as he recalled waving goodbye to Hugo.

That's when Father took him to live in the servants' quarters on Don Diego Castillo's *hacienda*. He was eleven years old.

Medina shifted position against the cross. His rear felt numb. Fili was taking a long time, whatever she was doing. He tamped some tobacco in his pipe, lit it, and let his mind drift.

He recalled the first time his father took him into Don Diego's *casa grande*. Up until then, he hadn't realized how poor they were. The sight of the huge rooms, the vast array of coats and pants and boots in a closet the size of his aunt's house, the stores of food in the kitchen pantry, the smell of meat served on platters to the Don's sprawling extended family, astonished him.

His father's job consisted mostly of greeting guests and members of the household at the door, smiling and bowing and taking their coats, cleaning and polishing their boots, taking care of the Don's riding gear, knife and gun collection, and making sure that when the Don wanted something or went somewhere or arrived from somewhere, everything was in perfect order. To prepare for these duties, Father had to go to a changing room every morning and put on his uniform: white frilly shirt, tight gray pants that stopped at the knee, matching gray coat with squared-off shoulders and no buttons, white stockings up to his knees and polished black shoes with silver buckles.

Mariano's job was to stay out of the way and not embarrass his father, a role he was more than happy to play.

Mariano was a shade darker than his father. He'd never paid much attention to this, but in the Don's *hacienda*, he began noticing skin colors and wondering about his own looks. Whenever he got the chance, he'd examine himself in mirrors or wavy window glass and notice that his nose was broader than his father's thin beak, his lips thicker. He started rubbing agave squeezings on his face because a servant girl named Chiqui told him it would keep his skin from browning in the sun.

Medina touched his face and smiled. That treatment hadn't done him any good. Father's face, while light, was always strained, often twitching from nervousness. His eyes would dart about, ever watchful that nothing be found out of place, ever fearful that Don Diego would find something amiss. Only after the Don retired for the night, ascending the grand staircase to his bedroom while twisting his handlebar moustaches and humming some Spanish tune, did his father's shoulders slump and his face relax.

Medina remembered meeting Father in the changing room, watching him put away his costume, slip into his homespun cotton shirt, pull his frayed wool pants onto his spindly legs and slip his feet into worn sandals. Then they would trudge down the hill to the servants' quarters, well out of sight of the big house, eat a simple meal of beans and tortillas, and curl up on pallets on the dirt floor of their adobe shack.

The Don was not cruel or harsh, but that was because he scarcely noticed Father at all. Not so for the Don's oldest son, Ricardo, who took pleasure in ordering Father around. Ricardo was a couple of years older than Mariano. He'd swagger in from a horseback ride with his friends, the red streak in his hair flopping like a cock's comb, sit down in the big hallway chair and stick out his legs, one at a time, for Father to pull his boots off. The boots came up to his calves and were hard to dislodge, so Father had to straddle young Castillo's leg and pull hard. Once Ricardo flicked a quirt over his father's upended rump, to the amusement of his sneering friends. From a crack in the pantry door, Medina remembered watching this with a strange mixture of awe and shame, amazed at the power young Castillo wielded, humiliated at the powerlessness of his father, mortified by his own helplessness.

Staring now at his father's grave, he crossed himself. *Father, you did the best you could.* He sighed and shook his head.

He remembered hiding places in the big house, closets and crannies where he could wedge himself away from anyone's notice. He'd rush quickly to complete the chores his father assigned him, slipping in and out of rooms noiselessly as a wraith. On occasions where he was forced into the company of his betters, he'd hide behind his father's legs or stand still as a post beside a wood armoire or a straight-backed chair, and become part of the furniture. He was good at being invisible. Young Ricardo's eyes seemed to look right through him. Which was fine.

Working in the Don's stables had been his salvation. Father had arranged that assignment on a day when the Don was in a good mood, pleased with Father's perfect repair of a prized set of dueling pistols that had misfired during a practice session.

For the first year at the stables, cleaning stalls and hauling hay, water and manure were his main tasks. He didn't mind. When Ricardo came with his friends to ride, he'd melt into the background. But gradually, under Omar's tutelage, he discovered he wanted to learn more about the ways of horses. Omar. He remembered how the old Turk knelt on a small rug five times a day and mumbled incoherent passages from a book he kept on a shelf flanked by candles.

The old man loved his work, and Mariano was avid to learn. He soaked up Omar's teaching like moss soaks up water. He learned how to calm a nervous animal or subdue an unruly one. He learned the role of a groom, how to behave deferentially with the Don and his guests, how to stand just so off to the side and help ladies and gentlemen mount up without seeming to exert himself and giving them the illusion they were doing everything on their own.

Even with Ricardo and his friends, he established an uneasy but acceptable presence. On those occasions when they came to the stable to ride, he took extra pains to be efficient and deferential, averting his eyes, bowing, and humbling himself. Mostly they ignored him if he did things correctly.

His duties grew to the point that by the time he was fourteen, Omar trusted him with most everything and was able to take longer naps and leave work earlier, in keeping with his advancing age.

Fili's voice pierced the morning quiet.

"*Hola! Hola?* Are you still here?"

"Yes, coming."

He rose and walked stiffly back toward the crumbling house with its hidden memories and its flapping piece of tin on the roof. It struck him again that the house was warning him away.

35

FILI'S STORY

During the brief time he'd spent by the graves, Fili had transformed herself part way back into the beauty he remembered as a young man. Color infused her cheeks. Her lips were darkened with some sort of rosy paste. Her hair was combed, shiny with something she'd put on it. She led him to the wood bench on the porch at the front of the house and sat down. Medina lowered himself on the other end. Between them sat two tin cups of juniper berry tea.

She raised a cup. "You were good with the riding lessons."

"Thank you. It was Omar, I only passed his teaching along to you."

She smiled. "Still modest."

Her magic dimples appeared for a moment, then faded. As a stable boy he'd taken care not to overstep his bounds, to keep the proper distance, look at her chin rather than directly into her eyes. Show deference. What caused him to avert his eyes now was not modesty, but shame. His last memory of this woman was her floundering in the water, stripped and vulnerable, calling for him to help. Now here she was—amazingly—living in his father's home.

So many questions. What happened to her after he ran from Fili's pool? Had he been blamed for whatever they did? Had she defended him against Ricardo's accusations? Had the Don believed her? How had she ended up here? How to begin?

He finally said, "Omar. Did he find you? Help you after those boys, your half-brother..."

She spit out her tea with such violence that it very nearly hit Medina's knee.

"Ricardo! That slimy shit! He cheated me out of my home, the turd. My horse, my inheritance—everything!"

Fili's words came in short bursts, like blows of flint on steel. What startled Medina as much as her rough language was the glow that inflamed her eyes. Blue-green orbs of hatred. In place of that dimpled smile was a snarl so fierce it caused him to recoil.

"That *mierda* of a half-brother hated me from the very start," she went on. "Insane with jealousy. He knew he couldn't talk to the Don directly about me. So he tried every other way to cast doubt on me. Undermine me."

She twisted a strand of hair around her forefinger. Her hands were scrubbed clean and her skin gave off a fresh, yucca-root smell.

"I tried to win him over at first. Convince him I meant no ill. Tried to tell him that my mother was no threat, either. That she would keep her place. That she had no designs on the *hacienda*. You saw we were *simpatico* to him, yes?"

Medina nodded, although he had little memory of that.

After a pause, he asked, "Who is she? Your mother."

Her eyes softened. "She is dead. Not long ago. Just before your father was killed." Fili took up her cup, then set it back down without drinking, face in a frown.

He reached out to touch her forearm. "I am sorry. What happened to her?"

"Who knows? Some disease that whores get. There was no doctor to say." Her eyes hardened, defiant. "Yes, she was a whore. A beautiful, Spanish whore. Daughter of a rich *hacendado* who threw her out because she fell in love with a..." here she paused and looked him up and down. "A stable boy."

Medina withdrew his hand. He didn't know what to say.

"You are surprised? Be careful who you fall in love with." She gave a harsh little laugh and looked away, tossing her hair back over her shoulder.

"So my grandfather, fine citizen that he was, had the stable boy beaten near to death and tossed out in the desert somewhere. No one ever saw him again. And my mother...well, she was only sixteen. No home. And there are not many occupations open to a disgraced, cast out young woman. Then Madame Castaneda found her and recognized what a prize she would be. Light skin, blond hair, eyes like mine. She set her up on the top floor, the elite floor, of her Santa Fe bordello. She rented my mother out to her highest paying customers."

"And that's where Don Diego found her?"

"Yes. Yes, indeed. Not only found her. Fell in love with her. Right away—on the first visit, according to her. You would, too, yes?"

Fili had this disconcerting way of asking questions and not waiting for an answer. Medina had none, in any case.

Fili lifted her feet to the bench, hugged her knees, resting her chin on them. Her eyes got a far-away look. She was still slender, and the long skirt that pressed in around her sitting form revealed hips that had not broadened in the way of most women past thirty years who subsist on corn and beans.

"He bought her from the Madam," she continued. "God knows what price. He set her up in a nice home in Santa Fe—our home. That's where I grew up. We had real beds. Real furniture. And oh, the dresses! The Don was generous. When he visited he brought me those sweet candied figs you can only get in the traders' shops. And necklaces from France. Imagine!" She shrugged and waved as if saying goodbye. "They are all gone now.

"My mother taught me how to please men. How to please the Don. I learned to curtsey. To say 'if you please.' Fetch his special pipe he kept at our home, know what he wanted before even he did, and bring it to him before he could ask. She was determined that I not be cast out, as she was. That I would learn to be a proper lady. So the Don would treat me like a daughter."

"Were you? His daughter?"

"Yes. I have his small ears. And his bearing. The way he walked, small steps, with arms that hung straight instead of swinging. He used to call me his little straight arm."

Medina studied her face as it softened into remembrance. It was becoming almost beautiful again. He found himself caught up in her story.

"So he, the Don, brought you to the big house?"

"It was my mother's doing. At first he resisted. Not proper, he'd say. My wife is an invalid, he'd say. But my mother kept at him, week after week. Whispered lovelies into his ear, made him laugh. Opened him up like a sack of tortillas. As my fifteenth birthday approached, my *quinceañera*, she made up a story about me that he could use with people. That I was an orphan child of his dear cousin in Spain. That my parents had died during a trip to Mexico City. That I had no home. How could anyone object to taking in a waif like me?" She raised her palms like a child wanting to be picked up.

"So that's when you came to the *casa grande*?"

"Yes. No one believed the story, of course. The Don himself kept mixing it up. Told different versions of how my parents died. In a horse accident sometimes, then from bandits on the Camino Real. He would call me his daughter in unguarded moments. People overheard. The servants joked about it."

"Omar told me you were the Don's daughter," Medina said.

"Omar was nice. So were you." She tilted her head and looked at him more closely, taking him in, as if really seeing him for the first time.

Medina felt himself blush. He changed the subject.

"Ricardo. He hated you."

Her face went hard again.

"That prick. That little red rooster. He had this crazy idea that I was out to take over the *hacienda* from his father. That somehow my mother, a whore, would be brought in to displace his mother. Absurd! The Don would never do something like that. Although you could understand why he found my mother attractive, compared to his own wife. That poor woman. Drab as a post, unlovely as a rock. A political marriage. She spent most of her time in her room. Made a deer look brave by comparison. They had no respect for her. Not even the servants. Maybe that's why the little Don was worried. He couldn't count on his mother to stand up for him."

She paused a moment to focus on Medina. "You saw how he treated your father? What did you think of that?"

Medina swallowed. "I was...ashamed. Of my father."

"You should have been furious, fuming mad. Should still be."

Yes, Medina thought. *I should have been a lot of things.*

She lowered her knees, crossed her legs, tucked her feet back under the bench and leaned toward him. She'd gone from looking beaten down to looking like a volcano about to explode.

"Ricardo hated that the Don gave me school lessons. A tutor—you met her, an educated woman named Miss Elizabeth. She taught at the Catholic school. He hired her to teach me. I was learning to read, to write. Even to do accounts. That's what bothered my half-brother the most. That I might learn to keep the *hacienda's* books. She gave me a ledger book to practice in. I used to flaunt it, show it to the little Don. Say things like, 'see, the *hacienda* made good money last month.' His face would turn red as his topknot."

She barked out a mirthless laugh, then paused. "That was a mistake. I tried to be nice to him at first. My mother warned me, when I would see her, which wasn't very often. Warned me to keep on his good side. And I did for a while. But he would have none of it. Enemy. That's what I was to him.

"He stole my doll once, a gift my mother made for me. I brought it to the big house to remind me of her. It was made of fine silk, a light pink, sewed just so into arms and legs and stuffed with cotton. It had a sweet face sewn on, blue eyes and blond hair made from yellow yarn. It disappeared one day. I looked and looked for it. Then it showed up in my bed after a couple of days. Tucked under a blanket with only its head showing. I took off the blanket. You know what I found?"

Medina shook his head.

"He cut a slit in between her legs, and stuffed a corn cob in there. Wrote "*PUTA*" on her little bare chest."

Whore. Medina felt his own anger rise.

"Bastard."

"Yes." She nodded, then gave him a look.

He met her eyes and let them linger.

"That day at the pool. When he followed you. What did he do?" He hadn't intended to ask this question, not wanting to draw attention to his own cowardly response, but out it came.

She rose from the bench and paced in a tight circle under the overhanging *vigas*. The frayed straps of her sandals, thin-soled from long use, had worn little grooves in the tops her feet.

"You saw some of it. The first part. I saw you hiding in the rocks above."

"I am sorry I ran away."

Her eyes measured him. Then she shrugged.

"It would not have mattered. There were three of them. You were just one boy."

"Fifteen. I was old enough to..." *To do what, exactly? Run at them? Throw rocks?* "I could have led them away from you, at least. Made them chase me." It stung that she dismissed him as a mere boy, but it was also a relief to hear she bore him no resentment.

"You became their scapegoat." She stopped pacing and stared hard at him. "They blamed you for what they did to me."

Medina waited, the unspoken question hanging between them.

"He raped me."

Medina held her eye for a moment, then looked away. He remembered her being thrown in the pool, naked, sputtering, calling to him. But he had run before witnessing the aftermath. He didn't want to hear more.

She told him anyway.

"His two bully boys held me down. Each one grabbed an arm and a leg. They spread me apart. My half-brother climbed on top. I screamed and screamed until my voice gave out. Tried to bite him but he was too quick, too strong. They had the courtesy of dragging me to that little grassy place. More comfortable for them than the rocks. Nice of them, don't you think?"

Embarrassed, Medina could only shake his head.

"The Don was waiting for me when I finally dragged myself home. They had practiced their story. So they each said the same thing when he questioned them separately. They said they found you and me together. Not a rape, they said. Willing lovers. They had all the details worked out. We had been swimming together, naked, in the pool, they said. Then we kissed, walked arm in arm to the grassy area, and made love. And sure enough, my virgin blood was there, on the grass, for the Don to see as proof. That, and the fact that you had run away. A sure sign of guilt. Did they ever catch you?"

Medina felt his anger rise, hot and throaty.

"I found Omar, told him what had happened. He saw the danger right away. Knew my version of the story would not be believed. Three against one. He told me to run like I never ran before, like a pack of wolves were after me. I made it here to Arroyo Hondo, when they caught me."

"They told the Don they killed you."

"They would have, if some men, some *Americanos*, hadn't stopped them."

"What happened?"

"It was like with you. His two friends held me, one on each side, while Ricardo went at me. Hit me again and again until his own hands were too sore to hit anymore. Left me bleeding in the road."

He winced at the memory of Ricardo's gloved fist smashing into his face, his stomach, his groin. Her hand was suddenly on his face, hot to the touch, a flame of shared anger.

He said, "What happened to Omar? I was worried about him."

"He had to leave the *hacienda*. Ricardo drove him out. I heard that he died. Old age."

"Where is he now? Ricardo, I mean."

"He is the Don now. The old Don died not long after I was sent away." She locked her gaze on him, hard as agate. "Ricardo deserves to die."

Medina slowly nodded his agreement.

"One thing he said was true," she said. "Ricardo, I mean."

"What?"

"He said that weeks before he and his friends followed you out to the pool, they had become suspicious of you. They noticed you were watching me. Like a lovesick goat. That much was true."

She reached over and cupped his chin in her hand. His own hand met hers and lingered there.

Yes, that much was true.

She drew him to his feet. "Come inside," she said, her voice low and urgent.

36

PLEASURE AND PAIN

The pallet on the floor was surprisingly soft. He wondered what she had stuffed it with.

"Goose down," she said, as if reading his mind.

He let her push him down onto it, lift his legs one by one and pull off his moccasins. She reached for his tomahawk, but he pulled it from his belt and set it on the hardpan floor, along with his knife. He raised his hips as she untied his leather belt and pulled his buckskin pants off. Moving back a step, she watched his face as she pulled her blouse over her shoulders and cupped her breasts in her hands, displaying them as prizes he might have won in a card game. They were cream-white—he remembered how they'd flashed in the sun that day at Fili's pool—with tiny, rose-colored nipples the size of gooseberries. She pulled her skirt down, then tugged off her *camisa*, and stood there for a long moment stroking the astonishing auburn patch between her legs.

She knelt beside him, knees against his side, worked his shirt up to his armpits and bent to kiss his stomach. He felt himself twitch into hardness. Her mouth found his.

"You taste like mint," she said.

He could only nod, dumbstruck.

She grasped his hand and guided his fingers into her. She was already wet. Then she took him in her hand. A low moan escaped him.

Her aggressiveness astounded him. He'd found satisfaction with other women—Indians in hospitable lodges mostly, an Irish whore once at Fort Laramie—but he had always directed things. This was something new.

An image of Takánsy floated into his mind. He remembered her rubbing his injured limbs with her concoctions, kneeling beside him on his sick bed much like Fili was doing now, him getting hard. He tried to force the image away, but it hovered there like an accusation. Idiotic. Takánsy was lost to him. Why couldn't he put her out of his mind?

He felt himself go soft. Alarmed, he squirmed under her touch.

"Mariano." She spoke firmly, like a school teacher. "Your mind, let it go into the clouds. Close your eyes and float. There is no moment but this moment."

And so he did. He let her sweep him away, restore his desire, take him into her. She moved in ways he'd not thought possible, as she brought him to an explosive release. Then, after lying on top of him long enough for his breathing to return to normal, she pulled away from him with a little sucking sound, flipped onto her back and pulled his fingers into her again.

"My turn," she said.

She guided his hand, showed him how to touch her just so, how to slide his finger across her faster and faster until she heaved and cried out and finally shuddered to a stop.

She sat up and leaned back against the wall, legs stretched apart, a flush blooming on her skin. He rose to a sitting position and regarded her, his mind a riot of questions. Can this be real? He had let her take him, and for a few moments he'd escaped into a fantasy world, following her lead. But why had she done this? He let his eyes roam over her body. Fair skin, still firm despite some encroaching wrinkles, a tiny roll around her waist. And bruises on her shoulder and inner thighs. There was more to know of her story.

She plucked her skirt off the floor and wrapped it around her shoulders and torso.

"That was nice, yes, my stable boy? You liked it?" She gave him a wan smile, not enough to activate her dimples.

He nodded and reached for his shirt. The sun streamed through the front window, but the air inside the thick adobe walls was chilled.

He said, "You learned all this from Madam Castaneda."

It was not a question. Her expertise, her deft handling of him. There was no doubt.

"Not the last part," she said. "That was my own doing."

"So that's where you went—to Madam Castaneda's house— after the Don threw you out?"

"Where else? My mother had to return there, to the Madam. We lost our house even before the Don died."

"Why did you come here?"

She gave a bitter laugh.

"The little Don started visiting the bordello. Started asking for my mother. It gave him pleasure to fuck his father's whore. Then his father died. Don Diego fell off his horse and broke his neck. Dead, just like that." She snapped her fingers. "Ricardo then became the Big Don. And soon, he decided he wanted me, the pig. The first time he came for me I barred the door to my room. He had a fit trying to get in, shouting and cursing. He was drunk, thank God. Madam Castaneda steered him to some other poor girl, but later she came to me, furious. Said she was the one who would choose who could take me. told me I had no say in the matter."

"He did that to you?" Medina said, pointing at her bruises.

"Ha! That came later." She leaned away from the wall, eyes again catching his, firing up again, blue-green flames.

"My mother got us out of Santa Fe right after that. Left Madam Castaneda. Last September. She and two others came up here to Arroyo Hondo. Set up their own small bordello for traders going in and out of Taos."

"But...this is even closer to Ricardo. Wouldn't he...?"

"My mother thought closer would be safer. That Ricardo wouldn't visit whores near his own home. Everyone would know. Too public, too scandalous. But that sonofabitch has no shame."

"So he found you."

"Two weeks ago. He found out we were in the new bordello. He came in one night when I was asleep. Him and his two toughs. They held me down and did me like they did at the pool. Laughed as I screamed. Then they beat me." She pointed to the fading purple-green insults on her body.

He felt her anger growing in him, warming his exposed limbs. He was vaguely aware of his teeth grinding together.

"At least my mother didn't live to see that. She died not long after coming here. First thing I did was look for your father. Antonio. He and my mother had become friends. Your father promised my mother before she died that I could come here, as a safe haven. Then he was killed. Forced to serve in the Governor's militia. After Ricardo's attack I came here. No one knows except Luisa, my friend at the bordello."

She looked around the bare room then at the down sleeping pad. A twisted smile played at her mouth. "Some haven."

"What do you mean? Did my father..."

"No, no, he was a good man. Kind. Would not hurt anyone, not even bad people. Too good, really."

She started twirling her hair with her finger. "My friend Luisa will quietly send customers to me here. I will take them on."

"Aren't you afraid the Little Don will find you?"

"Yes. But I have to eat." She let that sink in, like a heavy stone.

"Your father and my mother were friends. Both victims of the little Don. They had a sad kind of kinship. Like with you and me."

Then she fixed him with those hard blue-green eyes, daring him to look away.

"So will you help me?"

"Help you what?"

"Kill him."

37

RUN, GET AWAY

Medina's first impulse was to flee. The urge was so powerful that his body jerked as if she'd stuck him with an awl. Inside his head the familiar voice shouted, *run, get away!* He raised his hands to his ears to block the words, then quickly lowered them, realizing how ridiculous he looked.

"Mariano, are you all right?" He felt her hand warm against his suddenly cold shoulder.

He brushed her hand away, jumped up and began dressing, jamming his feet into his pants as if he were stamping out a fire. Anger welled in him, anger at her manipulation of him, anger at his own cowardice, at his father's subservience. He strove to turn it against Ricardo Castillo, conjuring up the new Don's sneering smile, his aristocratic nose, the streak of red in his hair. He imagined grabbing that hair, circling the base of it with his knife, hearing the satisfying rip as he tore the scalp off in one mighty yank.

He paused, his pants at half mast.

"How?" His voice came out like a raven's croak.

She appraised him through veiled eyes, choosing her next words carefully.

"I have a plan...the *beginning* of a plan." She rose and began pulling on her own garments. "But we must not rush. He is a careful man. With bodyguards. Let us think more about this. I will go to market, get some food. We will eat. We will celebrate. Bring some of that whiskey from Turley. We will rest, spend the night."

He finished dressing.

She leaned in to kiss him on the cheek, ruffle his hair with her hand.

Like teasing a stable boy. He pulled away.

She grinned, grabbed a sack and walked out the door, a spring in her step.

Later that afternoon, as the setting sun once again kindled the dull town of Arroyo Hondo into a flaming version of itself, Medina made his way back to his father's house with a small bottle of Turley's whiskey brought to him by Chepe Luis.

He'd asked his childhood friend if he'd mentioned his visit to his father's home.

"No, not even to Candelaria," was the reply.

"Good," Medina said. "Don't tell anyone about my visit. Not Turley, not anyone. And tell Candelaria and your children that they must forget they ever saw me."

Chepe Luis looked puzzled.

"The reason? You do not want to know. For your own safety and that of your family, forget I was here."

Killing Ricardo Castillo. Could he do it? Common sense told him to mount up and get the hell out of there. *Suicide! That's what she is asking. Manipulating me with her blue-green spell. That was what her lovemaking was all about.* He thought of Papín. In the realm of salesmanship, he and Fili would have been a match for each other.

Yet the lure of vengeance was there, too, undeniable, growing inside him. She had skillfully played on that, goaded him into a fury, made him feel their joint humiliation, laid bare the intimate details of her degradation at Ricardo Castillo's hands. In turn it caused him to relive his own vicious beating by the new Don of *Hacienda de los Arboles*.

Yet a bond had been forged between him and Fili, there was no denying it. He wanted to hear her plan, be part of it. Maybe it could be done. Maybe it wouldn't be suicide.

Besides, what kind of life did he have to return to? Gambling away his earnings in the hovels of El Pueblo? Drinking away his disappointments? The life he'd imagined with Takánsy—becoming a respected business man, settling on beautiful Thompson's Creek, fathering her children—that life was gone from him, thrown away by his own choice.

Little would be lost by teaming up with Fili. And what might be gained? Self-respect? Courage? Banishing the fear that had too often caused him to turn tail and run away? An end to the bad dreams that troubled his sleep.

When he arrived at his father's home with the whiskey, he found Fili stacking her market purchases on the table: some rice, beans, a winter squash, a chunk of goat meat. She greeted him with a nod and a questioning look.

He stared at her for a long moment, holding her gaze, then said, "I agree to kill him."

"You are sure?"

"I am sure."

She gave him a grave smile.

"It's not only for revenge, you know. He is a danger. The other girls at the bordello, they are afraid of him. He is... not normal."

He thought of the servants at the *hacienda*, boys and girls, young prey for Ricardo Castillo's sadism.

"I will do it without you," he said. "I have my own reasons."

"You will need me. Otherwise, it is not possible. He is too well protected."

She prepared their meal in a clay pot and set it aside while she went out and lit a fire in the *horno*. When the flames subsided into glowing coals, she set the pot on to cook, came back inside and beckoned to him. They sat down together on the pallet with their backs resting on rolled-up blankets propped against the wall.

Fili gazed at the open door, her face a mask of concentration.

"The Don is coming to the bordello tomorrow. He has been yelling at my friend, Luisa, about me. He is enraged because she will not tell him where I have gone. He threatened her. Yesterday he told her he would close down her house. Beat her."

"How do you know this?"

"I just saw Luisa. At the market. She is still waiting for me there. I will tell her to let the Rooster Don know I am here."

He leaned forward in alarm. "You want him here?"

"Of course. We can't kill him in his *casa grande*. Or in Taos, or on the street. He never travels alone."

"You think he will come here alone?"

"No, he will have his two cousins with him. They will do as they usually do. Hold me down. He likes it that way."

"But how..."

"You will be here, waiting. Your horse and gear will be hidden in that old corral and shed down the hill. Eusebio's old place. You will have your weapons primed. That big rifle you carry on your saddle, that pistol in your belt. I will have my knife ready. I have been sharpening it. They will put their weapons aside. They won't be expecting you." Her voice grew more excited as she spun out these details, as her vision of events became real.

"But what if they bar the door? How will I get in?"

"You will be in here, with me. In there." She pointed to a corner of the room covered by a curtain suspended from a viga and hanging clear to the floor. He had thought it was merely a wall covering.

"You will stand on that bench behind the curtain. Well hidden. They always set their rifles aside so they can grab me and hold me down. When the time is right, you come out and shoot the two thugs. But don't kill the little Don. I want to slit his throat myself."

Medina nodded. *Yes, that might work.*

She pulled him to her, kissed him wetly on the lips, drew him into another round of lovemaking. Cementing the bargain. He put that thought out of his mind and willed himself back under her spell, gave himself to the pleasure of her, blotting out past and future, enjoying the moment, the luxury of skin-on-skin, the smell and taste of her. He could, he conceded, grow fond of her. If they lived.

Then they ate. She retrieved the cook pot from the *horno*, brought it inside, ladled the contents into wooden bowls. The goat stew was delicious. She had fancied it up with some asparagus shoots she'd harvested from a secret garden his father had shown her, by a bend in the creek. Medina was ravenous.

"Lovemaking gives you an appetite," she said.

She rose, slipped a blanket over her shoulders and walked to the door.

"I go back to the market now. To speak with my friend. To give her instructions."

"Does she know I am here?"

"No. She does not know of our plan."

"Why are you so sure the Don will come?"

"I am not absolutely sure, of course. But he is wanting me, and Luisa will tell him. She has to. For her own safety. We shall see." With a little wave, she eased out of the door and closed it behind her.

He sat there for a while, then rose from the pallet and walked over to the alcove. He pulled the curtain aside. It exposed a niche about three feet deep and three feet wide recessed into the wall, with a bench set against the back. Half way up the wall was shelf big enough to hold a child's pallet, and above that, a rectangular opening covered by a *rebozo* with faded red and yellow stripes. He drew the fabric aside. Through it he could see his parents' graves.

A sudden rush of memory hit him. The cracks in the adobe above the window opening were the same jagged lines he'd traced with his finger as a child. The pattern in the wood of the overhead viga resembled a goat, a knothole its eye. The shelf was where he'd slept as a five-year-old. Before his mother died. He reached for the wall to steady himself.

Something terrible leapt into his consciousness, a dark thing kept hidden all these years, a creature at the back of a cave suddenly bounding out.

38

THE ALCOVE

He remembered lying on that shelf, wanting his mother. He was hungry. His five-year-old stomach, twisted up with an empty feeling, that demanded her immediate response. Where was she? *He rubbed the sleep from his eyes, thought about calling for her, but remembered she would be angry if he cried, and so he summoned all his child willpower to keep quiet.* Why didn't he smell tortillas cooking? Why didn't he hear her humming as she patted the corn masa into flat cakes?

His chubby finger traced the familiar cracks in the adobe above the small window. He thought about the new-born lamb in the corral outside. He rubbed his blanket with his hand, held it close to his face and stuck his thumb in his mouth. This eased his hunger for a while, until the need to pee, combined with the gnawing of his stomach, impelled him to push back the blanket and ready himself to climb down from the shelf onto the bench.

Then came the terrible cry. The scream that made him forget about eating or peeing or anything else. The cry that caused him to tug the window curtain aside and witness the horror that would be walled off in a corner of his brain, sealed safely away for so many years.

The memories came to him in bursts, lightning flashes revealing monstrous images. Mother staggering out from behind a tree on the hill, making that unearthly cry, hands outstretched, a stick poking out of her back. Another stick flying out from the trees and lodging in her shoulder as she fell forward onto her knees and started crawling toward the house. The second stick wobbling obscenely back and forth each time she moved. Sharp cries coming out of her mixed with whining noises like a dog makes, and a panting, rattling sound in her throat like he heard once when Father killed a goat.

Watching from the window, he tried to scream but no sound came out, only a repeated whisper of "Mamá Mamá Mamá," because something told him he must not make a sound.

Then came the men running from behind the tree to catch her. The first had black and red paint on his face and the second had a white face with dark patches under his eyes and their arms and chests had paint too, strange dots with jagged lightning marks, and their legs were bare with leather flapping about their middles and bows in their hands and arrows poking out of some kind of holder on their backs and he realized the sticks in Mamá's back were arrows.

Mamá turtle-crawled toward the opening he peered through, close enough to fix him with a stare that however brief, carried the indelible look of death and despair that would lie buried in the depths of his brain forever.

In that same terrible moment she choked out the words, "Run! Get away!"

*Then she turned toward the corral, as if to lead the men away from him, and resumed her screaming, and the man with the red/black face swung one leg over her shoulders and grabbed her pretty long hair and yanked her head back and clamped it between his knees and... no-no-no...his copper-colored hand had a knife in it, and he stuck it under her chin and sawed it around the inside of her jaw until her tongue was exposed and he pulled out her tongue and cut it off and tossed it into the sand and the blood gushed out onto his hand and her screams turned into gurgles and...*oh Mamá Mamá Mamá*...the blood,* *the blood and there was a black bloody hole where her chin used to be and that copper-colored hand with the knife and the blood spilling over it filled up his whole head and he must not have seen this, must never see it.* Ever again.

     Mamá struggled to her feet and tried to walk over to the corral and they laughed—laughed!—as she tried to open the corral gate and sank down to one knee, and they walked slowly over to her talking to each other and then the knife came out again and red/black face grabbed her hair and the knife cut around the top of her head and... no no no...blood came out of the cut and when he grabbed her hair and pulled there was a ripping sound like when Father would skin a deer, and where her hair was there was a white patch turning red and he was screaming again...no no no...and no sound came out.

     The men left her there in the dirt beside the corral and walked down to the horses and mules in the next corral farther down the hill, and he felt he must go to her, but he remembered her voice saying run, get away *and so he crawled out of his blanket and off the shelf to the bench and rushed to the door and let himself out and ran into the bushes where he crouched down and changed himself into a small rabbit and didn't move and didn't breathe and looked down to see Mamá trying to crawl away but she could barely move and her arms and hands were scratching in the dirt and he wanted to run to her, but at the same time he didn't want to touch her and get her blood all over himself, and he knew the men must not see him and he must not cry or move and must disappear and become part of the bush, and everything started getting dark and he closed his eyes and refused to see what happened next and refused to think of what happened before.*

39

THE KNOCK ON THE DOOR

The touch of Fili's hand on his shoulder made him jump as if he'd been stung.

"Mariano, you are all right? You don't answer."

He swiveled around. Dumbstruck, he could only shake his head. How long had he been standing there in the alcove? He hadn't been aware of her coming in.

"Mariano! What is wrong?"

He blinked, forced himself to respond. "*Perdón.* What did you say?"

"I asked you to move your horse and gear. Down to the next house with the corral. The abandoned one. No one should see that you are here."

She stood before him in her *rebozo*, auburn hair still showing signs of the tangled aftermath of lovemaking.

"I just returned from the market, from talking to my friend. You were standing so still. A tree stump. What were you thinking?"

He swiped his sweaty palms over his eyes.

"Remembering." His voice wavered. He fought for control. "When I was a child. My God, I…"

She waited for him to continue, but no words came.

"Your face," she said. "A bad memory. You are shaking."

He raised his arms and opened and closed his fists. He realized he was still naked. What a sight he must be.

"Cold," he said. "My clothes."

"Are we still in this together?" she asked.

He shook his head to clear it, to bring himself fully back to the present, to reassemble the details of their plan, his part in it.

"Mariano?"

Finally, he nodded. "Yes. I will be ready."

He stepped around her to retrieve his clothes. He needed time to think. Still trembling, he slipped on his pants and shirt and cinched his belt into place. Running his hands over his tools helped steady him. He tucked them into his belt one by one—tomahawk, Green River skinning knife, pistol, powder and ball, pipe and tobacco. He pulled on his moccasins and felt the reassuring shape of the dagger hidden in his right moccasin top. He lifted his rifle from where it leaned against the adobe wall, stroked its steel barrel, took into himself some of its hard coldness, and headed for the door.

"Mariano?"

Fili had the uncertain look of someone about to be abandoned.

"I will be back shortly. As you said, my horse and gear must be hidden in that old shed down the way. Make yourself fetching. We will want Don Ricardo's attention to be full on you, yes?" He nodded at her, gave her what he hoped was a reassuring smile and let himself out into the dimming light of the late afternoon.

Inside the shed, he fed and watered Don Justino, tied him to a manger, groomed him and left him saddled, ready to ride. He would have to get away fast to stay ahead of Governor Armijo's troops once the deed was done. As he made his preparations, he felt increasingly ready for the danger ahead, more ready, somehow, than he'd ever felt before. More able to resist the voice in his head that urged him to run. *This time he would act as a man. This time Ricardo Castillo would die.*

He would be running again, but not in panic. This would be a carefully planned escape over the border, over familiar terrain, back to El Pueblo where the Mexican forces had no jurisdiction. He would be careful to keep out of sight of villagers. He worried about Chepe Luis, worried that the authorities would question him, beat him. He hoped his friend would remember not to say anything to Turley or others about his visit.

He walked backward toward the house, brushing out his horse's prints with a mesquite branch as he went. He doubted the little Don would notice, but Medina's years of trapping and dodging trouble had made him careful.

In the evening he and Fili ate together in silence, lost in private thoughts. When they finished, he rose and put his Hawken rifle, primed and ready to fire, in the alcove behind the curtain. He looked around to make sure nothing of his was evident to a wary eye.

Fili poured water into a basin, washed and oiled her hair, combed it into glossiness, and rubbed something on her lips that brought out a slightly darker rosy color. She dressed herself in a white blouse and a black skirt with a red border. Underneath the skirt, she cinched a thin belt around her waist with a small scabbard in the back holding a five-inch dagger.

"We will have to be alert to anyone's approach," he said. "I'll take the first watch."

"He won't come until tonight."

"Maybe, but we must be ready. You rest now."

She nodded and lay down on the pallet. She closed her eyes, but her breathing never deepened. She turned over, then back again.

"It's no use. I can't sleep." She rose, began pacing in a tight circle. Then they sat down together and waited.

Two hours later they heard the clink of a bridle bit from somewhere out in front.

They tiptoed over to the door and peered through a crack. Medina stared, unbelieving. There in front of the house, astride three horses, sat the stair-stepped, long-faced, hollow-cheeked, scraggly-bearded Strong brothers, Lester, Lem and Lew.

The men dismounted, tied their horses to bushes and advanced on the house, long rifles held in the crooks of their arms, tall Lester in the lead.

"*Carajo!*" Medina whispered. "How did they come here?"

"Who are they?"

"Traders. From Missouri. Probably not really traders. I guided them to Taos from El Pueblo."

"Get rid of them!" Fili hissed. "They will spoil everything."

"Move back. Don't let them see you."

Medina stepped toward the door just as Lester's big knuckles rapped against it, three solid knocks that echoed against the adobe walls. Medina's right hand felt for his tomahawk while his left opened the latch. The door swung inward.

Lester stepped back forcing Lem and Lew to move to the side. Three sets of eyebrows arched up over widening eyes.

"What the hell?" Lem said.

"You!" Lew said.

"How did you get here?" Lester said.

Instead of lowering his gaze, Medina moved forward into the door frame, stared directly into Lester's narrow eyes and spoke in hard-edged English. "This my father's house. Why you are here?"

Lester blinked. "There's supposed to be a whore here. Light skinned, pretty hair."

"Who told you that?"

"Don Ricardo Castillo. Not more than a couple hours ago. Said we should stop on our way back to...say, who in the hell do you think you are to be grilling me like some army sergeant? Where's the woman?"

"She's in there somewhere," Lem chipped in. "I can smell her."

As if in an army drill, three long rifles were simultaneously lowered into firing position, not yet pointing directly at Medina, but close enough. Medina keenly felt the absence of his own rifle, hidden in the alcove behind the curtain.

"Shit, you haven't been fucking her, have you?" Lem said.

"Mexican fucking a white woman?" Lew said.

"Step aside." Lester said. "We're coming in for a look."

He thrust a big hand into Medina's chest. Medina staggered back. The room suddenly felt very small as the three barged in and closed the door behind them.

Fili stood in the corner opposite from the alcove. As the men's gaze left him to seek her, Medina edged back toward the curtain concealing his Hawken.

"Well aren't you the pretty one," Lester said with a show of his fine white teeth. "Just like the Don said."

Medina was again struck by how the man's cultivated speech contrasted with his rough appearance. He groped behind him and felt the edge of the curtain.

"Nice bonus he gave us," Lem said. "She's the best looking thing we've seen in three months."

"Bonus my ass. He owed us big time after the deal we gave him on those trade goods," Lew said.

"What we got in return was plenty," Lester said. "A good look at the Don's *hacienda*, his miserable defense force. Not to mention the real lowdown on Governor Armijo's troops. And now this." A low chuckle rumbled out of him, echoed by each of the brothers in turn.

Lester lowered his long rifle, leaned it against the door frame and stepped toward Fili.

"Well Miss, let's have a better look at you." He grabbed her wrist and pulled her away from the wall.

Instead of resisting, Fili gave him a coquettish smile and swirled around like a dancer, drawing his arm around her as she pressed into his body.

"You first? You are *mas guapo*, the most handsome."

Lester's teeth flashed again as he laughed his low laugh.

"Speaks the King's English, too," he said, then added, "I'm the oldest, so I always go first." He turned to his brothers. "Take that little Mexican outside. If he tries to run, shoot him. I'll let you know when I'm done. Don't worry, I'll get her nice and ready for you."

The voice in Medina's head at that moment was not his mother's. It was a deeper growl from somewhere dark and primitive. *Kill them.*

Fili reached out and pulled Lester's face around to focus on her beguiling smile.

"Don't worry about him. He was my old stable boy," she said. "He always wanted to fuck me, but I never let him. Poor as a *peón*. Let him watch so he can see how a real man does it." She reached for Lester's waist and began unbuckling his belt. "How rich are you, Mister American? I'm worth a lot." She yanked his pants down past his knees, exposing white, hairy thighs that were startlingly spindly in comparison to the rest of him.

Medina watched Lester's face register surprise, then confusion, then embarrassment. The toothy smile disappeared. Color rose in his cheeks.

Then it was Lem and Lew's turn to grin.

"Lester likes it better when they fight him," Lew said with a wink. He was the shortest of the three and the one closest to Medina.

Lester bent down to retrieve his pants. His brothers looked at each other, pointed at Lester's white legs and began to laugh. Medina groped for the curtain behind him, eased it aside and reached into the alcove. His right hand closed over the rifle's cold barrel. Slowly, he drew it forward to his side.

Then he froze. Lester's eyes were on him.

"Behind that curtain!" Lester shouted, still bent over, one hand pointing while the other clutched at his pants. "A rifle! That little Mexican shit. Take him outside and shoot him. Or better, stick him with a..."

He never finished his sentence. In the moment the brothers' focus switched to Medina, Fili reached behind her back, pulled out her hidden blade and plunged it into the side of Lester's neck. He was still partially bent over, trying to pull up his pants, neck exposed like a lamb at slaughter. Her hand yanked the knife down through vessels, windpipe and skin, and a bright gusher of blood fountained out.

"Fili, no!" Medina shouted too late. Then everything became a blur, noise and confusion.

"She stuck me!" Lester's voice barely gurgled.

Medina brought his rifle forward and raised the long barrel toward Lew just as Lew's weapon swung toward him. As he ducked to one side, Medina saw Lester fall backward, hands clutching at his throat in a futile attempt to staunch the gout of blood, his rump hitting the floor with a thud, legs still entrapped in his lowered pants. At the same time the barrel of Lem's rifle swung toward Fili who leapt at him with drawn knife, fire in her eyes, teeth bared like fangs.

Medina pulled the trigger and dove for the floor. A roar filled the room, too loud a sound for his Hawken to make on its own. He landed in a shower of adobe chips and rolled away from the wall as someone screamed, "Shit!"

Smoke billowed into a gunpowder-scented cloud that stung his eyes and made it hard to see. He cast the Hawken aside, jerked his tomahawk from his belt and scrambled toward the sound of boots shuffling on hardpan. He clambered over a body, still twitching on the floor, and launched himself at the standing figure emerging through the smoke. The stock of a Kentucky long rifle glanced off his shoulder and grazed his head. The arc of the swing carried the rifle butt over him, past him. He jumped to his feet and buried his tomahawk in the side of the man's skull. A grunt at the impact, and the man slumped to the floor. It turned out to be Lem.

Medina gulped the smoky air.

"Fili. Fili!"

Tomb-like silence filled the room.

He flung open the door. Moonlight filtered through the smoke as it streamed outside. He turned back into the room. Fili sat on the pallet, legs spread, back against the wall, regarding him. He rushed over, knelt beside her and took her hand in his. It was limp.

"Fili?"

Her eyes found his for a brief moment, then lapsed into a stare. She blinked once. He leaned close. Her breath came in little gasps.

"Fili, can you hear me?"

No response.

His knees, close against her thigh, felt wet. He looked down, saw the blood pooling next to her, spreading out from behind her. Panicked, he grasped her shoulders.

"Fili, stay with me!" He pulled her toward him. That's when he saw the gaping hole in her back, torn flesh, the broken end of a rib. He pushed her back against the wall.

Her head began to loll to one side. He took her chin in his hand and guided her face toward his. Her eyes met his once more, then jerked to the side, focused on something beyond him, behind him. He whirled around.

Lew staggered toward them, eyes wild, lips a frothy spew of bloody foam, his right hand clutching his stomach where Medina's rifle ball had found its mark. His left hand held a long knife above his head.

Medina leapt up, ducked under the wildly swinging blade and stepped to the side.

The momentum of the Missourian's swing carried him to his knees. His scream gurgled through the welling blood in his throat.

Medina kicked him in the stomach. The knife clattered to the floor. He grabbed Lew's hair from behind, jerked his head back and with his own skinning knife, slit the man's throat. He guided the slumping body to the side, away from the pallet.

Panting, he jumped back over Lew's body to kneel beside Fili. Her head now sagged forward onto her chest. No sign of breath stirred in her perfectly still form. He cupped her chin in his hand and tipped her head back against the wall. The fire had faded from her eyes. They stared straight ahead, unseeing, blank as pale stones. He let her head fall forward again and scrabbled backward on hands and knees.

A low moan escaped him, the only sound in the still room. His stomach heaved and spewed out the remains of Fili's meal into the spreading pool of blood on the floor—*so much of it!*—adding the smell of vomit to the reek of gunpowder and evacuated bowels that poisoned the air with the stench of death.

He scrambled to the door, flung it open and lurched outside. Gulping fresh air, he slammed the door shut and collapsed on the bench against the wall. By the time his breathing returned to normal and his whirling head began to clear, the moon had disappeared behind the western horizon.

He buried her during the night in a shallow grave scraped out of the hard desert soil next to his mother's resting place. It was daunting work, the broken shovel his only tool, and by the time he finished hours later, his body dripped with sweat despite the cold night air. He fashioned a crude cross out of juniper branches and stuck it in the ground, propped up with some large stones dragged to the site. If he'd known how to write, he would have scratched out something like, "*Here lies Filomena, murder victim of Ricardo Castillo.*" Instead, he bowed his head, crossed himself, and asked Jésu to welcome her to a better place. He mumbled what he could remember of last rites, lamenting all the while that there was no priest available to speak the proper words.

Surprisingly, no one showed up at the house that night. The sounds of rifle fire must have been muffled by the thick adobe walls. He went back inside, dragged the Strong brothers into a pile on the floor and covered them with every scrap of tinder he could find, wood from the bench he'd chopped up with Lew's huge knife, the sticks beside Fili's *horno*, the corn stalks from outside, wooden bowls and eating utensils. On top he added the saddles and gear from the Strong brothers' horses, still tied outside. He found a can of cooking lard on a shelf on the rear wall and emptied it onto the ghastly pile.

He untied the Strong brothers' horses from the bushes in front of the house, removed their halters, slapped them on the rump and sent them trotting and snorting into the night. Then he ran to the corral where Don Justino waited and led him back to the house. Inside, he kindled a blaze at the edge of the heap on the floor. Gradually the lard caught fire and spread to the wood. Smoke billowed out toward the door.

A snorting Don Justino carried him away as the brown, acrid smelling smoke began to rise into the dawn-lit sky.

He headed east, away from the settlement and up into the piñon-juniper forest. Once hidden in the trees, he turned north toward the border and safety. That night he made camp on a small stream that fed the Rio Culebra, the river of snakes that coils into the Rio Grande. He rubbed down Don Justino and staked him out to graze. Exhausted, he lay down under a blanket without bothering to set up his canvas tent.

As he gazed into the night sky, he fought to ban the horror of his father's house from his mind. He must drive the blood and the stench and the mask of death on Fili's face into the same dark cave that contained the memory of his mother's torture and death. Every time an unwanted image flashed into his mind he muttered *vaya, vaya*, begone, over and over like a chant, until he could refocus his thoughts on something else, like the route he would travel in the morning, his strategy for escaping to El Pueblo.

It didn't work.

Images of his mother, his father, and Señorita Fili kept forming in his head. He tried to picture them while they were still alive, but their death throes elbowed their way in and he had to chant them away. It was like trying to turn a buffalo stampede with useless spells.

At one point, desperate for a distraction, he conjured up a picture of himself as a young child trying to shrink into invisibility in the old Don's *casa grande*. He'd always been ashamed of himself as a little boy, frightened and cowardly, ready to run at the sight of his own shadow. He studied his child-self in his mind's eye, saw his frightened eyes, trembling chin, his small hand clutching the back of a chair, cringing behind it.

Tears pooled in the corners of his eyes and spilled down his temples. He tried to stifle a moan, but it turned into a sob that grew into a crescendo of shoulder-shaking, lung-squeezing, body-wrenching cries that left him gasping for breath. He pressed both hands to his mouth to stop himself, which succeeded for a moment while his breath came in little repeated jerks. But the sobbing returned, again and again, and he finally gave into it, letting it wash through him, exhaust him. It was the first time he'd cried since leaving Taos as a fifteen-year-old youth.

Finally, his eyes emptied of tears, his body drained, he fell into a deep sleep.

40

VALLEY OF FOG

The rising sun seared Medina's eyes as he rode east across the flat plain of the San Luis Valley toward the pass in the mountains he must cross to reach the Arkansas River. Gray fog, released by the melting night frost, wisped low over the landscape ahead of him. Don Justino snorted, as if giving voice to Medina's unease. Above the gathering grayness, on the eastern horizon, the sun knifed cold and unforgiving through Mosca Pass in the Sangre de Cristo range. Many more hours must pass before he could escape this treeless exposure, cross the pass once again and return to El Pueblo, the border, and safety.

His mind replayed his strange loss of control the night before. His eyes were swollen as if they'd been blasted by desert dust. To have cried like a baby—not just cried, but wailed, helpless in the grip of some relentless force—alarmed him. Had he suffered some kind of fit? He was glad no one had been there to see him.

He now felt calm, more at peace than he'd felt in a long time. He took a deep breath. His body felt light, relaxed, almost euphoric. Something had shifted, but he wasn't sure what. He wished he could find someone to tell him what it meant. But there was no one. And best to keep it to himself. Maybe it belonged in the cave with the other memories.

He glanced down at his hand and wiggled his sawed-off finger inside its furred glove. His hand felt numb, then began to prickle. It was freezing cold, one of those sudden weather changes of early spring. He removed his glove and rested his hand on Don Justino's warm neck, which bobbed up and down in time with the horse's long stride. Don Justino had been his rock and refuge since he left Fort Bridger.

He crossed himself and prayed for the safety of Chepe Luis's sweet family, prayed that Chepe Luis and Candelaria would not be questioned about the burnt corpses in his father's house. If they were, he hoped God would give them strength to deny any knowledge of Medina's presence in Arroyo Hondo.

He glanced backward, as much to rest his swollen eyes from the sun as any expectation of seeing anything through the fog. As near as he could tell, he'd successfully evaded pursuit. Riding parallel to the road between Taos and El Pueblo, he arrived at the turnoff toward the east that ascended La Veta Pass, the most traveled route. A clump of trees marked the junction. There he paused before continuing north toward the much less traveled trail over Mosca Pass. He reined Don Justino into the grove, dismounted and relieved himself against the rough bark of a cottonwood. He sat down to rest and soon dozed off.

Then he heard the riders.

The creak of leather, the clank of metal, the rowling of spurs, the thumping of horse hooves. He jumped up, placed a restraining hand on Don Justino's nose and peered cautiously from behind the tree. Fog hid them, save for one long moment when not fifty paces away, he was able to see Ricardo Castillo passing by in front of a dozen riders. The Don's horse was a huge, white animal prancing along under an enormous black saddle weighed down with so many silver ornaments that it would have brought a normal horse to its knees. Castillo's black leather boots gleamed even in the dim light. Gloves with long, fringed cuffs held the reins, leather encased his body like armor, a jewel-handled sword hung from his belt, a red collar rose around his now beefy neck. On his head a plume of exotic feathers swept rakishly back from his Spanish military hat. Underneath the hat, Castillo's lock of red hair hung down to his shoulders, swaying in rhythm with the horse's mane. Behind him the riders bore swords, lances, muskets. A small army.

As the riders disappeared into the fog on the La Veta Pass road, Medina felt a strange calm. No fear clutched at his throat. Instead of running away, he considered how he might take them on. His mind was clear, rational, calculating. But there were too many of them. He would have to let them pass, for now. But one day, somehow, Medina would find a way. One day.

He waited quietly until the sounds of snorting horses and clanking arms faded into silence. Then he mounted Don Justino and resumed his northward course until he turned east toward Mosca Pass.

Soft shoots of frost-covered April grass were beginning to force their way up through last year's faded growth. The greening understory glowed in places where brush strokes of slanting sunlight penetrated the ground fog. The fresh smell of growing grass mingled with the familiar odor of winter decay.

Facing into the sun once again, he squinted at the trail ahead. Instead of bearing straight across the flatness, it wound forward in gentle curves, two ruts through the grass, as if its original maker had been unsure of his destination, with later travelers following sheep-like in his path. The shifting ground fog opened and closed like a ghostly curtain, toying with his ability to see the trail ahead.

The image of Fili's pale, blood-drained body and the gory carnage that surrounded it kept clawing its way into his head. Banish it! He must keep trying. He had kept the scene of his mother's murder at bay for years. Surely he could do the same with Fili's death.

Takánsy's image slowly replced it. Standing in her beaded dress, holding out his medicine package, looking at him with smiling eyes when he took his leave. He shook his head to clear it. He knew he needed to move on, stop dwelling on the past and get along with his life.

Stop gambling, stop drinking, carve out a place for himself in the world as it is, as it will be. Better to think about his discovery, nearly a year ago, of Thompson's Creek, a not-too-big, not-too-small stream the Fremont party crossed as it wound its way through the foothills north of St. Vrain's fort.

While Fremont camped at the Thompson crossing, Medina had followed the river upstream to hunt game. He discovered that the stream cut its way through an impassable box canyon before winding gently through red sandstone hogbacks onto the plains below. Riding along its banks under the shade of towering cottonwoods, he'd felt a strange sense of peace. After leaving Fremont, he'd camped there for three nights.

That's where he should go now. Say goodbye to El Pueblo, claim his horses from Charlie Autobees, and start a new life on Thompson's Creek. Unfortunately, the spot was far away from the trails used by caravans heading to Oregon. Not a great place to make a living.

Still, it was a wonderful place for the imagination. He pictured himself sitting beside a campfire in that lovely spot, brewing rich coffee, Don Justino grazing nearby. Then, unbidden, an image of black tresses and luminous gray eyes gazed at him from the other side of the campfire. Damn! Thoughts of Takánsy kept intruding at unexpected times.

Backlit by the sun, shimmering curtains of ground fog danced in front of him, pulling apart then together again like deranged ghosts. A shape materialized in the track several hundred paces ahead, then disappeared. Don Justino jolted to a halt, ears twitching forward.

Medina squinted into the shifting vapor. A bush? A lone buffalo? At its next parting, the foggy curtain revealed a figure on a horse. Two figures. Moving toward him. The curtain misted shut before he could be sure.

Guiding Don Justino off the trail with his knees, he lifted the Hawken from its resting place across his saddle to a higher perch on the pommel. Some twenty paces off to the side, he dismounted behind a low willow bush, the only cover available. Covering Don Justino's quivering nose with his hand, he waited.

Time dragged. Had they stopped? Left the trail to loop around him? His nervous eyes scanned his fog-draped cover. Had the figures been a mirage? His imagination?

Don Justino snorted.

An answering snort, close by. Two riders materialized out of the vapor, followed by a pack mule laden with a bundle wrapped in canvas. The lead rider, tall and bearded, sat atop a high-stepping black horse.

The second figure, draped in a blanket, rode a gray gelding. *Diós Mío!* THE gray gelding. Its rider tossed a tress of long black hair over her shoulder, pulled to a stop alongside the other rider and fixed Medina with a gray-eyed stare.

Medina's rifle slid from his hands onto the ground as a familiar voice reached his ears.

"*Mon amí,* it is you, sure enough."

Papín.

The Frenchman dismounted and in a few long strides reached Medina and embraced him in a back-thumping bear hug. Medina thumped back, but his attention never left Takánsy. A blood-red blanket bundled her against the cold and formed a backdrop for her hair, which spilled down over her shoulders in a dark cascade. Her face remained composed, her eyes grave. Was she glad to see him?

Papín pulled back to look at him, claiming Medina's attention.

"I see you kept your hair away from Captain Jack's Utes, no?" Papín laughed and gave Medina's shoulders an exuberant shake.

Dazed, Medina asked, "Why you are here? On this trail?"

"To find you."

"To find me?" Medina shook his head to clear it.

"Yes." Papín nodded, stepped back and wagged his finger in mock peevishness. "And you are not easy to find. At Bent's Fort they tell me I find you at El Pueblo. At El Pueblo they tell me you coming back over Mosca Pass. I wait for a day, then I decide to come over pass to look for you. Why not? I know the trail well, no?"

Medina's confusion grew. "But why?"

Papín drew him closer and whispered in his ear, "I have a proposition for you, my friend. A trade."

A trade? What sort of trade would bring Papín this far out of his way? Medina's inventory of goods was hardly bigger now than when he left Bridger's place. A few horses from Charlie, some tack, a short stack of trade blankets left by Goodale as collateral for the beaver pelts he took to St. Louis. Nothing more.

Recovering, Medina said, "My friend, it is good to see you again after all this time. We will have some stories to tell, yes? But I'm curious...what is it I have that you seek?"

Papín smiled his cagey trader's smile.

"We will speak of it when we smoke. But first, come and greet Takánsy. She has been long in the face since you left. No one else will let her test those poultices and foul-smelling drinks on them." He grinned and pulled Medina toward the gray gelding.

At closer range, Takánsy's face looked fuller, her cheekbones less well-defined. She swung her leg over the gray's rump to dismount. Her movement seemed labored.

Medina stopped short. The reason for her slowness shouted at him from beneath her blanket: a swollen belly lifted the red folds in the unmistakable profile of pregnancy.

She patted her stomach. *"Sorpresa,"* she said, using one of the Spanish words he had taught her.

Surprise indeed. The shock of seeing her like this caused his breath to catch in his throat.

She dropped the reins, walked to him and reached for his hands with both of hers. They felt warm, smooth, and smelled of sage.

"Your eyes are big, like seeing a spirit." The corners of her mouth crinkled for a fleeting moment. She squeezed his hands as if to show him she was not a mirage, then dropped them and stepped away.

Medina searched her face. He felt an urge to draw her in, wrap his arms around her and bury his face in her neck.

He heard himself say, foolishly, "This is you?" He glanced at Papín.

The Frenchman doffed his fur cap, exposing his bald head, bowed at the waist and smiled.

"Back together at last, after what, nearly two year, no? You have the wolf look, like you want to eat her."

Medina stammered, *"Perdóname,* it is just that I...the surprise, you see, I was not expecting..." He felt his mouth slide into a foolish grin.

Papín stepped forward and put a hand on each of their shoulders, forming a triangle.

"My friend, seeing us is big shock for you." He chuckled and wagged his head from side to side like a school teacher scolding a dim-witted pupil. "If we are attacked by grizzly at this moment, you will be useless." He bent to retrieve his friend's rifle and placed it in Medina's hands. "Come, let us be on our way. We will ride with you back toward El Pueblo. When we camp tonight we will smoke the pipe and tell of our adventures, no?"

Medina thrust the Hawken into its scabbard and swung into the saddle. As he led them across the plain, he kept craning his head around to make sure he hadn't imagined them. There they were, trotting along behind him, real as Don Justino's swaying gait that carried him closer to the pass.

The fog thinned, then burned away in the warming sun. Ahead loomed the huge hills of sand piled up at the base of the mountains, the great dunes that never failed to widen his eyes in sheer wonder at their improbable presence. Today they felt more like an obstacle. He led them around to follow the stream that skirted their sandy edge. The water, not yet swollen with the spring rise, flowed down from the mountain pass they yet had to cross.

They climbed past the tree line, wound through the boulder fields and finally crested the summit, still patched with dirty snow.

Once on the east side, heading down, Medina looked for a campsite. Impatient to talk, he soon found a grassy clearing ten paces wide, ringed by cottonwoods on one side and a bend of the Huerfano River on the other. From this secluded spot they could watch the trail to El Pueblo winding up and over a rise to the south. Anyone on the trail would not see them, screened as they were by willows and brush.

They dismounted, unsaddled, removed their packs, and picketed their horses. Despite her swollen middle, Takánsy moved with ease, her body and slender hands graceful as ever. She refused Medina's offer to help with a friendly shake of her head.

Medina built a small fire, Takánsy set some water on to boil, Papín dug coffee beans, jerky and some hard tack biscuits out of his pack. It felt as if they had been sharing a camp for years, as if they were family members who knew each other's camp duties. They cleared places under the cottonwoods for their blankets and strung up canvas to guard against the chance of rain. Then they sat down to eat.

41

THE TRADE

Their campsite smelled of new grass where their horses had disturbed the tender shoots. Alder buds unfurled along the stream bank. The river gurgled with the first small surge of early snow melt, a silver shimmer in the moonlight. Their faces flickered in the firelight, Papín's animated, Takánsy's composed. Medina kept glancing her way, searching for some sign of her mood. No ghost stare, but no hint of her special smile either. Contentment? Maybe.

They chewed the last of their buffalo jerky supper and edged closer to the fire. Pipes were drawn out of pouches, tobacco tamped into place, tiny embers placed on top, air sucked through, smoke blown. The ritual seemed to take forever. Medina, fox pipe clenched in his teeth, toyed with the frayed end of a rope, waiting for Papín to divulge the reason for this meeting.

Casually, as if this were no more than a social visit, the Frenchman brushed a bit of jerky from his beard and recounted his visit to Fort Hall in the spring, five months after Medina's departure.

"Fields and his wagon train were still there, edgy as hungry dogs, keen to head west at first snowmelt. He still had your horses, but no cows. I supplied the cows, sure enough." Papín winked. "The same cows the Crows stole from him. When he saw them, his eyes pop out, like this." Papín made his eyes bulge, laughed and slapped his knee.

"Did he pay?" Medina asked.

"He stomped around and shouted and cursed, made a big show, but finally he paid. No choice. He said, 'Not one more day in this hellish place.'"

Medina forced a smile. Fields' fantasy of an Oregon paradise must have grown more vivid with each passing day in the Fort Hall mud season. Not that Medina wanted to hear any more about the wagon train. He removed his pipe and rubbed his jaw to relieve its tightness.

Papín rambled on, telling how he'd unloaded other items on the wagoners at a good price. How he and Takánsy had remained at Fort Hall until fall, trading with Oregon-bound travelers. How the number of wagon trains had grown as Papín predicted, and how his forecast of their needs had resulted in a tidy accumulation of plunder.

Medina shifted his weight to ease the numbness in his legs. He fussed with the frayed rope end.

Papín talked on. "Then word comes from one of my brothers in Missouri. Pierre." He paused to tap another wad of tobacco into his eagle-head pipe and light it with a glowing red ember. "They set up a crossing on the Blue River in Nebraska Territory. A toll bridge. Pierre said thousands of pilgrims will be moving through come spring. Going to Oregon. Thousands! They gather in Kansas City, buy all manner of things they don't need and forget the things they do. At the Blue they figure out what's what, and no one is around to supply what they need, or pick up what they leave behind. My brother, Pierre, ask me to come, set up trading post at Blue River crossing."

A ring of smoke, birthed in Papín's rounded mouth, wobbled out into the night air. Papín watched it rise and break apart on the edge of his hat brim.

"A trader's paradise, the Blue. A hundred times better than

Fort Hall. A thousand!" His eyes got a faraway look as he drew in another puff of smoke and expelled it slowly back into the night air.

Medina's own pipe lay cold in his hand, burnt out. Papín gripped Medina's arm.

"Yes, we went there. She and I." He nodded toward Takánsy. "Spring and summer of '43. Even starting from scratch, I clear twelve hundred dollars. I remember one wagon train, a Captain Brady in charge, he..."

Medina cut in. "You came looking for me. Why?"

Papín glanced up, eyebrows raised, then broke into a grin.

"Ah, my friend, you are losing the patience, no?" He leaned close, and using his most confidential whisper, said, "There is a problem. She does not like it there. She will not stay."

Medina glanced at Takánsy, serenely adding small twigs to the fire.

To Papín he said, "So you decide to return? But why here, along the Arkansas? So far from Fort Bridger."

"Not return, exactly." Papín shifted closer, his breath stirring the air close to Medina's ear. "This brings me to the proposition I bring you. *Mon ami*, how you would like to take her on? As your wife. For a fair trade, of course." He eyed Medina and rubbed his hands together.

Medina forced the muscles in his face to remain still. He looked at Takánsy. Her wide eyes locked on his, the corners of her mouth lifting ever so slightly into that knowing smile. Suddenly, he knew. This was her idea, her wish. But how could this be? He'd abandoned her, chosen to honor Papín instead of keeping his promise to her, urged her to go with him then broken his word. Had she forgiven this betrayal?

She shifted position, one hand on her heavy belly.

Medina pointed the stem of his pipe toward her and asked Papín, "Your child?"

The Frenchman knocked the ashes from his pipe and tapped in a new wad. A smile spread across his face. "It won't be my first. Travel the north country and you will find, what, six or seven little Papíns, no? They all are in good hands, just as this one will be."

Medina nodded, remembering Takánsy's healing touch.

"So what do you say, *mon ami*? You get her, plus a bonus. A little one to amuse you when you return to your lodge." Papín's smile turned into a soft chuckle as he gave Medina a gentle push in the chest. "And think of the extra pair of hands when you open your own trading post. A bargain, sure enough."

Despite himself, Medina's thoughts crept under the buffalo robes to imagine the moment of the child's conception, of Papín enjoying the pleasure of Takánsy's body. It was stupid to feel jealous. Yet the image sent heat up his neck.

"You hesitate," Papín said. "I can always return her to Bridger's place. But I am thinking, well..." His hand gripped Medina's arm. "Let us be honest. From the moment you first see her in your training corral that day, your eye has been on her. You try to hide it, but your face betrays you, no?" He smiled and squeezed Medina's arm.

Medina shrugged, looked down, nodded assent.

"You could have stolen her from me when you left Bridger. She was ready. But you chose honor. For why? You prove to be good friend. So I have come a long way to find you, to bring you a chance to finally have what you have long wished for."

"No, I..."

"Do not deny it. My friend, your face, she tells the truth. So let us trade. Why not?" He released Medina's arm, raised his palms in an elaborate shrug, and leaned back, waiting and smiling.

The Frenchman's matter-of-fact approach helped settle the tumult in Medina's head. He wanted her, child and all, that much was certain. But his bargaining juices now flowed hot, and Takánsy's knowing glance had given him a card to play.

"Good. Let us be honest, as you say. You must admit you do not travel these many miles only to do me a favor. This is her idea."

Papín's trader face stayed still save for a slight twitch of his left eyelid, but it was enough. Medina pressed his advantage.

"What is stopping her from leaving you and going with me without a trade?" He said it with a wink, to take off the edge.

Papín was ready for him. "You want the best for her, no? Best for her means a good price, something to set tongues wagging among the Bridger women. What will that old gossip, Jenny, say if she finds out our Takánsy is handed off for no trade, like worn-out buffalo robe?"

Medina felt his own smile widen. When it came to bargaining, no one could top Papín. No wonder his brother wanted him as a partner.

"One more thing. She will not go with you without a priest's blessing—an annulment. For that, I must agree, no?"

There it was. Papín's trump card.

Medina pictured Takánsy's wooden cross, the daily prayer, the rosary beads. Yes, she would want to stay right with Jésu. He twisted his face into what he hoped was an expression of uncertainty, as if weighing the arguments.

He said, "But annulment requires..."

"A reason, yes. Beatings. Infidelities. To these sins I will confess."

"But it takes more..."

Papín raised his hands, palms toward Medina, in a gesture asking for patience.

"It takes a priest. A compliant one. And it so happens that such a priest awaits us in El Pueblo. A Jesuit Blackrobe. A timid man, very open to suggestion, especially when he partakes of the sacramental wine. I travel with him from Westport. For me he will annul our marriage, and do a new one for you. For a price, of course." A fox grin spread on the trader's face. "He owes me big."

To this, Medina had no reply.

"So let us get to business, why not? I have gone to much trouble. I cannot go back empty handed. I am thinking horses. You have an eye for the best, and I am told by a Monsieur Autobees you have some good ones, no?"

Medina threw in his hand and raised his arms in surrender. He owned six horses in El Pueblo, two fine animals he had hand-picked from several herds at a high price, plus the four he would get from Charlie for taking the Strong brothers to Taos. Papín wanted all six, with six blankets thrown into the bargain. An unheard of trade for a woman. When word got out, men would look at him as if he had gotten kicked in the head. But they would look at Takánsy, too, and be impressed. A fair exchange, he decided.

"You win, my friend."

They knocked the ashes from their pipes, rose, embraced, and clapped each other on the back, sealing the bargain.

Papín pulled Medina toward the edge of the clearing, away from the fire where Takánsy sat. He gripped Medina's shoulders and gave him a penetrating look.

"One thing you should know, my Spanish friend. You are

right about one thing. This idea, it comes from her. For two years I am swallowing my pride, ever since realizing that, well, her heart was yours instead of mine. I saw it happen, even before you rescue her from those Utes. In truth, she was never mine, sure enough." He sighed and knocked the ashes from his pipe.

Medina looked away, embarrassed. This was turning into a confessional.

Papín continued, "I, on the other hand, lose my heart to her when I first see her, back in her village. Oh, she came with me willingly enough. But I think, at the time, her heart was dead to me and I could never awaken it." Then as if noticing Medina's discomfort, Papín winked, patted his head and pulled off his badger fur cap. "Maybe it was my no-hair, upside-down face. In hair, you have unfair advantage."

Medina remained serious.

"What happened to her back then, before you met her?"

"She refuses to speak of it. Her father, a crippled-up big man named Ironhand, told me she disgraced him by losing a horse race, then disgraced him even more by refusing to marry some young brave. I am guessing he set a bride price too high, the selfish old gopher. Still, I gave him plenty for his daughter. But believe his story? I do not." Papín shook his head and looked into the darkness.

Medina remembered Takánsy's strange ritual at the stream.

"Do you know why she scars herself?"

Papín shrugged. "Again, she does not say. Her young man died in a raid on the Blackfeet, so maybe that had something to do with it. For why she is the way she is. Or was. You seem to have lit a spark."

Papín's melancholy left Medina unsure of what to say.

"I am sorry," was all he could muster.

The quick smile returned to Papín's face.

"No need. I have brought her to you. I am ready for new life. And I have six excellent horses to begin, no?"

Medina nodded. Papín had a resilient spirit.

"You have done what many would not do. Thank you."

Papín stepped back, swept his fur hat onto his hairless head, and bowed at the waist.

"You are welcome. Now I go patrol the borders of our camp.

Never let one's guard down, with wolves and savages about." He looked at Takánsy and back at Medina, winked and strode into the darkness of the cottonwood grove.

Medina returned to the fire pit. Only coals glowed where the fire had burned. Takánsy fixed him with luminous eyes. He felt awkward in her gaze and was grateful for the darkness. He stepped over to kneel at her side.

"Takánsy. You heard? Our bargain?"

She nodded.

"You are...you agree?"

Another nod, this time with a hint of smile crinkling the corners of her eyes.

"I hope so," he said. "But I cannot understand why. After I left you without...after I broke my word."

She reached to cup his chin in her hand. "Your choice was true. It making my heart glad and sad, all at once."

Medina took in a deep breath. "But Papín. Now you have decided to leave him. Why?"

"Papín is good man. He sees the hole growing in my heart, from missing you."

He grasped her hand, held it against his lips, kissed her palm. "*Diós.* I could not get you out of my head." He felt dizzy.

She kissed him full on the mouth, then pulled back and gave him her full, brimming smile, radiant, unrestrained.

The sound of a branch snapping signaled Papín's return. Medina felt so dazed he forgot to let go of Takánsy's hand. Papín saw them that way, grinned, and turned back into the trees.

"The first watch, I will continue," he said.

Later, as Medina lay on his back under his blankets and peered through the cottonwood branches into the star-dotted sky, he marveled at life's strange turns. God's doing, or Fate's? He crossed himself in silent thanks, just in case it was God's. But at thirty-two winters he was old enough to know that blessings are often mixed, and wondered, even at that moment of elation, what trials God—or fate—would place on the other side of the scales in the months and years ahead.

42

BEGINNINGS

She pressed into him, her hand stroking the back of his head, her voice murmuring, low and sweet in his ear. Her belly swelled under his hand like a warm melon, surprisingly firm. Inside he could feel faint stirrings of the tiny creature that would soon emerge, howling and waving its arms, into their new world.

Takánsy grasped his hand and pressed it more firmly into her roundness.

"Two moons, maybe three, and I shall be a mother." She reached for his head and pulled his face toward hers. Her eyes gleamed; her face glowed in the reflection of the rectangle of sunlight that brightened the adobe wall opposite the room's only window. The window's two iron bars formed a silhouette on the wall in the shape of cross. A blessing, she had said, on their union.

Outside in the plaza of El Pueblo, a rooster crowed. The handle on the crank of the well squeaked a morning song. Someone—Sycamore?—called a greeting to someone else. The scent of smoke from cookfires drifted into their window.

"To act as father to his child, does it bother you?" Takánsy held his head as if she wanted to see as well as hear his answer.

"Papín is good friend. No. It does not bother me."

She pulled his lips to her breast. He took the nipple in his mouth and felt it, and himself, grow hard again. She guided him into her, and he thrust, more slowly this time, savoring each motion and prolonging the rush at the end.

The first time he'd tried to go slow, concerned for the life in her belly. But anticipation of that moment, so long in arriving, undid him. She had clamped her long fingers over his mouth to stifle his cry. Her lovemaking seemed enthusiastic enough, accompanied by low moans and a satisfying shudder at the end. Still, he sensed a reserve in her, a withholding, a less than whole-hearted giving. Not surprising, he supposed, this being their first time, her being with child, and their location in an unfamiliar adobe hut in a town full of strangers. Give it time, he thought, give it time.

Papín had left the day before with six fine horses and one timid priest in tow. His momentary melancholy during the previous night around the campfire had vanished. He was all bustle and purpose and back-slapping joviality, looking forward to his new position as head of what would become "the largest trading post on the Oregon trail." His showman's mind conjured new ways to display trade goods on shelves using arrangements no traveler could resist, new tricks to encourage travelers to stay overnight in tents for a fee, new ways to spread the word in Westport and Independence that his trading post would be a "must stop" along the route.

Medina took in Papín's words like a horse feasting on spring grass, digesting them slowly, storing them for later use. His avid attention spurred Papín to divulge ever more details about his plans for the future.

Only at the moment of parting did Papín show a hint of sadness. He'd kissed Takánsy on the forehead and both cheeks, gripped her shoulders in his hands, and looked at her long and hard.

"Till we meet again," he had said.

Takánsy, eyes glistening, gave his arm a squeeze and said, *"Merci, cherie,* thank you."

After Papín's departure, she turned to Medina, a slight smile on her lips, and taking his hands said, "We are husband and wife."

Her look suggested immediate consummation of that state, as did her firm grip on his arm as she led him back to their adobe room, provided as a wedding gift by Charlie Autobees. Medina, skin tingling, tried to calm himself. He felt under her spell, as if she were the one in charge. So different from the despairing woman he first encountered at Fort Bridger, a soul adrift, unable to run from the Woodpecker's raiders even when she had a chance. Now she radiated a new strength of purpose, a strength he found a little intimidating.

For one thing, she insisted they return to the north country before the baby's birth. This announcement came just before they knelt before a rough plank altar to exchange vows in front of the skinny priest Papín had bribed. The ceremony took place in El Pueblo's church, a squat adobe room which looked like all the other squat adobe rooms, save for a rustic cross with a crooked crossbeam that was nailed above the door.

"My child must be born at Bridger camp," she had said. "Close to Jenny and the others."

Surprised by her boldness, he argued, "That is too far, and such travel, it will be dangerous for you and your baby." He pointed to her stomach. "And here I can have work to do, for Charlie. He will pay me. Then we go north later."

She shook her head.

He tried to stare her down, but her eyes stayed fixed on his.

He said, "Tim Goodale, he is coming here soon from Saint Louis, with money from the beaver pelts. My share."

"Señor Tim will find us. He will speed like race horse to Bridger's. Jenny waits there, not here."

It was hard to argue with that. In the end he backed down. Takánsy's unexpected determination raised his ire, and he struggled to keep his own stubbornness under control. He didn't want tension to spoil their first intimacy, skin on skin, under the buffalo robes.

In that, at least, his expectations were more than met. They lay together now, he on his back and she on her side with her breasts pressing into his arm. He sighed in hazy satiation.

"Mariano?"

"Takánsy."

She giggled at the sound of it, and flung her bare arm across his stomach. She fingered his chest with her tapered fingers.

"You are a no-hair," she said. "Like Indian."

He laughed and reached for the soft mound between her legs. "And you," he said, "are a yes-hair, like a silky mink." He thrilled at the firmness of her body, the muscle lines so well-defined.

She pulled his hand from her and brought it up to her face.

"And you are strong, like buffalo bull, and you have to stop now, or you will kill me." She smiled and traced the curve of his mouth with her fingers.

A warm wave swept over him. Now that it was allowed, he couldn't keep his hands off her. He let his fingers roam. They traveled down the curve of her spine, traversed the roundness of her hips and found her elbow folded at her side. From there they ascended the perfect smoothness of her arm. Near the shoulder they tripped over the scars.

He said, "Why you do this?"

She stiffened and withdrew her arm. "A small sacrifice I make..." Her voice trailed off. "You do not need to...you can just... love me."

She pulled his face to hers, but he resisted.

"Why? What sadness makes you hurt yourself?" He recalled the sect in Taos whose members, the *Penitentes*, would flagellate themselves during the annual pilgrimage to the Virgin's shrine, raising scars on their backs. "You are a *Penitente*?" he asked, and immediately felt foolish, seeing the answer in the look of puzzlement on her face. Still he persisted. "What happened to you?"

She turned away, her bare back now a wall.

"Mariano. We have new life. We must not speak of old life." Her voice, flat as stone, conveyed finality. Medina imagined her ghost stare, as stark and unseeing as on the day of their first encounter.

He sighed. Secrets. We all have them. Best forgotten. Maybe now, in a new beginning with Takánsy, he could forget Fili, his mother and father, Chepe Luis, the little Don. He could put those beasts back in their caves.

He stroked her back, felt her muscles relax, felt his own

unease dissipate as he sought to rekindle their closeness. Soon, he drifted into sleep.

Out of the black nowhere, hands came for him, blood-covered hands pinning him to the floor while other hands sawed at his hairline and sliced at his throat, and, unable to move, he screamed and jerked and pushed away the hands until he heard her voice say, "Mariano, Mariano, what is wrong? Stop! You are with me," and he realized it was her voice and her hands and he sat up, shuddering, his breathing hoarse, and wrapped his arms around his knees.

She brushed her fingers across his sweating forehead and drew him close.

"What was it, *mi querido*?"

He shook his head. "A nightmare. Pardon me for waking you. I will be all right."

"A spirit visit? What was it?"

"Someone was trying to scalp me. A foolish dream." He lay back down and pulled her to him. "Sleep. Let us go to sleep again."

She snuggled against him and soon he heard her breathing change into the regular rhythm of sleep.

His own fall into unconsciousness came much later.

234 David M. Jessup

Epilogue

Near Fort Bridger, April 12, 1857

Don Justino's knees wobbled. The horse staggered to regain its balance, then with a sigh, went down on its front knees. Its rump swayed in the air for a moment, then toppled like a slow-falling tree next to the lodge-sized boulder behind which Medina and his horse had taken shelter.

Medina pulled on the lead rope. The horse could not lift its head. It gazed up at Medina with great, apologetic eyes. It blinked a few times to ward off the snow that whirled down on them in the lee of the boulder.

The howling storm had sprung on them during a hunting trip south of Fort Bridger, upstream along Black's Fork in the Uinta foothills. It would soon grow dark. Remorseless wind drove tiny daggers of ice sideways into their bodies. He'd found protection behind the boulder. But for Don Justino, shelter had come too late.

A lump swelled in Medina's throat. He shouldn't have brought his aging horse on this trip. How many winters had they been together? *Twenty?* The horse had been only five, entering its youthful prime, when it carried him up Black's Fork into Bridger's camp past the spot where he'd first met Takánsy. Born him along on tireless strides during the grueling pursuit of the Ute raiders. Two years later, in 1844, the magnificent roan had brought him back to Bridger's, accompanied by his new wife, pregnant with Papín's child. Over the next thirteen years, Don Justino had carried him across ridge and mesa on countless hunting trips, trading forays, and scouting assignments. Both Papín's son, Louie, now twelve, and Antonio, his own ten-year-old boy, had learned to ride on Don Justino's strong back. Now that great back lay still under a mounting mantle of snow.

Medina unsheathed his knife. He could barely feel it in his numb fingers. Time was short. He knelt beside his horse's head and gently brushed snow off the animal's neck. He stroked its roughened winter coat. He made the sign of the cross and tried to murmur a few words of goodbye, but they caught in his throat. Grasping the knife in both hands, he drove the blade deep into Don Justino's pulsing jugular. A gusher of blood, black in the half-light, spewed onto the snow. Don Justino barely twitched.

Is there an afterlife for animals? Medina wasn't sure, but just the same, he prayed for Don Justino to go there. He got to work, his own survival at stake. He slit the horse's belly and pulled the steaming guts out into the whiteness. The stench did not linger in the wind-whipped air. Wrapping his blanket tight around his body, he crawled into the bloody cavity of Don Justino's carcass and pulled the flaps of belly skin as close together as he could. The wind screamed, clawed at the warm carcass in frustration, unable to reach him. Feeling returned to his hands in sharp pricks of pain. He thanked Don Justino for this final gift. Finally, he dozed.

It was almost dark when he woke. Out of immediate danger from the still howling blizzard, Medina thought of Takánsy. Due to deliver her third child at any moment, she would be just now finishing her evening meal. Or so he hoped. He didn't like the idea of her being caught in this blizzard while out harvesting dry frozen currents from the bushes upstream from their lodge. An image of her ungainly form, belly swollen, slipping and falling in the snow, nagged at him.

This damnable place and its cursed winters! Bridger's had been their home off and on for most of the past thirteen years. Four years ago, in 1853, Jim Bridger had abandoned his fort to an armed gang of Mormons, who set up their own fort nearby to defend their strange religion against the U.S. government. In response, Uncle Jack Robinson rallied the mountain men and their Indian wives and allies who had been living at Bridger's to establish a new trading camp close by. Takánsy moved with them.

Takánsy seemed rooted there, strange for an Indian— particularly a Flathead, a people somewhat more rooted than most, but still wanderers. Medina supposed it was her attachment to Jenny, who still maintained a lodge in Robinson's camp while Goodale roamed.

Takánsy's stubbornness galled him. He had tried to convince her to move. Sometimes she'd travel with him, but only for a few months at a time. Then she'd look at him calmly and say, "I will return to Bridger's now," and off she would go, leaving him to catch up after he finished his current business.

Business, he reflected, had been good. It sometimes shocked him to think about how his life had changed since leaving El Pueblo. Invisible no more, he asserted himself with confidence, put himself forward as an expert guide to army and civilian expeditions, hovered no longer in the shadow of Tim Goodale or anyone else. He commanded respect. He'd successfully operated a ferry on Green River, and with Papín as his internal mentor, accumulated a sizeable amount of plunder through the barter of trade goods. He never picked fights, but didn't shrink from them, either. His reputation as a marksman had grown, and despite his small size, his quickness and skill with a knife had silenced several bullies who had crossed him. Best of all, the horrors of Arroyo Hondo haunted his dreams less and less as time passed.

Around him the wind continued to howl. He drew his knees closer to his chest. His blanket, along with his rib-caged enclosure, retained enough body heat to keep him from freezing. The rank smell of bloody carcass faded, as odors do, when breathed repetitively.

His thoughts drifted away to the valley on Thompson's Creek far to the south, the one he'd explored during the second Fremont expedition. Winters there would be pleasant compared to this. But it was far from the great trails that traversed the plains and brought immigrants, armies and traders close enough for him to earn a livelihood. Sighing, he flexed his fingers and toes to keep his blood circulating. Someday, he thought, she'll be ready to move. Maybe this storm will convince her. But he doubted it. Hadn't her last two pregnancies, both in winter, ended badly? Bloody lumps of stillborn children, buried under rocks in the cold ground. If those stillbirths hadn't persuaded her to move, what would?

For weeks after each of those failed birthings, the ghost stare had clouded her face. She once tried to cut herself, but he'd stopped her. Instead, determined to do penance, she made a solemn vow to stop training horses, or even riding them, except for pulling a *travois* when they moved somewhere.

He found her self-punishment deeply vexing. She loved horses. Why would she deny herself this calling? It was bad for business, too. When he wasn't guiding or scouting, he still had requests to train horses and mules for travelers. He needed her help. His frustration equaled Papín's, who had wanted her to race horses. Medina had shouted at her, cursed and stomped about, demanding to know why. All he got in response was, "It is to atone for my sins." That, and the tight-lipped, vacant stare. A shutting away as final as the stiffening limbs of his dead horse.

The snow continued to drift over him, flakes caught in the vortex created by the boulder as the wind howled overhead. His body warmed under the thickening white blanket.

He recalled Takánsy's first two birthings, the successful ones. Papín's son slid silently into the world on a calm summer day shortly after they returned to the Bridger encampment from El Pueblo. Standing outside the birth lodge, Medina hadn't heard a sound. Alarmed by the absence of a baby's squall, he violated custom by poking his head through the lodge door to find out what was happening.

Jenny had waved him away with a dark look.

"You'll put a hex on him," she said. "Go away."

Papín's child had turned out to be a boy. Louie, they agreed, should be his name, to honor the boy's father. But the boy couldn't have been more unlike his namesake. For one thing, as an infant, he didn't cry. Somber, restrained, the opposite of outgoing, Louie seemed destined to become anything but a trader. He seldom laughed, and his play consisted mainly of watching other children play. Only after studying a situation for hours, sometimes days, would he join a game.

David M. Jessup

To Medina's satisfaction, however, the boy was thoughtful, obedient, and learned well. During Medina's stays at his wife's lodge between trips as a guide or a trader, Louie would watch him build a snowshoe or repair a trap, eyes solemn, refusing repeated offers to participate. Later Medina would come upon the boy sitting by himself repeating the motions with surprising skill. To Medina's further satisfaction, the boy was helpful. He never refused a request, always obeyed a command. He possessed what Medina considered a son's greatest virtue: respect.

Medina's own son, Antonio, lacked that virtue. Born three years later on a blustery September day, the baby had come into the world squalling and hadn't quieted much since. Medina had no trouble hearing his arrival into the world, nor could he miss the child's noisy presence in camp as he grew.

Naming his boy had been an issue. Medina insisted on Antonio, after his father. He wasn't sure why he insisted on this. More from tradition, he supposed, than any feeling of veneration or respect. Takánsy argued for the name Pablo, after St. Paul, the bearer of the gospel to the nations. Medina had prevailed, at least on the surface. But after the boy learned to talk, he would sometimes respond to a reprimand by saying, "My name is Pablo, not Antonio."

The brazenness of Antonio's defiance shocked Medina. The small boy would stand with feet planted, arms crossed, narrow black eyes flashing under darkened brow, as if daring his father to act. Not even sending the boy sprawling with a hefty cuff seemed to curb his rebelliousness. Medina suspected Takánsy of providing her son with this alternative name, thereby fostering his son's misbehavior. But she always used "Antonio" in Medina's presence.

Now ten, the younger boy led his boisterous playmates into increasingly daring adventures. As long as the adventures remained lighthearted they were tolerated, even appreciated, by the people in the camp. Like when they stuffed an old buffalo skin with dried grass, adorned it with the bleached skull of a bear, and rigged it up to plunge down from a tree branch in front of Peg Leg Pete out for an evening walk.

But sometimes the pranks turned annoying, even dark.

One day they put crawdads in some ornately beaded moccasins belonging to Uncle Jack Robinson, just before he presented them as a gift to the chief of a visiting band of Shoshones. On another, they tortured one of the camp dogs by setting fire to a straw belt they had fastened about its waist.

"It is what Indian boys do to prepare themselves as warriors," Antonio argued.

"We are people of Jésu," Takánsy replied. "We do not torture." Her vehemence surprised Medina.

Medina hoped their next child would be somewhere in between Louie and Antonio in temperament. If the child survived, that is. He listened to the blizzard's roar, muffled by his bloody shelter. The wind seemed to be lessening. Listening to it, he again grew drowsy, and finally fell into a troubled sleep.

The next morning, after digging out of the crusted drift and snowshoeing back to Bridger, Medina found Takánsy huddled inside the birthing lodge, the fire gone out. In her arms nestled a newborn. The baby, a little girl with startlingly lush dark hair and wrinkly brown skin, latched onto Takánsy's nipple like a tiny goblin, eyes closed, miniature hands rhythmically kneading, oblivious to all but the life-giving softness of her mother's breast.

Takánsy's weary smile greeted him. "Look, how beautiful she is. Perfect." She rolled back the robe far enough for him to see the infant's wrinkled little body and count her fingers and toes.

Medina touched the foot of the rabbit-sized creature, who responded with a momentary pause in her sucking. So fragile. He covered them and stooped to rekindle the fire. That's when he noticed the afterbirth piled beside the tipi wall.

"You are all right?" Medina asked. "Why is Jenny not here?"

"The storm. Too loud. No one could hear. And this little one is coming fast." She smiled down at the newborn and stroked her glossy head. "Yes, I am fine, and your daughter is, too, thanks be to Jésu. And you?" she asked. "This storm? I am worrying."

"I am fine," he said.

"Louie and Antonio?" she asked.

"Those boys. I see them digging out from Jenny's lodge when I come into camp. The snow, it is deep." He blew on the struggling flame, feeling irritated at Goodale's wife. Jenny had assisted with the birth of both his sons and had been on hand for the stillbirths, as well. He had repaid her with generous gifts. But now, after helping nurse Takánsy through a pregnancy fraught with illness, the plump Shoshone woman was missing.

"We are lucky this time," he said.

Takánsy crossed herself. "Blessed."

He felt her eyes on him. Even after all this time, their gray depths still cast a spell. He would spare her the news of Don Justino until later. He looked again at the baby.

"A girl," he said. "I think she will be beautiful. Already she is. Look at all that hair."

"She is my prairie flower," Takánsy said, using an impossible to pronounce Salish word.

Medina stiffened. "Marcelina, or Lena, short name. You agreed, remember? If it was a girl."

"Yes. Lena." But the upturned corners of Takánsy's mouth signaled a private inclination to use two names for the girl.

"Lena," Medina repeated for emphasis. He wondered what other disagreements might arise between them as this child grew.

Wind gusted hard against the tipi, lifting the entry flap and blasting them with an icy swirl of snow.

"*Carrajo*," he muttered as he bent to secure it. "This wind! This cold. Not a place for this beautiful child." He turned, knelt and grasped Takánsy's hand. "You remember my telling you the place I found, Thompson's Creek, to the south, near St. Vrain's Fort? A rocky creek runs there, no mosquitos. Not wind, snow, cold, like here. A better place for our children. We go there to live."

Takánsy pulled back. "My hand, you are hurting it."

He relaxed his grip. "*Perdón*, I did not mean to. There we build a strong house of logs. Big lodge. Warm in winter, cool in summer. We raise fine horses. Cattle. What do you say?"

She studied him with her solemn gray eyes. "My husband, your heart is strong on this."

"Yes."

Her eyes roamed around the canvas interior of her lodge, lingering briefly on each item hanging from the poles, a fox pelt, parfleche bag, copper pot, shirts with her beadwork, rawhide skins, as if recalling a story from each. Then they settled on the tiny girl at her breast. She stroked the infant's dark hair. The child let go of her nipple and erupted with a thin little burp.

They both laughed.

"Maybe we are going there," she said. She patted his hand. "When our daughter is old enough to travel. I will pray on it."

"In the fall, then?"

Her nod signaled agreement.

He smiled, leaned toward her, brushed her lips with his, then each eyelid as it closed in anticipation of his kiss, as if banishing the ghost eyes of his first memory of her astride the gray gelding beside this same creek so many years ago.

David M. Jessup

AUTHOR'S NOTE

Mariano Medina, Takánsy, Tim Goodale and Louis Papín, along with many other characters in this book, were real people who roamed the American frontier in the 1840s and 1850s. Mariano Medina was born in Taos, New Mexico, in 1812 and died in Colorado in 1878. According to the Zethyl Gates biography (*Mariano Medina, Mountain Man*), Medina met his future wife, Takansy, in the early 1840s, and later acquired her from Louis Papín, a French trader, for the price of six horses and six blankets.

There is conflicting information on the founding date of Fort Bridger. Most historians say 1843, others date the beginnings of the encampment in late 1842. I chose the earlier date to compress the time between the Fremont expedition and the fictitious meeting of Medina and Takánsy at Bridger's.

Not long after Lena's birth in April 1857, Mariano Medina embarked on the adventure that would seal his place in history. Later that year, President James Buchanan dispatched twenty-five hundred U.S. Army troops to put down the "Mormon Rebellion" in Utah. As the army marched across Wyoming Territory, its progress was slowed by Mormon guerrilla attacks. With supplies depleted, the army finally arrived at Fort Bridger in November, only to find it burned to the ground. Instead of continuing into the Mormon stronghold at the Great Salt Lake, the troops holed up for the winter close to the smoldering ruins of the fort.

Captain Randolph Marcy was ordered to lead an expedition six hundred miles to the south to bring in supplies from Fort Massachusetts in the San Luis Valley, which had been annexed by the United States after the Mexican-American war in 1846.

On November 27, 1857, Marcy set off with forty soldiers and twenty-four civilian guides, packers and herders to cross the Colorado mountains in the dead of winter. Among them was Mariano Medina, Tim Goodale, and Jenny, the only woman on the trip.

The snows were unusually deep that winter, slowing progress. Instead of thirty days, the exhausted troops were still bogged down on the wrong side of Cochetopa Pass by mid-January. Most of their sixty-six mules had died or had been eaten. Jenny's beloved horse was also sacrificed to feed the starving members of the expedition, much to her distress.

When they reached the top of Cochetopa Pass, Captain Marcy sent Medina and another Mexican guide on ahead to Fort Massachusetts, one hundred miles farther south, to bring back a rescue party. Eleven days later, Medina returned with fresh horses, additional supplies, and the joyous news that help was on the way. The expedition was rescued. The only casualty was a starving soldier who ignored the admonition to avoid eating too much of the food that, if consumed slowly, could have saved his life.

From Fort Massachusetts, Medina was sent back north to report on the fate of Marcy's troops and inform the army that help was on the way. He arrived at Fort Bridger in March, and Marcy brought in fresh supplies in June. Medina then guided the army from Fort Bridger into Utah. The troops, unopposed, marched into Salt Lake City on July 26, 1858 to install a new governor, appointed by the President.

Later that year, Mariano Medina took his family south to establish a trading post on the Big Thompson River near what is now the town of Loveland, Colorado. The tragic death and secret burial of his daughter, Lena Medina, in 1872 is the subject of my first novel, *Mariano's Crossing*, to which this book is a prequel.

Onto these bare historic bones I have grafted an entirely fictitious body of events, motives and personalities, including the characters of Curfew, Captain Jack, the Castillo family, and the Strong brothers. Fleshing out the facts of history is what is fun about fiction.

David M. Jessup

ABOUT THE AUTHOR

David M. Jessup co-owns Sylvan Dale Guest Ranch in Loveland, Colorado, where he introduces grass-fed cattle to guests, and guests to the ways of both the old and the new West. A history buff, he is passionate about preserving open space, battling invasive weeds, catching wild river trout on a fly, singing cowboy songs, and telling stories about the American West—some of them true. He and his wife Linda spend part of the year in Maryland exploring the world with their grandchildren.

Jessup is a popular speaker at book clubs, schools and community organizations on topics such as cattle ranching, sustainable agriculture (*Git Along Little Microbes*), land conservation, flood recovery (he's been through two floods on the Big Thompson River in Colorado), fiction writing and the history behind his novels (*Fact to Fiction*). His talks are sponsored by the Heart-J Center for Experiential Learning, *www.heartjcenter.org*.

Mariano's Crossing, his first novel, was selected as one of three finalists for the Colorado Book Award in literary fiction. He also won first place for mainstream, character-driven fiction in the Rocky Mountain Fiction Writers Contest and was selected as a finalist in the Pacific Northwest Writers Contest and the Santa Fe Writers Project.

Jessup's blog, *Beef, Books and Boots*, contains stories of ranch life, articles on sustainable grass-fed beef, and reviews of his favorite books about the American West.

His website is *davidmjessup.com*

The ranch website is *www.sylvandale.com.*

Book Discussion Questions

Historical fiction sometimes suffers when authors dwell too much on historical fact at the expense of a good story. On the other hand, fiction can sometimes veer too far away from the facts. What kind of balance between fact and fiction do you find in *Marino's Choice*?

What are the main goals Mariano Medina is striving to attain? What motivations—both conscious and unconscious—fuel his efforts to continue the struggle toward these goals?

What happens to Mariano when he becomes discouraged and loses hope?

What are the sources of Medina's attraction to Takánsy?

What are the central dilemmas faced by Mariano Medina? What values influence the choices he makes? How does the past influence his choices?

What is your favorite scene in the book, and why? What major emotion does the scene evoke in you as a reader?

How do both Mariano's body memory and his mind help Mariano cope with early childhood trauma? How do they hinder him?

What parallels and differences exist between the period leading up to the 1846 U.S. war with Mexico and current border issues?

What did you learn about the time period in which this story unfolds? What surprised you about Fort Bridger, El Pueblo and Taos that you didn't know before?

David M. Jessup

CPSIA information can be obtained
at www.ICGtesting.com
Printed in the USA
BVOW06s0032041216
469722BV00005B/17/P